B. J. HOFF

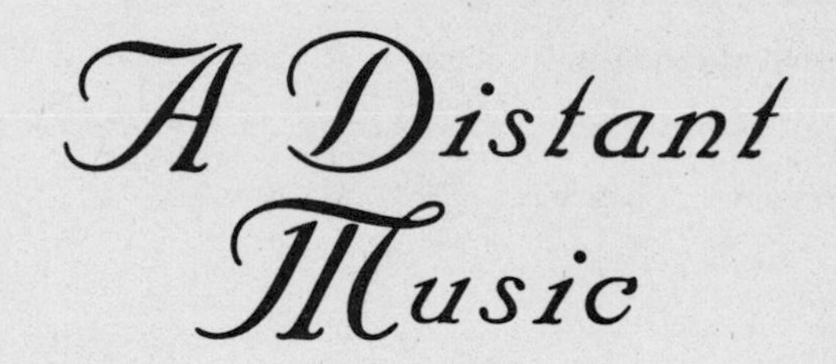

HARVEST HOUSE PUBLISHERS

EUGENE, OREGON

Scripture verses used in the main text are from the King James Version of the Bible. Scripture verses in "What God Says About Hope" are taken from the HOLY BIBLE, NEW INTERNATIONAL VERSION®. NIV®. Copyright© 1973, 1978, 1984 by the International Bible Society. Used by permission of Zondervan. All rights reserved.

The verse appearing on p. 226 is taken from the New King James Version. Copyright ©1982 by Thomas Nelson, Inc. Used by permission. All rights reserved.

Published in association with the literary agency of Janet Kobobel Grant, Books & Such, 4788 Carissa Avenue, Santa Rosa, California 95405.

A portion of this novel was previously published as *The Penny Whistle.*

Cover photo © Rubberball Productions/Index Stock Imagery; Thinkstock/Index Stock Imagery

Cover by Koechel Peterson & Associates, Inc., Minneapolis, Minnes

A DISTANT MUSIC
Copyright © 2006 by BJ Hoff
Published by Harvest House Publishers
Eugene, Oregon 97402
www.harvesthousepublishers.com

Library of Congress Cataloging-in-Publication Data

Hoff, B. J., 1940-
A distant music / B.J. Hoff.
p. cm. — (The mountain song legacy ; bk. 1)
"Portions of this novel previously published as The penny whistle"—T.p. verso.
ISBN-13: 978-0-7369-1404-8 (pbk.)
ISBN-10: 0-7369-1404-8 (pbk.)
1. Teacher-student relationships—Fiction. 2. Coal mines and mining—Fiction. 3. Poor families—Fiction. 4. Sick children—Fiction. 5. Mountain life—Fiction. 6. Musicians—Fiction. 7. Kentucky—Fiction. I. Hoff, B. J. 1940- Penny whistle. II. Title. III. Series.
PS3558.O34395D57 2006
813'.54—dc22 2005020466

Printed in the United States of America

08 09 10 11 12 13 14 / BC-MS / 13 12 11 10 9 8 7 6

For Dana and Jessie,

who taught me everything I know
about how young girls think and how young women
make their mother proud time and time again...

And for Jim,

who could teach even Jonathan Stuart
a few things about what it means to be a *good man.*

Acknowledgments

Many thanks to Nick Harrison, Carolyn McCready, Kim Moore, and all those at Harvest House who played such a vital role in breathing new life into Maggie MacAuley and the lovable inhabitants of Skingle Creek.

And, as always, with appreciation to Janet Grant, sainted agent and patient friend.

To My Readers:

A few years ago I wrote a novella entitled *The Penny Whistle.* It was a story about two young girls, Maggie MacAuley and Summer Rankin, and their efforts to restore the hope…and the health…of their beloved teacher, Jonathan Stuart. Ever since the publication of *The Penny Whistle,* I've continued to hear from many of you, asking for "the rest of the story."

What a gift it is to any writer to realize that readers have come to love the characters in her book so much that they want to know more about them. To my great pleasure, I can now thank you for your patience and respond to your requests for "more." With this new book, you're about to renew your acquaintance with Maggie, Summer, Jonathan Stuart, and many others in the small Kentucky mining town of Skingle Creek. And I'm happy to tell you that *A Distant Music* isn't so much the "rest of the story" as it is the *beginning* of the "rest of the story." I hope you enjoy it…there's more to come.

God's blessing upon you all,

Prologue

When the Music Stopped

The harp that once through Tara's halls
The soul of music shed,
Now hangs as mute on Tara's walls
As if that soul were fled.

Thomas Moore

Northeastern Kentucky
November 10, 1892

Maggie MacAuley could pinpoint the exact day when the music stopped in Skingle Creek.

It was the same day some no-account unknown stole Mr. Stuart's silver flute. The same day Mr. Stuart seemed to give up. The day he began to change.

The only schoolteacher who had ever stayed for more than a few months, Jonathan Stuart had arrived fresh from the state university almost six years ago. The town knew little about him, for he never talked much about himself, only that he had grown up in Lexington.

How or why he had ended up in a little mining town like Skingle Creek was anyone's guess, but to everyone's surprise, he had settled right in and stayed put.

Maggie had been only six years old when Mr. Stuart came to town, but she could still recollect his first few weeks at the school and how the people of Skingle Creek had wagged their tongues about "that new teacher" and how he was a "different cut," a "city fellow." The older students, like Maggie's sisters, Eva Grace and Nell Frances, claimed to have known right from the start that their new teacher was indeed "different."

Of course, Eva Grace and Nell Frances were inclined to think they knew just about everything.

If truth were told, not a soul in Skingle Creek—child or grown-up alike—had ever come upon a man like Mr. Stuart.

Maggie figured their teacher must be what was meant by a "gentle man." His smile was gentle. His voice was gentle too, and words seemed to fall easy from his tongue. His laugh was quick to come but never rowdy. Even his walk was quiet and unhurried. He had a way of making it seem as though whatever he happened to be doing at any particular moment was the most important thing he had to do all day.

He also had a way of making all the students in the small one-room schoolhouse feel as though they were the most important people in the world. At least in *his* world. Maggie had never seen Mr. Stuart in a rush, nor had she ever known him to lose his patience with the slower learners. Although he had himself a fine gold watch, he seldom took it out of his vest pocket, except when it came time to change from one class to another or to ring the dismissal bell. If time was of much importance to him, he seldom showed it.

He never raised his voice, not even when Lester Monk—who everyone knew was the pokiest boy to ever set his feet to the floor in the morning—lumbered through his sums or went to stuttering when he tried to read more than two or three words in a row. Mr. Stuart would just smile and nod, as if to encourage Lester to keep on trying, that he was doing fine, and that they had all the time in the world.

Maggie was pretty sure any other teacher would have bawled Lester out something fierce or maybe even smacked his hand with the ruler and made him stand in the "dumb" corner. But not Mr. Stuart. He treated all his students the same, even Lester.

Eva Grace said he was by far the best teacher they'd ever had. Nell Frances disagreed—she *always* disagreed with their older sister just because Eva Grace *was* older. And prettier. A *lot* prettier than either Nell Frances or Maggie herself. Prettier, even, than their mother, who Da said was the "best-looking woman in Rowan County."

One thing Maggie's two sisters did agree on was that Mr. Stuart was a great storyteller. And just like every other lesson he taught, his stories almost always had a Point, unlike the tall tales of their Great-Uncle Ruff, whose yarns were known to be the most far-fetched throughout the county.

He was a great one, Mr. Stuart was, for making a Point.

His stories were also crammed with enough excitement to make a body's heart hammer and enough adventure to satisfy even the older boys in the schoolroom. Sometimes he told them stories from the Holy Bible, and Maggie had noticed that he never had to read these stories but seemed to know them all by heart. Sometimes the stories were about animals or people who had lived long ago. "Folk tales," Mr. Stuart called them.

But no matter what kind of tale he told, there was always a Point. It wasn't that he would come right out and say what it was. They just knew by the way he would end the story and stand there, watching them with a little smile, that he was looking to see if they had got the Point.

Many of the teacher's stories had to do with God and how He loved people and all the creatures He had made—even toads and spiders, which Maggie thought must take an awful lot of love. Oftentimes, Mr. Stuart's stories seemed to have a Point about being kind to others, even to those who weren't nice to *you*. Some stories made a Point about gossip. Others were about envy, and how it was wrong to resent folks who had more money and possessions than others.

That particular Point wasn't much of a problem in Skingle Creek.

Except for Dr. Woodbridge and Judson Tallman, the mine superintendent, everyone in town was fixed about the same when it came to money: nobody had any.

Skingle Creek was a company town where everyone took their living from the coal mines. According to Maggie's mother, it wasn't much of a living. Ma said that what the company store didn't get on payday, the tavern did.

This was just about the only subject to spur a quarrel between her folks. Ma would nag Da to bring his wages home and not stop at the tavern, and Da would in turn call her a terrible scold and say how any man who worked twelve hours a day under the ground ought to be free to lift a glass or two on payday if he felt so inclined. It was his way, he would declare with a fierce scowl, of washing the coal dust from his soul. Maggie thought she understood what he meant by that. Hadn't she felt the same way those times when Mr. Stuart played his silver flute? Somehow the music seemed to wash the coal dust and all the other dingy thoughts and feelings right out of her soul.

The music was...a *glory*. A wondrous thing entirely. Sometimes it was like a graceful bird, winging up and over the clouds. Other times it was more like shiny coins tumbling out of an angel's knapsack. And sometimes—and to Maggie these were the best times of all—it was like a happy waterfall, pouring down from heaven itself over the town, washing away the ugly black dust that coated the unpainted company houses, the laundry on the clotheslines, and even a body's hair.

During these special moments Maggie could almost pretend the whole town and even life itself had been washed clean and made new by the music from Mr. Stuart's silver flute. But now the flute was gone, stolen by somebody who either didn't know how important it was to its owner...and his students...or somebody who didn't care.

Meanwhile, from the looks of him, Mr. Stuart was getting sicker and weaker by the day. Of late, he seemed to scarcely have the strength to write their assignments on the blackboard.

For a long time now, Maggie's mother had insisted that Mr. Stuart was "sickly." And recently some of the other grown-ups, like their neighbor, Pearl Callaghan, had also taken to remarking how the teacher just kept getting "poorer and poorer," that there wasn't "enough of him to stand against a strong wind."

It shamed Maggie to admit it, but up until lately, she and the other students hadn't paid all that much attention to their teacher's poor health. Mr. Stuart had always been a lean man—thinner than most, she reckoned—but then almost everyone in Skingle Creek was on the lean side. Other than the Woodbridges and the Tallmans, no one in town got enough to eat to make them fleshy.

Still, even though she couldn't actually pinpoint the exact day when Mr. Stuart's health had taken a turn for the worse, Maggie could recall when the light had seemed to go out of him, when he no longer smiled as often or whistled softly to himself, and when instead of walking up and down the aisles to help them with their papers, he had taken to sitting at his desk most of the day.

He had even stopped telling his stories with a Point. Most of the time now, he merely assigned the class a number of pages to read on their own or a row of sums to figure by the next day.

The fact was that since the morning he discovered that his silver flute had gone missing, Mr. Stuart hadn't been the same at all.

And neither had anything else.

One

Jonathan's Children

Even the children are old in such a place.

From the diary of Jonathan Stuart

Jonathan Stuart watched the faces of the children as they filed into the classroom and slid behind their desks.

He had always thought of them as *his* children, as if they were a special gift, temporarily entrusted to him by Providence—and accompanied by an almost frightening responsibility. As his gaze came to rest on first one, then another, he couldn't quell the bitter question that had nagged at him for days now: *Who among them could have done such a thing?*

And why?

He found it unthinkable that any one of his students might have had so little regard for him or for something that belonged to him. Yet he realized that in all likelihood the one responsible for the theft of the flute was right here, in this classroom.

He watched Kenny Tallman take his seat—and discounted him

almost immediately. The narrow, bespectacled face was that of an unhappy child who, in spite of belonging to one of the few financially comfortable households in town, never seemed quite at ease with the other students—or with himself, for that matter.

The boy glanced up, giving the uncertain smile that never failed to touch Jonathan's heart. No, not only did this reticent youth have no reason to steal from his teacher, but of all the children in the room, Kenny was probably one of the very few who wouldn't have had the daring—nor the motivation—to attempt such an exploit.

Jonathan had long wondered about the Tallman boy's home life. Quieter than any other student in the class and possessed of a reserve that gave him a presence much older than his years, Kenny seemed to be liked well enough by the other children, though he was something of an outsider. Perhaps it had to do with the fact that his father, Judson Tallman, was superintendent of the mines and known to be a hard, uncompromising man. Certainly, he was one of the least popular men in the small community.

He and his son lived alone at the foot of "the Hill," as Dredd's Mountain was called by the miners, in a neat, two-story house. Tallman periodically hosed their home down to rid it of the coal dust that blackened it and every other dwelling in town. Some of the miners were known to joke that Tallman's frequent hosing of his house was the mine super's effort to wash away his sins. Others would counter that nothing but a flood would accomplish *that* feat.

Kenny's mother had left Skingle Creek before Jonathan arrived. Although she'd been gone for years, rumors still circulated as to why Charlotte Tallman had abandoned her family.

Jonathan had heard most of the tales by now, but the one that seemed destined to survive all the others was that Tallman's wife had fled to escape her husband's cruelty. Speculation was that Judson Tallman might have ill-treated his wife, perhaps had even been violent with her. But rumors often ballooned into flagrant exaggerations, and Jonathan fervently hoped for Kenny's sake that such was the case with the stories about his father. A man who would mistreat his wife would almost certainly be capable of the same abuse toward his son.

Two of the older boys who had been whispering between themselves when Kenny came in now turned their attention his way. Billy Macken, a tall, heavy-shouldered youth who delighted in tormenting the younger children, muttered something to his buddy beside him. Orrin Gaffney, another troublemaker, leaned forward to Kenny, seated in front of him, and thumped him on the shoulder. "Billy wants you," he said, smirking.

Kenny looked around.

"Pick up my pencil, Four-eyes," the Macken boy ordered.

Kenny looked at him and then at the floor. "Where? I don't see any pencil."

Billy grinned and dropped a pencil to the floor. "*That* pencil, Weaselface."

Jonathan rapped his pointer on the corner of his desk, but neither youth seemed aware of his presence. He waited, deciding to see how the Tallman boy would handle the situation.

Kenny stared at the pencil on the floor for a long time. Finally, he bent over and picked it up, handing it to Billy without looking at him.

Jonathan wasn't surprised. Most of the younger children gave in to Billy Macken's bullying. The boy was the biggest student in the room and had an air of meanness about him that, combined with his size and rough behavior, was nothing less than intimidating.

He'd been held back more than once, and so he was one of the older students in the room. At fourteen he could have gone into the mines—it wasn't unusual for much younger boys to leave school and join their fathers in the coal mines. But Jonathan suspected that sheer laziness had kept Billy aboveground so far. Laziness and an overly indulgent mother, who had apparently talked her husband into letting their son stay in school for a while longer.

Jonathan tried not to warm to the idea of the Macken boy leaving school, even though it would make his days considerably easier. Billy had routinely rebuffed every attempt to interest him in learning. The boy was a daily discipline problem and a continual aggravation to the other children. Even so, Jonathan was loath to see Billy or any other boy go into the mines at such a young age. But if something didn't change, and change drastically, he was going to have to fail the boy again this year, and no doubt that would be the end of Billy's education. He couldn't see Buck Macken holding still for his son to stay out of the mines much longer.

He went to the boy's desk, waiting until he had his attention. "Billy, I want you to go outside and come in again, this time with a different attitude."

The boy met Jonathan's eyes with a defiant sneer, but finally he stood and sauntered down the aisle to the door.

Jonathan sighed and, ignoring the urge to give Kenny Tallman a reassuring pat on the shoulder, turned and went back to sit down at his desk.

When he glanced up again, he saw Lester Monk trudging up the aisle, brushing snow from his hair. The boy stumbled—a common occurrence with Lester—and shot Jonathan a self-conscious grin as he righted himself and squeezed in behind his desk.

Jonathan smiled back, studying the boy. Certainly Lester's family could use the money that an underhanded sale of the flute might bring. But somehow Jonathan couldn't envision the plodding, awkward Lester as the culprit. The youth simply didn't have the imagination to concoct such a scheme, much less the mental acuity to carry it off. Lester was clumsy, often inept—but he was no thief. Of that Jonathan was confident.

Behind Lester came Maggie MacAuley and little Summer Rankin, great friends who, admittedly, were two of Jonathan's favorite students. Both of them looked his way and smiled. Even though he had always tried to discipline himself against the folly of having favorites in the classroom, it was hard not to be partial to these two, different though they were in age and temperament.

Maggie MacAuley, with her riot of fiery copper hair and sharp little chin, was probably the brightest child in the one-room schoolhouse. The girl was unfailingly cheerful; her quick, eager smile would have melted the ice under Dunbar's mill in mid-January. Moreover, she had a keen wit, an insatiable curiosity, and a hunger to learn that challenged even Jonathan's love of teaching.

Maggie's parents were Irish immigrants, the family as poor as any other in town. Even so, Maggie and her two older sisters were invariably dressed in clean feed-sack pinafores, and the parts in their neatly combed hair appeared to have been cut with a straightedge.

Jonathan knew the MacAuleys to be good, principled people who did the best they could with the little they had. Maggie's father, Matthew MacAuley, was a leader of sorts among the miners—a man others respected and heeded, a man from whom his coworkers were likely to seek counsel.

It seemed to Jonathan that Maggie was very much her father's daughter. Possessed of a generous heart and a fiercely loyal nature, she could be counted on to help look after the younger children in the classroom and come to their aid whenever needed. She also exhibited a measure of common sense rarely encountered in one so young, a trait that more than once had led Jonathan to entrust her with considerable responsibility.

Yes, he was fairly certain that Matthew MacAuley's daughter was, like her father, a natural leader.

But not for a minute did he believe she was a thief.

As for poor little Summer Rankin, Jonathan's heart ached for the child, whose frailty seemed even more stark when reflected in the glow of Maggie's vitality. He found it absurd, and somehow obscene, to consider this small girl even remotely capable of wrongdoing.

Summer was a mere wisp of a child—a tiny, fragile creature whose white-blond hair and pale skin would have given her an almost spectral appearance had it not been for the angry flush of fever that more often than not blotched her hollowed cheeks. Jonathan had it from Dr. Woodbridge that the girl had a rheumatic heart and failing lungs. Of late, she was out of school more than she was in, and even on the days she was present, a distracted, distant stare glazed her eyes, causing Jonathan to wonder just how aware she really was of her surroundings.

Nine years old, Summer lived midway up the Hill in a rough-hewn cabin crammed with people, both children and adults. Jonathan almost always came away from his visits to the Rankin home feeling somewhat dazed by the number of family members who seemed to inhabit that cramped, raucous dwelling. Aging grandparents, aunts and uncles, and three of Summer's siblings—all under the age of six—lived there. It struck him as truly remarkable that a delicate, dreamy child like Summer could exist in such shabby bedlam, albeit an apparently *happy* bedlam.

For a time, until he had come to know both children better, Jonathan had puzzled over the bond between Summer Rankin and Maggie MacAuley. The twelve-year-old Maggie was as strong and self-assured as Summer was frail and shy.

While Maggie preferred rousing stories of adventure and sensible, precise lesson assignments, Summer responded mostly to art and music. In fact, this fey child was the only one of Jonathan's students he had ever allowed to touch his silver flute. A shyly whispered plea in the fall of the year had moved Jonathan to comply, even to demonstrate the basic rudiments of technique. To his amazement, within minutes Summer had managed to evoke a simple but plaintive folk melody he'd played for the class upon occasion.

But that had been months ago. These days, the girl had neither the breath nor the energy to play. Indeed, Jonathan suspected that most of Summer's strength now had to be conserved for the mere effort of existence.

A condition which he was beginning to understand all too well...

He watched the child take her seat, his throat tightening as she smiled up at Maggie MacAuley, who bent over the desk to button the top of Summer's sweater before scooting in behind her own desk. Maggie was fiercely protective of her ailing little friend. Even those inclined to bully the younger children were reluctant to incur Maggie's wrath by teasing or otherwise harassing Summer.

The weight pressing on his heart squeezed even harder as Jonathan questioned just how much longer Maggie's young friend would *need* her protection. He could almost see the girl failing. He wondered if Maggie saw it too, and he rather hoped she did. Otherwise, it would only go harder for her when she had to face the truth.

One after another the children slipped into their seats, Jonathan dismissing each as a potential thief with little more than a glance. These children were better than that. Other than Billy Macken and Orrin Gaffney, he couldn't believe any one of them was capable of deliberate treachery—or cruelty. For surely it might have been cruelty that motivated the theft. As much as he tried to avoid the thought, there was always the possibility that the flute hadn't been stolen for its monetary value at all, but rather to deliver a personal wound to him.

In that event, the offender would be someone with a grudge against him or, at the very least, someone who disliked him intensely. Was it possible that one of the children—*his* children—could actually bear such animosity toward him without his knowing?

Billy Macken now walked back into the schoolroom, and Jonathan's eyes went from him to Orrin Gaffney. Was it possible?

While the very idea appalled him, Jonathan wasn't in the least ignorant of human nature's capacity for meanness or duplicity. His years of association with children and their families had introduced him to a dismaying range of cruelties, of which both the young and their elders were capable. He had lost his youthful naïveté and much of his earlier belief in the innate goodness of man some time ago.

Yet with all their faults, these children were like family to him. Indeed, he loved them almost as much as if they were his family, in no small part because he had recognized their need for love and attention.

Much of the time, even the two troublemakers, Billy and his chum, Orrin, could evoke an aching compassion in him. He made a determined effort to dismiss his suspicion of the two. He mustn't judge them without evidence. Who could say what motivated their rebellious behavior, aggression, and spitefulness? Certainly, they shared the same needs and the same deprivations as any of the other students in his schoolroom.

It hadn't taken Jonathan long to realize that the children of Skingle Creek had known little in the way of affection or gentleness in their young lives. Nor had they been exposed to much in the way of beauty or the arts. This dark cavern of a town, carved from the bottom side of a mountain, seemed to exist in the shadows. If the coal dust from the mines hadn't smudged the face of the entire community, the lowering gloom from the surrounding hills would have. It was a gray, hopeless place in which to live, and sooner or later, many of those within its confines became a gray, hopeless people.

Survival seemed the only real ambition of the town's residents, their only visible achievement. Many were uneducated, even illiterate. The men—and most of their sons—broke their backs and punished their lungs by hammering and picking away in the bowels of the earth. They seldom saw daylight except on Sunday, going belowground before dawn and emerging, half-blind and hunched, well after sundown.

Although they created small joys wherever and whenever they could, for the most part mining families seemed to live grim, even bitter lives, from which escape was virtually impossible. The mining company had structured a brilliantly ruthless system that worked entirely to the company's advantage.

It was a system that bordered on enslavement. Not only did the company own the store that represented the miners' only source of food and clothing, but they also provided the only clinic where medical treatment could be obtained. They even owned the building that presently housed the school.

The truth was that the company owned the town.

And, for all intents and purposes, the miners themselves.

Two

The Collection

I set my face to the road here before me..

Padraic Pearse

A month after the silver flute turned up missing, Maggie MacAuley decided that something had to be done about Mr. Stuart.

He looked as thin as one of the racing dogs Garth Miller kept down in his barn. Only the day before, Lily Woodbridge had said he looked "faded," and though Maggie disliked agreeing with anything Lily said, she would have been hard-pressed to argue.

Indeed, Mr. Stuart was beginning to remind her of her mother's good Sunday tablecloth, which at one time had been bright and colorful, with mouthwatering pictures of loaves of bread and blue milk jugs on it. Now it was faded from so many launderings that it had hardly any color left to it. Ever since Lily's remark, Maggie would sometimes find herself gripped by the fanciful thought that when she looked up from her books she might find Mr. Stuart gone, faded away like the designs on that tablecloth.

He was terrible quiet these days—so quiet that sometimes they almost forgot he was even in the schoolroom. He was still strict with the lessons, still gave them proper instructions, but more and more often now he allowed them to work by themselves instead of holding what he called "class discussions."

Of late he was so...distant...that he didn't even seem to notice when the pesky Crawford twins or Billy Macken and Orrin Gaffney acted up. If they became too rambunctious, he would just look at them with his sad, tired eyes, and pretty soon Dinah and Duril would cease their mischief, as if they knew their teacher didn't have the strength to settle them down. Billy and Orrin, of course, only pretended to behave. As soon as Mr. Stuart turned his back, they started up with their mischief again.

He was like a man who was drifting away from himself, leaving only a shadow behind to keep order in the schoolroom.

Maggie was determined to find a way to help the teacher be himself again, to make things in their school the way they used to be. But an unsettled feeling in the pit of her stomach told her she'd better be doing something soon or it would be too late.

It snowed most of the morning, so Maggie and the other children had to stay inside for lunch. But early in the afternoon the sky cleared, and Mr. Stuart sent them outside to take some fresh air. Now everyone was standing around the school yard, their breath spiraling up like the smoke from the coal chimneys that fogged the town.

"We have to do something about Mr. Stuart," Maggie said, tugging her knitted gloves up over her wrists as far as they would go.

Summer Rankin bobbed her head up and down, puffing her fair hair into a halo around her cap. "Mr. Stuart is bad sick." She started to add something more, but instead broke into a fit of coughing. These days it seemed that Summer was nearly always coughing.

"It's his heart," said Lily, her face pinched in a wise-old-owl expression. "My daddy said he could tell from just looking at him that his heart is bad."

As the daughter of Skingle Creek's only doctor, Lily offered every comment as though the entire town had been holding its breath, just waiting to hear from her. Maggie had heard *her* da say that Lebreen Woodbridge was "little more than a quack" and probably ought not to be doctoring even hogs or chickens, but Lily took on as though the man made house calls on the governor himself.

Never one to tolerate Lily's airs, Maggie offered her own observation on Mr. Stuart's state of health. "His heart is *broken,*" she said, ignoring Lily's sour look. "He's that sad because he doesn't have his flute anymore. The music has gone out of him."

Junior Tyree, whose daddy was the town junkman and garbage hauler, dug the toe of his shoe at a rock embedded in the ground. Junior's people were the only black folks in Skingle Creek, and as a rule he didn't have much to say about anything that went on—which was just as well, since some folks probably wouldn't have paid him any mind. To Maggie's way of thinking, however, Junior showed more sense than lots of the white people in town. She for one had learned to pay attention on those rare occasions when Junior volunteered an opinion, which he looked about to do.

"He's gonna leave," said Junior, studying his foot as he went on raking the toe of his already scuffed shoe on the rock. "Teacher won't be staying around here much longer. He prob'ly thinks one of us took his flute."

That remark just about made Maggie take back her opinion of Junior's good sense. "Don't talk crazy, Junior Tyree! Mr. Stuart would not think any such thing. He knows we wouldn't steal his flute."

Junior looked up, his dark brown eyes squinting at Maggie. Junior always squinted, for though he could scarcely see the tip of his own nose, he was either too poor or too proud to wear spectacles. Maggie figured him to be too poor. Indeed, of them all, it seemed that Kenny Tallman was the only one who could afford eyeglasses.

"How you figure?" said Junior. "Who else is he gonna think done it 'sides one of us?"

His statement brought on an angry buzz from the others. "You better just hush, Junior Tyree!" Lily Woodbridge pushed up to Junior, hands on her hips, blond sausage curls wagging. "You don't know anything!"

Her eyes narrowed. "Or maybe you do. Maybe it was *you* who stole Mr. Stuart's flute, and that's why you're so sure he suspects one of us."

"Oh, be quiet, Lily," Maggie muttered.

Junior might have said a dumb thing, but he wouldn't have stolen Mr. Stuart's flute, and Lily knew that just as well as anyone. Junior was just like his daddy, Ezra, and didn't Da always say you could trade Ezra Tyree's word for gold, he was that honest?

"It seems to me that we need to be working out a plan to help Mr. Stuart instead of standing here quarreling at one another," she said pointedly.

She looked at the others—first Summer and then Lily, Lester, and Kenny. The problem was too big for the lot of them, she knew. But her mother always maintained that you had to start where you were or you'd never get anywhere at all.

That being the case, Maggie took a deep breath and proceeded to speak her mind.

"I've been thinking," she said, waiting until the others quieted before going on. "We can all of us see that Mr. Stuart is ailing bad. He's always been peaked, but he's even more sickly since his flute went missing. If we could just have found that flute, he might be feeling better by now, or at least not any worse."

"But we *didn't* find it," Kenny Tallman pointed out.

Maggie shot him an impatient look. "Like we don't *know* that?"

Kenny pushed up his eyeglasses a little higher on the bridge of his nose. "Well, I just mean it's not as if we didn't try. We looked everywhere we could think of."

"So then," Maggie said, "it occurs to me we might want to replace the flute."

She might as well have announced that they were going to blow up Dredd's Mountain with a firecracker, the way they were all staring at her.

"Listen now," she said in a rush, "Mr. Stuart's birthday is coming up. December 22, remember? That's almost Christmas. I was thinking that somehow we might give him a birthday present *and* a Christmas gift." She paused and then added, drawing out the words to emphasize them: "A...brand...new...flute."

They gaped at her as if she'd lost her wits entirely.

But Maggie wasn't about to give them a chance to start arguing. "Losing the flute has got a lot to do with Mr. Stuart's misery, don't you see? Isn't he always talking about how important music is? Remember last spring, when we were practicing the songs for the Easter program, how he said he wouldn't even like to think about life without music?"

Now two or three began to nod, and Kenny Tallman again spoke up. "He said he reckoned music is to the soul like food is to the body."

"I recollect what he told us that one time," Summer Rankin ventured softly, "after he played that song about Kathleen... Kathleen..."

"Kathleen Mavourneen," Maggie finished for her.

Summer nodded. "He said music is like the voice of the heart."

Some of the others exchanged looks, but no one said anything until Junior Tyree spoke up. "Mr. Stuart, he said he figured music was p'urt near in-inde*pen*sable."

"Indis*pen*sable," Kenny corrected promptly.

"Yeah," said Junior.

They were quiet for a time, thinking their own thoughts.

"A silver flute must cost an awful lot of money, I expect." Summer broke the silence and then coughed.

Maggie hunched her own shoulders against the sound. These days when Summer coughed, it sounded like crockery breaking somewhere deep down inside of her.

"How much, do you figure?" asked Junior Tyree.

Summer shook her head, her hand still covering her mouth as the cough subsided.

"A *fortune*, I bet," Lily declared with a dramatic roll of her eyes. "Probably thousands of dollars."

"Maybe not *thousands*," Kenny Tallman said, frowning behind his thick spectacles. "But a lot."

"How much is a lot?" Maggie asked, interested only in facts, not guesswork.

Kenny twisted his mouth to one side, thinking. Maggie knew she could depend on his answer. Kenny might be peculiar-like, kind of nervous and fidgety much of the time, but he was smart all the same. Real smart, especially when it came to money.

Maybe because he was one of the few in Skingle Creek who even knew what money looked like. Kenny and the hoity-toity Lily Woodbridge.

"A new flute like the other one," Lily put in, "would cost at least a thousand dollars."

Maggie found little encouragement in the fact that Lily had lowered her earlier judgment of *thousands* of dollars.

As if he'd read her mind, Junior Tyree piped in. "Might just as *well* be thousands for all the chance we got of comin' up with that kind of money."

Kenny Tallman looked at Lily with a frown. "What do you know about the price of flutes?" he said.

"I *know,*" Lily drawled, propping her hands on her hips and eyeballing Kenny as if daring him to question her further.

As usual, Kenny was too smart to egg Lily on. Instead, he just shook his head and turned to Maggie. "Most likely, a special flute like Mr. Stuart's would cost hundreds of dollars at least."

Maggie pulled a face, her mind running ahead. "Well, it seems to me the thing to do is find out exactly how much we *can* come up with. Kenny, you and Lily and Junior go talk to the older crowd over by the pump."

Maggie wasn't about to approach the older students. Her sisters, Nell Frances and Eva Grace, were always hanging out with this group, and lately they thought they were too important to give Maggie or anyone else the time of day. Besides, Billy Macken and his buddy Orrin were over there too. Maggie kept out of their way as much as possible.

"Me and Summer—Summer and *I*—will go see what the others think."

She stopped, glancing at Lester Monk, who hadn't said a word but was clearly expecting to be included. "Lester," she said with a sigh, "you come with us. We'll ask the Crawfords and Sammy Ray Boyle how much they can give."

"The Crawfords ain't going to have nothing to give," Junior said. "They don't even bring their lunch pails anymore, not since their daddy broke his leg in the mine."

Maggie had forgotten about the Crawford twins' bad luck. Not that she had much sympathy to spend on those two. Duril and Dinah Crawford were just about the biggest nuisances in school. Duril could be downright spiteful sometimes, and Dinah wasn't much better. Still, they were Mr. Stuart's students just like all the rest of them, so they ought to be included.

"Well, ask them anyway," she said. "We need to ask everyone. Lester, go and find us a jar. There ought to be one in the supply pantry. Look on the shelf with the paper and paints."

Lester grinned big, as if pleased to be useful, but he quickly turned sober. "What if Mr. Stuart sees me?"

Maggie waved off his concern. "Just tell him we need it for outside. He won't care. And get a *big* jar, you hear?"

"I'll ask my mama and daddy to help," Lily volunteered as Lester took off at a run. "I'm sure they'll want to *contribute.*"

Maggie looked at Summer and rolled her eyes at Lily's big word, but she held her tongue. Meanwhile, Kenny Tallman nodded in a way that told Maggie he would ask his daddy for help too.

Silently, Maggie began to tick off the possibilities if all the grown-ups were to make a donation, and her spirits brightened considerably. Not that she or any of the others could expect much from home, of course. Only Kenny and Lily had parents who could afford to part with their money. But she was almost certain that her older sisters would give something from their egg fund, and maybe she could even convince her da to put in a little.

As for herself, she had saved almost five dollars from cleaning the Carlee sisters' house every other Saturday over the past few months. She tried not to think about the fact that she had been saving her wages for Christmas.

Besides, she had already bought Summer's gift—a scarlet hair ribbon for her friend's "angel hair." She could hand make her other gifts as she had in the past. A new flute for Mr. Stuart was more important than store-bought Christmas presents.

Every little bit would help, so she must do her part. If everyone chipped in something—why, there was no telling how much they might end up with!

Their first attempt at a collection was not a huge success, but neither was it a total failure. The problem was that scarcely anyone had any money, except for Lily Woodbridge and Kenny Tallman. Miners were paid largely in the paper scrip that could then be traded at the company store for goods. But it wasn't of much use for a collection.

Lily, of course, made a great show of unknotting her handkerchief and putting in "what little she happened to have"—which turned out to be only ten cents! Kenny, however, had seventy-five cents, of which he kept only fifteen and put the rest in the jar, promising to bring more the next day.

The older students hadn't been much more help than the younger ones, but at least everyone had put in a little something. Everyone except for Billy and Orrin, who claimed the collection was a dumb idea and refused to give a cent. Duril and Dinah made light of it too, but everybody knew they didn't have anything to give. Maggie thought the least they could have done, though, was to keep their ignorant remarks to themselves.

She consoled herself with the thought that everyone had agreed to go home and ask their parents for help, so by next week there ought to be more money for the jar.

"So, then—that's what we'll all do," announced Lily Woodbridge right after school let out. "As soon as we get home, we'll ask our parents to contribute. *Some* of us," she said with deliberate emphasis, "should be able to bring in more in a few days."

The look she angled at Maggie seemed to imply that this would almost certainly not be the case with the students whose fathers worked in the mines.

Maggie squirmed a little, acknowledging to herself that Lily was probably right.

Da had all he could do—and didn't he remind them of it often enough?—just to keep food on the table for them. Maggie feared she already knew how he would react to the idea of putting money in a jar for a musical instrument.

Still, she had to ask. This was her idea, after all, and everyone else was going to try, so she must do her part too. But after she said goodbye to Summer at the foot of the Hill and turned toward home, she began to pray mightily that she wouldn't be one of the few whose folks couldn't—or wouldn't—contribute.

Three

Waiting for Matthew

A copper-skinned six-footer,
Hewn out of the rock...

Joseph Campbell

Eva Grace! Nell Frances! Come give me a hand now!"

Kate MacAuley balanced the baby on her hip as she set the table. Wee Ray was teething and fussy, and earlier she had nearly let the pot of potatoes cook dry while she tried to distract him from his sore gums.

The girls walked into the kitchen, and she handed the cross little tyke to Eva Grace to feed, and then she sent Nell Frances to the wash-room with the towels she'd heated in the oven for Matthew and a bar of new soap. "Mind you don't forget to put the old soap scraps in the bucket," she told Nell Frances.

Matthew claimed he was the only miner in Skingle Creek whose wife heated his bath towels in the winter, but of course that wasn't so. Kate happened to know that she wasn't the only woman in town who indulged her man, though to her way of thinking Matthew MacAuley might deserve the extra attention more than most.

Now that the baby was out of her arms and wouldn't be chilled, she went to open the kitchen door. The damp November evening was quiet and tinged with the odor of wood smoke and the more acrid smell of burning coal. Most of the morning's snow had melted off, but the porch steps were still coated with a dusting of white.

As Kate stood listening, the whistle from the mines sounded. She drew a breath of relief and silently gave thanks for another day of no cave-ins, no explosions, and then she closed the door and turned back to the kitchen. Matthew would be home soon, looking for his supper, and she still had the biscuits to flour.

As she worked at the stove, she glanced back now and then, watching Eva Grace, their oldest at fifteen years, dandle their youngest—nearly fifteen months—on her knee. Every so often the girl managed to get a spoonful of potatoes in her little brother's mouth.

"As soon as he's finished, change his didy and put him in his chair so you can help me. Your da will be tired."

"Da is always tired," the girl said, her tone careless.

Kate turned. "And I suppose you would *not* be tired, then," she snapped, "working under the ground for twelve hours a day, six days a week?"

Without looking at her mother, Eva Grace spooned another bite of food into Baby Ray's mouth. Then she pushed his bowl aside and got to her feet, tucking her brother into the crook of her arm. "I didn't mean anything," she said.

"Then mind your tongue."

After the girl left the room with the baby, Kate looked over her kitchen. The biscuits waited to be baked, the potatoes were done, the bacon frying.

A good meal.

It wasn't always so.

Again she went to the door and stepped outside, this time as much to watch for Maggie as for Matthew. Ferguson had asked the girl to work an extra hour at the company store tonight. Kate didn't like the child coming home after dark. But they needed the little money Maggie could add to the jar each week.

After another moment she saw the rows of flickering lights moving down the Hill from the mines, the lamps on the miners' caps appearing like a wave of lightning bugs.

But still no sign of Maggie.

Trying not to worry, Kate went back inside. By the time the bacon had crisped and the girls had returned to the kitchen, she heard Maggie running up the steps to the kitchen door and then stamping her feet dry. At the same time, the door to the washroom off the kitchen slammed shut, signaling Matthew's return.

Kate expelled a long breath of satisfaction. Her family was home.

Maggie had watched her da closely when he first arrived home, his face black with coal dust from the day's work in the mines. He was weary as always but did not seem overly cross. Even so, she would keep her silence until he came in from the washroom, scrubbed and wearing his after-work overalls. Perhaps she would even wait until after supper. His mood often brightened after he'd had his meal.

She helped to clear the table without being asked, which brought a quirk of her mother's eyebrow. Then she sat, trying not to squirm as Da drank the last of his tea.

Finally, Maggie could wait no longer. She wiped her hands down the sides of her skirt and cleared her throat. "Da? I was wanting to ask—" The words came spilling out in a rush, like marbles shaken from a sack.

Her sisters looked up, and Maggie hesitated, but only for a second or two. "Mr. Stuart's students are taking up a collection, you see."

Now it was her da who lifted an eyebrow, though he remained silent.

"For a new flute," Maggie hurried on, "to replace the one that was stolen—you remember, don't you? We're all of us asking our parents for help."

Her father said nothing. He merely pushed his empty plate a bit farther away from the edge of the table.

Maggie swallowed. "So, then, do you think you could give something for the collection?"

Her father turned a long, silent look on her. Maggie held her breath, aware that her mother was looking on with a troubled gaze.

"A collection, is it?" Da's face was pinched with the beginning of a scowl.

A gnawing took up in Maggie's stomach, but she managed to nod and smile.

He continued to stare at her. "Are you daft entirely, girl? When it's all I can do to feed the lot of you, you would ask for money for such foolishness?"

The angry red stain creeping up his neck should have warned Maggie to back off, but instead she hurried to explain, to make him understand. "But it's not foolishness, Da!" she blurted out. "Not at all. Mr. Stuart is sick and getting sicker since his silver flute was stolen. We only want to help by giving him back his music, don't you see?"

"What I *see*," her father said, his voice a low rumble, "is that your Mr. Stuart has apparently taught you nothing at all in the way of common sense!"

"Matthew—"

Maggie shot a hopeful look at her mother, but Da seemed bent on ignoring them both.

Maggie was not exactly afraid of her da. He never switched his children, as did some of the other fathers. But he was a big man, and with his unruly copper hair and dark red beard, he seemed terrible fierce when he was in a temper.

Even so, Maggie found his anger less wounding than his contempt. At the moment he was looking at her as if he might be raising himself a fool, and Maggie had all she could do to hold back the tears scalding her eyes.

She glanced at Eva Grace and then at Nell Frances for some sign of support, but neither met her gaze. Instead, they sat like two great lumps, staring down at their hands as if they had suddenly taken to growing claws.

Clearly, there would be no help from her older sisters.

She summoned what remained of her confidence, balling her fists at her sides and biting at her lower lip. "Please, Da, won't you just let me tell you about it? Everyone has pledged to bring what they can. I'll be putting in a part of my cleaning wages, and sure, Nell Frances and Eva Grace want to help with some of their egg money. But the only way we can hope to raise what we need is if the parents give too."

She had her sisters' attention now, all right. She could feel the two of them glaring at her. As for her mother, she had gone still as a stone.

Red-faced, Da looked from Maggie to her sisters, his big fists knotted on the table in front of him. "Now you listen to me, you girls, and you hear what I'm saying! This family has no money to give away."

He leaned forward, his eyes hard. "We all work at this house, except for Baby Ray, whose turn will come soon enough. We work to keep a roof over our heads and clothes on our back and food in the pantry. I expect if one our neighbors were hungry, we would give him bread enough to keep him from starving, but if I ever hear of any one of you wasting this family's hard-earned money on such folly as you've spoken of tonight, you'll sore regret it, and don't think you won't! I don't go breaking my back in the mines so my children can throw my wages out like garbage."

It was all Maggie could do to utter a word without strangling. Still, she risked his wrath with one more attempt. "Please, Da—it *wouldn't* be throwing money away! We only want to help Mr. Stuart!"

Her father banged one fist on the table. They all jumped, and from his high chair Baby Ray began to whimper.

"I'll see Margaret Ann by herself!" Da said, his tone sharp as he stood. "The rest of you tend to your lessons."

Maggie shriveled inside as her mother took Baby Ray from his chair and gave a nod to Eva Grace and Nell Frances, who followed her from the room. She was in for it now. Da hadn't called her Margaret Ann since last summer, when, in a frenzy to get away from a black snake, she'd accidentally sent several jars of green beans crashing from the shelves in the fruit cellar.

She sat as still as light, her face burning as if scorched by an iron, while her da stood watching her, his big arms crossed over his chest. Maggie waited for him to launch into one of what Eva Grace called his "word whippings." His face was a thundercloud, and he looked to be working up steam for a fierce scolding.

Maggie braced herself, gripping the sides of her chair, trying to swallow down the lump in her throat so she wouldn't shame herself by breaking into tears. But the tongue-lashing for which she tried to steel herself was slow in coming. Indeed, Da was keeping silent for an unusually long time, though his hard look never wavered.

"All right now, girl," he finally said, leaning over and planting both hands on the tabletop. "I think you had best tell me what this is about, for I'd be willing to wager that you're the one behind this business of a collection."

To Maggie's surprise—and great relief—his tone, while stern, no longer sounded angry. Did he mean to hear her out, then, instead of giving her a blistering "piece of his mind," as he was wont to do when riled?

Her hopes lifted a bit, and she took a deep breath. Perhaps, if she could make him understand just how desperate the situation was with Mr. Stuart, he might relent.

She chose her words with great care, telling him about the students' concern for Mr. Stuart. How he had changed, how he looked to be failing, how the loss of his treasured flute seemed to have broken something inside him and was draining the very life from him.

As she spoke, her da slipped quietly onto the chair across from her. He made no attempt to interrupt, but instead he sat ever so still as she went on.

Maggie explained that they had conducted a thorough search for the missing flute, but despite their best efforts they had turned up nothing except for chilblains and briar scratches. She also, with some reluctance, admitted to being the one who had initiated the idea for a collection.

"Don't you see, Da," she fairly pleaded as she finished her account, "we mustn't lose Mr. Stuart. We *need* him. All of us need him."

Da appeared to be thinking. For a long time he simply sat in silence, staring at his hands. Finally, he gave a heavy sigh and looked up. "Maggie, Maggie," he said, shaking his head. "I know you think me a hard man."

He waved away her attempt to protest. "You think me hard, and perhaps I am. But in this case, I'd be the first to agree that your Mr. Stuart deserves far better than he got. He is known to be a good man and a fine schoolmaster, and he is to be commended for his hard work with you and the other children. 'Tis a shame, a sorry shame, what was done to him, and may God have mercy on the black soul of the one who robbed the man. But don't you understand, girl?"

Maggie marveled at the softening of her father's face. To see him like this was such a rare thing that it was unnerving, to say the least.

"The poor man was not well even before this despicable theft, lass. Why, it's clear to everyone with eyes in their head that your Mr. Stuart is in very poor health, and he has been for some time."

Maggie flinched, wanting to argue the point even as something cold breathed through her at his words.

As if he had read her thoughts, Da raised a hand to silence her. "Listen to me, now, Maggie. Your teacher was poorly when he first came to us, and he has shown signs of failing ever since, though to give the man his due, he puts on a brave show of things. But he is exceedingly ill, lass. And the time has come for you and the other children to accept what cannot be changed. Even if by some miracle—and a miracle is what it would take—you managed to collect money enough to replace his stolen flute, I doubt the poor man would have the strength or the breath to play it."

Maggie fought to reject what he was saying, but she floundered as her own doubts began to gnaw at her.

Watching her father, Maggie saw that he no longer looked cross. Not a bit. To the contrary, the expression that had settled over his strong features was grave indeed.

"Ah, Maggie," he said now, his voice uncommonly gentle, "you must face things as they are, lass. There is no more music in the schoolmaster. Mr. Stuart is in a bad way. A dozen silver flutes wouldn't save the man now."

The tears Maggie had been choking back finally escaped. She heaved a sob and made to rise from her chair. But her father reached across the table to stop her. "Now, that's the truth of it, Maggie, and you must accept it for once and for all."

He held on to her hand, studied her, and then he added, "Even so, girl, your heart is right to want to help, and if I had an extra coin to spare, I would give it to you here and now. But there is naught, Maggie, don't you see? There is not a bit of money to spare. There never is. We're a fine, big family, and it takes everything we can earn just to make ends meet. I cannot—I *will* not—take food from my children's mouths to buy a flute for a dying man. A father cannot do such a thing, girl, and you must not ask it of me again."

Maggie knew he spoke the truth as he saw it. And hadn't she known all along the response she should expect? But hadn't she also heard her mother say, and say it often, that on occasion God had been known to do wondrous things entirely? She had allowed herself to hope that this would be one of those occasions.

Da patted her hand then, as if to comfort her. At least he had been kind and had not mocked her. Maggie couldn't remember a time when he had been so careful with her, so gentle with her feelings.

Because of this rare display of tenderness, she, too, softened. And because she somehow sensed that he was waiting for a word from her, she managed to tell him that she understood. "I expect what you say is true, Da. But I thank you for hearing me out."

He studied her for a moment before looking away. "Well...that's fine, then. That's fine."

He paused, and when he spoke again his tone returned to its more familiar gruffness. "Mind, if you can find an odd job or two in addition to your work for the Carlee ladies, you're free to use whatever you earn for your collection. But you're not to be neglecting your schoolwork nor your chores here at home."

As Maggie met her father's gaze, she was suddenly struck by the oddest feeling that he was the one who needed comforting, not herself. But Da was not a man to admit his feelings, and since Maggie could think of nothing more to say, she got up, said goodnight, and turned to leave the room.

She glanced back at Da and almost thought she saw a glimpse of the same sorrowful expression in his eyes that she had seen of late in Mr. Stuart's.

Four

A Jar of Wishes

Wish for a little or wish for a lot,
But always give thanks for the good things you've got.
The Wee Book of Irish Wisdom

Long after Maggie had gone, Matthew sat staring after her, thinking. Exhaustion dug deep into his bones, and his bad arm ached with a vengeance.

They don't know, he thought, *they haven't an inkling how hard it is simply to survive.*

Oh, he chided them often enough that they mustn't be wasteful, that there was no money for foolishness, nothing for "extras." The girls had no choice but to wear each other's hand-me-downs, and even wee Ray was clothed in the baby dresses and gowns his older sisters had once worn. Their house—the *company's* house—was furnished with odds and ends of furniture, none of which matched. Their food was simple fare: potatoes and beans and an occasional rasher of bacon or a chicken in the pot.

He raked a hand down his beard, and then he extended his arms in front of him and sat staring at his hands. The nails and creases of his knuckles were smudged with coal dust that would never completely wash away, his fingers thick and somewhat bent from years of picking slate or wielding a shovel.

Kate understood, of course. She knew as well as he that they lived from one payday to the next with only the smallest wad put by and with so much on tick at the store that they were never paid up in full. But even Kate didn't know that he lived in fear of some fool accident that could put him down for weeks or even longer, and then what would they do?

The other men never came out and said so, but Matthew knew they pitied him, having a household of women to support with the only male child still a wee tyke. Had his offspring been sons, they'd have been working the mines with him by now, adding their wages to his own.

That thought alone banished any regret he might have had for his lack of sons. He would not wish a life in the mines for any one of his children, and that was the truth. Moreover, he would do everything in his power to make certain his *only* son never had to go underground to make a living.

No doubt he was, if not entirely alone, at least one of very few to think this way. Most of the other men held that the more sons they had, the better, and they drummed it into the young boys' heads that there was no more noble or manly work. Many of the lads could scarcely wait to follow their das into the mines.

While Matthew prided himself on a good day's work, a job well done, he still hoped for something better for his boy. An easier life, a life of education and opportunity.

For himself, he had wanted nothing so much as a piece of his own land to farm. It seemed to him that if ever there was an occupation a man could wear like a badge of honor, it would be to farm the land.

But that was a young man's dream, a dream that was dying fast, for he was no longer young—and there was no land of his own in sight, not even a possibility.

It would seem that his Maker had consigned him to the mines for all time. And so long as he could provide for his family, it was a good enough life, he supposed. True, there were days when he groaned at the blast of the breaker whistle when it sounded long before dawn, dreaded the long trek down the road in the dark, knowing he would not see daylight again until the next Sunday came round.

But more than the long hours spent in the gloomy darkness several hundred feet belowground, and more than the choking dust and smoke and constant backache, what he disliked most about his job was that, as a foreman, he was responsible for the health and safety of the rest of the men. And boys. Boys who, for the most part, disdained an education. Boys who couldn't wait to go into the mines and stay there for the rest of their lives. The majority put their schooling behind them by the time they were nine or ten years of age, if not sooner.

Some of the lads—the breaker boys, especially—were little more than babes. Taddy Maguire and the little Pippino boy, neither no more than eight or nine, had been in the breakers for a good six months by now.

It was all too easy for families to get around the law that prohibited children under twelve from working the mines. A father would simply fill in the required age, pay the certificate fee, and his son was from that moment "employed" by the company.

Hard as it was to look after the safety of grown men, it was nigh impossible to protect the young'uns, who were often sleepy and frightened and careless.

Yet Matthew knew himself to be a good foreman, in part, he supposed, because he held few of the resident fears and superstitions common to many who worked belowground. He didn't spook easily, and he was big enough to haul a man out of trouble when need be.

The job had its advantages. He'd rather be the one doing the looking after than the one being looked after, and that was the truth. At least he was sober when he was on the job, and that was more than could be said for some of the men. And the foreman's wage had helped him to keep Kate and the children out of one of those "doublehouses," where the rooms were small as privies and the walls between the two families were paper-thin.

He scarcely noticed when Kate returned to the kitchen, so deep was he into his own thoughts. He looked up, and she rested a hand on his shoulder for a moment before proceeding to clear the table. When Matthew rose to help her, she shook her head.

"Sit and talk to me while the children are quiet."

Matthew watched her, taking in her easy, fluid movements. She was still slender as a girl, her waist not much thicker than when they'd wed nineteen years past. As always, her long reddish-blond hair—Kate's sister, Vivienne, called it "strawberry blond"—was fastened neatly at the nape of her neck with a piece of ribbon, a few strands of curl falling softly over her ears.

She was small, Kate was, a mere wisp of a woman. The top of her head scarcely reached his shoulder, and her hands were almost as dainty as a child's. But those soft blue eyes of hers could catch fire quickly enough when she was riled, all right, and her tongue was ready with a quick scalding if one of the girls—or himself—tried her temper past the boiling point.

As if she'd felt him watching her, she turned, and Matthew motioned her to him. She gave him a look but ventured over.

"The children will be wanting the table to do their lessons," she said.

"The children can wait a bit." He pulled her down onto his lap. "Besides, other than Maggie, when have those girls ever been in a hurry to do their schoolwork?"

Kate studied him, smoothing his forehead with her hand, much as she might have touched one of the children. "You look tired."

"A bit," he said, tracing the band of freckles over her nose with one finger and then running a hand down her back. She was so slight, so slender, that for a moment he felt chilled. There wasn't enough of her to withstand a strong wind.

"Well, at least you can rest after church on Sunday," she said, still watching him.

He shook his head. "The roof needs patching before we get deeper into winter, and I need daylight to do it."

"Oh, Matthew, you're worn out. Can't it wait?"

He lifted an eyebrow. "Winter's almost here, Kate. That roof won't take another downpour, much less a heavy snow. Besides, it won't be that bad of a job. Brian Scully offered to give me a hand."

They sat in silence for another moment. Finally she said, "Is Maggie in a pout?"

Matthew shook his head. "She's disappointed, of course, but she took it well enough."

"She's so worried for Mr. Stuart. She has a terrible crush on him, you know. As do the other two."

"The girl is twelve years old!" he sputtered. "And the other two not much more."

Kate shrugged. "Eva Grace is fifteen, Matthew—and Nell Frances will be fourteen in two months. It's hardly uncommon for a young girl to fancy herself in love with the schoolmaster. It happens all the time."

Again he arched an eyebrow. "Did it happen with you, then?"

"I didn't go to school, remember? You were the only teacher I ever had. And doesn't that just answer your question? It seems I *did* fall in love with my teacher."

It was little enough he'd been able to teach her, other than how to read and do simple sums. In other words, he'd taught her all he himself had known.

He sighed. "Our girls are bright, Kate. Especially Maggie. I want them all to have a proper schooling, not like us."

She nodded. "So do I, though I fear Eva Grace will trade the books for a husband at first chance."

Matthew pulled back a little and looked at her. "Not if I have anything to say about it, she won't."

She laughed softly. "If *you* have anything to say about it, Matthew

MacAuley, none of our girls will take a husband until they're old and worn out."

"Aye, and that would be soon enough."

Again, her gaze went over him. She was still smiling as she framed his face between her hands. "You're a good father, Matthew," she said softly. "A good father. A good husband. A good *man*."

He felt his face heat at her words, but he was pleased all the same. Kate wasn't a woman to offer praise lightly.

She always seemed to know the right word to say, the right thing to do, to lift his spirits. Even when he was unaware that a lifting was needed.

"I should finish in here," she said, getting up before he could stop her. "It will be bedtime before we know it, and the girls still haven't done their schoolwork."

Matthew stretched and got to his feet. "I'll give Sadie her supper and bring in some more kindling."

He went to stand beside his wife at the sink, scooping up some of the leftover potatoes and pouring a bit of bacon grease over them.

"And you always insist that *I'm* the one after spoiling the dog," Kate remarked, eyeing the tin of greasy potatoes.

Matthew shrugged. "The dog makes herself useful. She deserves to eat."

He saw her smile to herself and elbowed her.

"Stop it now," she fussed. "Go and call the girls."

He did fancy Kate's smile. After all these years, he still worked for it, still felt the warmth of it. At times, he struggled to tell her as much but could never find the words to say what he felt without making himself out to be a great fool.

Aye, he prized her smile, all right, so long as she didn't actually laugh at him.

Not that she would. Not Kate. She was careful of everyone's feelings, including his own. Might be she was *too* careful at times, especially with the girls. She tended to be soft with them, she did.

Perhaps because no one had ever been soft with her. No one except him, she'd told him not long after they were wed. She had never heard soft words, gentle words, from anyone but him.

That would have been reason enough by itself to treat her with care. But in truth, Kate was a woman with whom a man wanted to be gentle, a woman who should never be treated with anything but tenderness.

Faith, but he was a fortunate man. Even with three bickering daughters who now came bearing down on them in the kitchen, shoving and spatting with each other, he knew himself to be a man blessed.

Though it did take a bit of reminding every now and then.

Within a few days, Maggie had made an extra fifty cents sweeping up the company store two afternoons after school and another half-dollar ironing clothes for the Carlee sisters.

Feeling exceedingly virtuous, she'd given twenty-five cents to her mother from her extra earnings and then dropped the remainder in the collection jar, with Lily Woodbridge looking on closely.

Naturally, Lily had made a great show of things when her father, Dr. Woodbridge, contributed ten whole dollars. But for once Maggie hadn't minded Lily's uppity airs. She was too grateful to see the collection growing as it was.

She had been somewhat surprised—and disappointed—when Kenny Tallman admitted that his father had scarcely listened to his explanation about the collection, only to dismiss it as "so much nonsense." He had allowed Kenny only one dollar for the collection, and that grudgingly, from the sound of it. Maggie could understand *her* father's refusal to give what they didn't have, but everyone knew that Judson Tallman, as the mine superintendent, could afford more than a dollar.

Even so, Maggie couldn't help but be encouraged. In less than a week they had collected almost twenty dollars. Of course, they still had a long way to go. Twenty dollars probably wasn't even close to what they needed.

But what about the Bible story Mr. Stuart had related to them only this week, about how Jesus had fed an entire crowd with only five loaves and two fish—and had still had twelve full baskets left over? Maggie knew that she and her friends didn't have much chance of raising anything more than what they already had, but if the Lord could multiply bread and fish, He could certainly do the same with a jar of money, couldn't He?

If nothing else, perhaps they could find a store that would take their twenty dollars as a down payment on a flute and let them pay the rest on time.

She wouldn't give up, not for a minute. She would continue to pray that God would work in one of those mysterious ways Ma was always speaking of, that He would somehow turn the money and the wishes into whatever it would take to buy a flute for Mr. Stuart.

Five

Maggie and Summer

God bless the house where friends can enter,
where little is enough for all within.
Where the hearth is warm,
as is the welcome,
where there are no strangers,
but all are kin.

Anonymous

After church on Sunday, Kate gave in to Maggie's pleas to have her friend, Summer, come for dinner. The two girls skipped ahead of the rest of the family as they walked home. Before long, though, Summer couldn't keep up because of her cough and shortness of breath, and the girls fell back to a slow walk.

"Are you sure whatever that girl has isn't catching?" Matthew said.

He stopped long enough to shift wee Ray in his arms, and Kate reached up to tug the tyke's knit cap more snugly about his ears.

"I can't think how many times you've asked me that, Matthew—and how many times I've given you the same answer," Kate said as they started walking again. "Rose Rankin says it's nothing catching. According to Dr. Woodbridge, Summer has a bad chest. Her lungs are weak, and her heart too, from the fever she had as a wee one. It's nothing we need fear for ourselves."

She paused, dropping her voice even lower. "But she'll never get any better. Only worse."

Matthew made a sound under his breath. "I'd not be trusting anything that quack has to say."

Kate sighed. Ever since Matthew had broken his arm last winter, he'd blamed Dr. Woodbridge for the pain that continued to plague him, especially in cold or rainy weather. Kate secretly suspected that if he'd gone to the doctor first thing after the accident, his arm might have healed without the stiffness. But Matthew, being who he was, had spent hours helping the other injured men out of the shaft before looking after himself. By that time, the doctor had had to make a clean break before setting the bone. The result was that Matthew might always have an aching shoulder. And Lebreen Woodbridge would always be a "quack."

She shook her head, watching Maggie and her young friend as they trudged along in front of them. Poor little Summer was as pale as a glass of bluejohn, no bigger than a willow branch, and just about as sturdy. Kate could see a noticeable decline in the child almost every time she was around her.

How was Maggie going to cope, losing her best friend *and* their teacher? The girls had been as good as inseparable for close on three years now. Maggie had taken it upon herself to look after Summer almost since they'd first crossed each other's paths at the schoolhouse. Sometimes it almost seemed that they were blood sisters, so dependent on each other had they become.

And like most of the other children, they both purely adored their Mr. Stuart.

He *was* good to the children. Anyone could see that Jonathan Stuart was a good man, a kind man who cared about the students almost as if they were his own. He was forever going out of his way to give them some extra bit of learning or bringing things into the schoolroom to make it more pleasant for the children. It seemed he was never overly stern or demanding of the students in his charge, yet if her own girls were any example, the young'uns worked extra hard to gain the teacher's favor.

What was the likelihood, Kate had wondered more than once, of a town as small and poor as Skingle Creek being blessed with such a schoolmaster?

It weighed on her heart that what had at first seemed such a blessing would only make her daughter's loss that much more difficult to bear.

After Sunday dinner, Maggie and Summer escaped to the bedroom. Perched in the middle of Maggie's bed with Sadie napping at the foot, they launched into working on their Christmas card project for their parents and Mr. Stuart.

"Making Christmas," Summer called it.

Maggie frowned at her own efforts. The Three Wise Men she'd drawn on Mr. Stuart's card looked more like a trio of grasshoppers, and the star they were following resembled nothing so much as a lopsided windmill.

She glanced over at Summer. The younger girl had cut out of white paper a lacy snowflake and was carefully gluing it on a thin piece of starched blue material, which she had earlier trimmed into a perfect square. She had already finished a card for her parents: a heavy piece of brown paper, on which she'd sketched a lighted candle and stitched its outline with red and green thread.

Again Maggie scanned her own pathetic scene before setting it down with a long sigh. "It's awful."

Summer glanced up. "It's not awful," she said, studying Maggie's picture. "It just needs a bit more work, is all. Here, let me see."

Maggie watched, fascinated by how easily Summer managed to

turn the windmill into a graceful star and then change the three grasshoppers into the Wise Men they were meant to be.

"You're going to be an artist someday," she told her friend.

Summer smiled and then coughed. After a moment, she held up a much-improved version of Maggie's drawing and examined it. "No, I'm not," she said, her voice grating from the cough. "I'm going to be a teacher. Like Mr. Stuart."

"I expect you can be both, if you want to."

"I'd like that. I'll do the artist stuff just for fun, though, when I'm not teaching."

Maggie sighed. "I wish I could find something I was good at."

Summer seemed about to protest but got caught up in a coughing fit that shook the bed. Maggie turned her head away. She hated watching her friend fight for air when these spells came upon her.

When Summer finally got her breath back, she went on with her stitching as if nothing had happened. "You're good at lots of things, Maggie," she said.

Maggie sniffed her skepticism, but Summer seemed not to notice. "You're the best speller and the best writer in school. And you're better'n any of the boys when it comes to playing toss. You're the smartest of us all too."

Maggie pulled a face. "What good's throwing a ball or out-spelling the likes of Lily Woodbridge? That doesn't mean much, I reckon."

"You can out-spell Kenny Tallman too," Summer pointed out. "And he's the smartest boy in the whole school. And you tell the best stories of anyone I know. Your stories are even better than my daddy's."

Maggie thought about that. She reckoned she did do pretty well in the storytelling department. And she liked making up tales well enough. It was also pure pleasure to beat the boys out at spelling or anything else, especially playing ball. Still, she'd rather be artistic like her friend.

Summer began to pick up her artwork. "I ought to go now," she said. "Mama don't like me out in the night air. Can I leave my cards here? If one of the young'uns gets hold of them, they'll end up all ruined."

"Why don't you stay over? Mama won't care."

Summer hesitated, but after a moment she shook her head and continued to slip her supplies into one of the old flour sacks Maggie's mother had given them. "I better not. I cough a lot at night anymore, and I'd keep you and your folks awake."

Maggie clenched her hands behind her back until they hurt. The thought of Summer coughing so hard through the night brought a knot to her own throat.

She tried to laugh. "You know you wouldn't keep me awake. I can sleep through anything."

Summer smiled at her but again shook her head. "I reckon I better go."

"Well, then, for certain you're welcome to leave your Christmas cards here."

Maggie stood on the porch, hugging her arms to herself as she watched Summer turn onto the road. The wind was up, and she was cold, but there was another coldness, a different kind of cold, someplace inside her that had nothing to do with the raw wind of the evening.

Her mother called her twice, but not until Maggie lost sight of Summer altogether did she turn and go back inside.

Six

Faced with a Painful Decision

Whate'er for Thine we do, O Lord,
We do it unto Thee.

William W. How

After two weeks Maggie figured the collection was as big as it was going to get, at least for the time being. They had a little more than twenty-five dollars, and although such an amount sounded like a fortune, she couldn't help but wonder just how far it would get them in a music store.

A conference was held in the school yard at noon on Thursday, where it was decided that the next step should be to determine the actual price of a new flute. Maggie doubted that they'd raised nearly enough money for even a down payment, but she agreed that they needed to know exactly what they were up against.

Kenny Tallman wasn't doing a blessed thing to quell her nervousness. He seemed dead set on the idea that they were too far away from their goal to expect any respectable music store owner to take them seriously.

At times Maggie wanted to box his ears. Other times she couldn't help but secretly agree with him.

Even so, no one wanted to wait until they could accumulate more money. Indeed, they all appeared to be of the same mind, that to wait much longer might mean waiting too long. Mr. Stuart wasn't looking any better, and that was the truth.

In the meantime, they agreed to search for odd jobs about town to keep money coming in for the fund. That way, Maggie pointed out, they would be able to make ongoing payments each month, should they manage to acquire a flute on credit.

Without the contrariness of the Crawford twins, who had been out of school the entire week, it was fairly easy to reach a unanimous decision on how to proceed. All they needed now was an adult who would be willing to investigate what would be required to make the purchase and settle on the necessary arrangements.

Lily immediately volunteered her father, pointing out that since he had made the largest *contribution,* it was only right that he act as their "agent." It occurred to Maggie that if Dr. Woodbridge were successful, they would most likely never hear the end of Lily's carrying-on.

On the other hand, she reckoned she could put up with Lily's blather and any number of other annoyances if the doctor managed to bring home a flute for Mr. Stuart.

When the bell rang, signaling the end of the noon hour, Maggie and the other children entered the schoolroom in a state of high excitement. She could tell that most of the others were as jittery as she. The awareness that they were a step closer to the fulfillment of their plans seemed to stoke them like a furnace.

Had Summer been there, at her desk next to Maggie's, no doubt the two of them would have giggled over their shared secret throughout the afternoon. But, like the Crawford twins, Summer had been out of school all week, her lung sickness worsened by the cold rain and sleet that had fallen during the past weekend.

Maggie was rummaging among the clutter in her desk for her spelling book when Mr. Stuart caught them off guard by rapping his pointer to get their attention. Maggie glanced up, surprised to see that instead of listing the day's spelling words on the blackboard as he usually did during lunchtime, he had written only two names: *Mrs. Hunnicutt* and *the Crawford Family.*

Maggie stared at the board, puzzling as to why their spelling words had been replaced with these two names. And what did one name have to do with the other?

The Widow Hunnicutt was a nice older lady who lived in a log cabin on the Hill not far from the Rankins. The Crawfords lived in one of the company houses nearest the tipple. So far as Maggie knew, they weren't kin.

Mr. Stuart had put the pointer down and now stood gripping the back of his chair. His knuckles were white, as if the mere act of standing required a great deal of effort.

Still, his voice was strong enough when he spoke. "We have two special requests today, class," he said. "One is for the Crawfords—Duril and Dinah's family. The other is in regard to Mrs. Alice Hunnicutt. I want to stress that in both cases the needs are urgent, and I think we should do everything we can to help."

The entire class now sat quietly in their seats, intent on the teacher's words and sensing that this afternoon was going to be different from other days.

"Pastor Wallace and Father Maguire stopped by at lunchtime with some disturbing news," Mr. Stuart continued. "It seems that the Widow Hunnicutt is very ill and has also suffered a bad fall." He paused, his expression plainly distressed.

"Apparently, she was found to be...malnourished as well."

Some of the students glanced at each other. Maggie felt really bad for Mrs. Hunnicutt, of course. The elderly widow was known to be kind, especially to children. She recalled that once, when her own mother was abed with the pneumonia, the Widow Hunnicutt had brought them a tasty pandowdy and some blackberry jam from her cellar.

Mr. Stuart stood watching them. "Do you understand what 'malnourished' means, class?"

Lily was the first to reply. "It means the Widow Hunnicutt hasn't been eating right," she said, her tone edged with a hint of disapproval.

"It means she's had nothing *to* eat." Mr. Stuart's tone was sharper than usual. He even looked a bit angry, his face stained with more color than Maggie had seen for a long time.

"More than likely, she's been without food for several days," he went on. "And her coal bin was nearly empty."

Again there were questioning glances among the students. Maggie reckoned they were all of them wondering the same thing she was. Why would anyone's coal bin be empty in a town where coal was mined every day of the week except on Sundays?

"Mrs. Hunnicutt has been taken to the hospital in Lexington for treatment," Mr. Stuart told them. "The doctors believe she'll be all right with the proper care."

For a moment he stood studying his desk as if deep in thought. "I don't know about you," he finally said, looking up, "but I felt... *ashamed* when I heard about this. Such a gracious Christian lady—one of the town's oldest residents—living in such deprived circumstances. And it seems that things are scarcely better for the Crawford family. You know that Duril and Dinah's father was injured in the mine recently?"

Everybody nodded.

"Well, there's a new baby now, and neither the child nor Mrs. Crawford is doing very well. With Mr. Crawford unable to work for who knows how long, there's no money for food and medicine."

Maggie tried hard—though it took some real effort—to feel as sorry for the Crawfords as she did for the Widow Hunnicutt. And she *did* feel bad for the family, especially knowing that the new baby and Mrs. Crawford were both poorly. But she had to offer up a hurried prayer before she could muster an equal measure of sympathy for Duril and Dinah, bossy and annoying as they were.

She turned her attention back to Mr. Stuart and was struck by how hollow-eyed and sickly he looked. But his voice was still strong as he went on.

"Mrs. Hunnicutt is completely alone, as you know, but apparently she couldn't bring herself to ask for help. If Pastor Wallace and one of the deacons hadn't called on her when they did..."

His words drifted off, his meaning unmistakable.

Maggie swallowed, unable to shut out an image of the Widow Hunnicutt, cold and hungry in her tiny house, with no one to help. Mr. Stuart's voice drew her back to the classroom.

"Pastor Wallace and Father Maguire are asking for donations to help stock both Mrs. Hunnicutt's pantry and the Crawfords'. They're also hoping to collect enough to purchase coal and help pay Mrs. Hunnicutt's hospital bill."

A sense of uneasiness began to nag at Maggie as Mr. Stuart continued to explain.

"They understand that no one has a large amount to give," he said. "The dropping prices in coal have made for a difficult year. But Mrs. Hunnicutt's situation is most desperate, and so is the Crawfords'. If the town doesn't come to their assistance, the Widow Hunnicutt could lose her house and have to go to the county home. And I can't think what will become of the Crawford family."

Maggie saw that the teacher's hands were trembling on the back of the chair. "With that in mind," he resumed, "it seems only right that we take up our own collection here at school. Naturally, we won't be able to contribute a large amount, but anything will help." He paused. "And if you're worried about using scrip, I'm sure I can work out an arrangement with Mr. Ferguson at the company store to convert the scrip to cash money."

He glanced about the room, his gaze stopping to rest on Maggie. "Would you go to the supply pantry, Maggie," he said with a smile, "and get a container for us? There should be a tray or a jar on the shelves we can use."

Maggie swallowed, and then she slowly twisted out of her seat. As she trudged down the aisle, she met a number of anxious looks from some of the other students.

She figured they were all thinking the same thing. The collection was almost sure to be a huge failure.

No one had any money left, that was the thing. Not even scrip. They had given everything they could raise to their own collection for Mr. Stuart.

A collection he knew nothing about.

The tray reached Lester Monk last, who sat staring at it for a moment before digging down into first one pocket, then the other, only to come up empty-handed and red-faced. Maggie virtually held her breath as Lester shambled up to the front with the tray in hand.

Mr. Stuart had sat down at his desk, but now he got to his feet again, smiling as Lester handed him the tray, turned, and clogged back to his desk.

It occurred to Maggie that she had never seen Lester move quite so quickly, as if he couldn't wait to get away from the teacher.

As she watched, Mr. Stuart's smile faded, his features tightening. She had known the collection would be scant, but it was worse than she'd feared. After a nerve-racking length of time, the teacher upended the tray, revealing that it was completely empty.

Maggie felt a hot surge of shame rise up in her. Mr. Stuart stood holding the empty tray in one hand while gripping the edge of his desk with the other, all the while regarding them with a look of disappointment that made Maggie wish she could shrivel up into nothing and disappear entirely.

"It seems—" The teacher cleared his throat, and then again, as if something were lodged in it. "It seems that we won't be able to help just now."

For a long time he said nothing more. Then his expression seemed to clear slightly. "We can't give what we don't have, of course. But perhaps if we think about it overnight, we might recall having put away some savings to buy Christmas presents. If so, we might decide that we can spare at least a little something for Mrs. Hunnicutt and the Crawford family as well. In the meantime, some of you older children might consider volunteering to do odd jobs around the Crawford place, and for Mrs. Hunnicutt when she returns home."

He paused. "If she manages to *keep* her home, that is."

His studying gaze seemed to take in every student in the room, one at a time. "You do understand, I hope, that giving of your time and effort means just as much as putting money in a collection plate. Sometimes it might even mean more. When we have no money to give, we can still give something of ourselves—our time, a job that's needed, a word of encouragement. In fact, by giving of ourselves—and giving with love—we not only give a gift to the other person, but to God as well. I think there can be no finer gift than that."

He smiled at them then, not the forced-looking smile of moments before, but his usual warm, easy smile that said he cared about each and every one of them. "We'll leave the tray here on my desk for now. Perhaps by tomorrow some of us will find a little something to put in it."

He waited another moment, and then he flipped open his gold pocket watch and checked the time. After instructing Maggie's sister, Eva Grace, to drill the younger children in their arithmetic problems, he sank down onto his chair to hear the book reports of the older students.

Maggie sat watching him, feeling for all the world as if she'd just had the wind knocked out of her.

Seven

Disappointment

Disappointment has a bitter taste
that only hope can sweeten.

Anonymous

Jonathan made a show of reviewing his grade book, though he was actually studying the children as they gathered their books and papers, preparing for dismissal.

He supposed his disappointment was irrational. With only two or three exceptions, these were poor children. Their families struggled simply to keep them clothed and fed. There was no money for extras.

And even if there had been, the holiday season was upon them. It was only natural that they would hold tightly to the little they had in hopes of affording some inexpensive gifts for their loved ones.

What had he expected of them, after all?

Clearly, he had allowed his desire to help the Crawfords and Mrs. Hunnicutt to cloud his common sense. Even if some of the children *had* anything extra to spare, it wasn't likely they'd be carrying it on them. Besides, what little they might be able to collect, even with the help of their parents, almost certainly wouldn't be enough to make any real difference for those in need.

He traced over and over a triangle on a piece of scrap paper, berating himself for his reaction to the empty collection tray. They had seen his disappointment, of course. He would have thought he was beyond displaying his feelings to a group of children. After years in the classroom he ought to be capable of controlling his emotions in front of his students.

His family would help, he was sure. But it would take several days by the time he contacted them and waited for the mail to bring a response.

He thought of his own modest savings. The idea brought a tightening in his chest. The money he'd put by was to pay for his care...later.

The time was coming, no matter how he tried not to think about it, when he would no longer be able to work. The frequent pain, the shortness of breath, and numbing fatigue were almost constantly with him now. At times it was all he could do to drag himself home in the evenings and fall into bed. He hated the idea of being dependent on his parents for however long he might be totally disabled. If there was any way to leave his savings untouched, he really needed to do so.

The flute would have brought a tidy sum...

But the flute was gone. Still, he had to think of something. What had possessed him anyway, giving in to disappointment over the children's failure to come up with a collection when he hadn't yet decided on what *he* could do?

He drew a long breath and stood, anticipating the familiar lightheadedness and then waiting for it to clear as he dismissed the children. Most of the students were gone when he glanced toward the door and saw Maggie MacAuley standing there, watching him. Jonathan managed a smile for her, but her expression remained uncharacteristically solemn. Finally, she gave a small nod and turned to go.

Jonathan was thankful that she wasn't there to see him stumble in his weakness as he turned to bank the last of the fire in the stove.

As soon as the dismissal bell rang, Maggie and the others lost no time in assembling outside. To make sure Mr. Stuart didn't overhear them, they went all the way to the gate at the end of the school yard.

That's where the argument began.

To Maggie's dismay, some of the students seemed to have already made up their minds that the money in the collection jar ought to go to the Widow Hunnicutt and the Crawfords, rather than toward a new flute for Mr. Stuart. Lily Woodbridge quickly moved to squelch the suggestion, and for the first time she could recollect, Maggie found herself in agreement with the other girl.

"I positively will not go along with any such thing!" Lily warned, tossing her sausage curls. "That money is for Mr. Stuart's flute."

Maggie put in a word to signal her support of Lily.

Junior Tyree then commenced to make, what was for him, a lengthy speech. "I reckon we all want to do something for Mr. Stuart," he said in his usual slow drawl, "but it don't seem right somehow, spending all that money on a music instrument when other folks is going hungry." He finished on a quick breath, looking at no one in particular.

Something stirred in Maggie, an uneasiness she did her best to ignore.

"We took up that collection for one reason!" Lily snapped at Junior. "To replace Mr. Stuart's flute. The Crawfords and the Widow Hunnicutt are not our concern. We can't be responsible for *everyone!*"

A few heads nodded in agreement while Maggie grew even more uncomfortable. No one else said anything for a moment, until Kenny Tallman spoke up. "I think Junior's right," he said, pushing up his glasses a little higher on his nose. "It seems like it might be more important to buy food and medicine than a flute." He paused. "Even if the flute *is* for Mr. Stuart."

Maggie glared at him, but he didn't look back at her.

Everyone knew Kenny "liked" her, and over the past few weeks, Maggie had just about decided that she liked him back. He was, after all, the smartest boy in the room, smarter than even the few older boys who only *thought* they knew everything there was to know. He was clean, too, with his hair never mussed and his shirttail always tucked in. And he never acted stupid like the other boys, either. Kenny was quiet-natured and polite.

Now, however, Maggie wasn't so sure she liked him after all. And if he really liked her, wouldn't he be on her side about a matter of such importance? Wouldn't he at least pretend to agree with her?

To her further exasperation, even Lester Monk decided to voice his opinion. "Folks who is hungry need food," he said, his hair standing straight out in the blustery wind. "And sick people can die without medicine."

"Well, Mr. Stuart might die too, if we don't do something!" Maggie blurted out. "And we don't have time to start all over again with another collection."

The instant the words were out, she wished she could swallow them back. By a kind of silent agreement, they had all been careful not to give voice to the idea that Mr. Stuart might not be around much longer. That he might actually die.

Lily didn't seem to notice Maggie's blunder. "Since my daddy put in almost half of the entire collection, it seems to me I should have some say in what it's used for."

Her tone had gone all high pitched like a chicken's squawk now, the way it always did when she was fixing to take on. "And *I* say it goes toward a new flute for Mr. Stuart."

Even though Maggie agreed with her, she sensed that Lily's high-and-mighty airs were rubbing some of the others the wrong way. Hoping to avoid an all-out ruckus, she said, "I recommend we go ahead just like we planned. Once we've made a down payment on a flute, we can start up a *new* collection for the Crawfords and Mrs. Hunnicutt."

There was a ripple of approval, if not wholehearted enthusiasm.

Then Kenny spoke up again. "If you don't think there's time to take up another collection for Mr. Stuart," he said, still not meeting Maggie's gaze, "how do you figure the Crawfords and the Widow Hunnicutt can get by much longer? It sounds to me like they need help right now—maybe even more than Mr. Stuart does."

The debate continued back and forth, but they couldn't seem to settle on anything. At last Kenny suggested they take a vote, and on that much, at least, everyone agreed.

Until Maggie thought of something else. "Summer should vote too. It's only right."

Lily shot her a peevish look. "Why? She hasn't been here often enough to even know what's going on."

"I've *told* her what's going on," Maggie countered. "She ought to have a say in what we do."

"She probably didn't put anything in the collection anyway," said Lily. "Well—did she?"

"I don't know if she did or not."

In truth, Maggie figured Summer wouldn't have put anything in the collection, not only because she hadn't been at school, but because she wouldn't have had any money to spare even if she were well. Still, she didn't want to give Lily the satisfaction of proving a point.

"But even if she *hasn't* had a chance to give, she still can once she gets back to school," she said.

"Summer isn't coming back to school, and you know it!" Lily snapped. "She's too sick. She'll *never* be able to come back to school."

Maggie wasn't prepared for the way Lily had turned on her, and she was even less prepared for the other girl's mean-spirited words.

"That's not so!" she shot back.

"*Is* so! My daddy said."

Maggie had never wanted to light into anyone the way she wanted to go after Lily Woodbridge at that moment. She had all she could do to keep from smacking the other girl to wipe that smug, know-it-all look off her face.

"I don't believe you!" she burst out. "But no matter what he said, it doesn't make it so!"

"My daddy is a doctor, Maggie MacAuley. I expect he knows a whole lot more than *you* do. Summer is not ever coming back, so we don't need her vote. She doesn't count!"

Maggie flinched as if she'd been struck. She clenched her fists, blinking hard to stop the hot tears threatening to spill over from her eyes. "Don't you ever say that again, Lily Woodbridge! Summer does so count. She counts just as much as any of us! And don't you forget it."

A few murmurs of agreement went around the group, but Maggie was past caring whether anyone agreed with her or not. When Lily smirked and waved a hand as if to dismiss the lot of them, Maggie began to rock on the balls of her feet, ready to tear into the other girl.

Before she could make a move, however, Eva Grace stepped between her and Lily. "Maggie can talk to Summer tonight and find out what she thinks," she said firmly, looking first at Lily and then at Maggie. "Even if Summer can't be here, she's entitled to an opinion."

Maggie continued to glare at Lily, who finally gave another shrug and then took on a look of total indifference.

Finally, Kenny spoke up again. "So everyone agrees then? We'll meet again in the morning and vote our conscience."

Maggie felt him watching her, but she deliberately didn't look at him. At the moment all she wanted to do was get away by herself and try to think.

Maggie pretended not to notice that Kenny was following her down the road from school. She was still furious with Lily and still confused about her own feelings regarding the use of the collection. Any further opinions from Kenny would only unsettle her that much more.

She couldn't very well ignore him, though, when he came up alongside her.

"Are you mad at me?" he asked.

Maggie walked even faster, but apparently he meant to keep up with her.

"Maggie?"

"Why would I be mad at you?" she answered, her head in the air.

"It just seems as though we ought to first help Mrs. Hunnicutt and the Crawfords," he offered.

Maggie said nothing.

"Don't you think?" he pressed.

Maggie stopped and faced him. It was on the tip of her tongue to tell him what she really thought about his not taking her side in the school yard, but the idea of being spiteful to Kenny somehow didn't feel right. Kenny always looked so—sad. Even with his glasses on, his eyes often reminded her of her dog Sadie's eyes. Sorrowful.

Kenny was the only boy in school with eyes like that. Only Mr. Stuart had eyes as soft and sad as Kenny's.

"I don't know what the right thing is," Maggie said. "I just know we need to help Mr. Stuart too." She paused, trying to think how to make him understand. "It's not that I don't care about the others. I do. But I don't really *know* them. Mr. Stuart, he's...special. And he needs our help."

Kenny nodded. "I know. It just seems that the Widow Hunnicutt and the Crawfords might need our help even more."

Maggie drew in a long breath. "I reckon I'll just have to pray about it."

Kenny fidgeted a little and looked away.

"Do you pray?" she asked him.

Kenny shrugged, his gaze still elsewhere. "My daddy says only girls pray. And he doesn't believe it does any good anyhow."

Maggie stared at him. She couldn't imagine her own da saying something like that. "Doesn't your daddy believe in God?"

Kenny's answer was a long time coming. "I suppose not. He says people just made up God a long time ago because they were too cowardly to take care of themselves."

Maggie actually gasped. Was this what her da called *blasphemy*?

"Is that what *you* think?"

He looked at her. "No," he said, shaking his head. "Not really. Mr. Stuart says everything around us is living proof that God's real. And the Bible stories he tells us—you can tell he believes every word." He stopped. "If Mr. Stuart believes in God, I guess I do too."

Maggie nodded, relieved to learn that Kenny wasn't a blasphemer after all.

They started walking again. "Anyway," Kenny said, his voice low, "I didn't mean to side with the others against you. I just didn't know what else to do. We don't have enough money to help everybody."

They came to the fork in the road, where Kenny would go one way and Maggie another. "I reckon you're right," she said, stopping.

"About what?"

"About voting our conscience. I expect that's all we can do."

They parted then and turned for home. All the way down the road, Maggie worried over exactly how her conscience might tell her to vote.

It worried her even more to think that her conscience might have already spoken and she was just trying hard not to listen.

Eight

A Heavyhearted Night

We never knew a childhood's mirth and gladness...

Lady Wilde

Late that afternoon, after sweeping up at the company store, Maggie went up on the Hill to visit Summer.

As always, the Rankin cabin seemed to be running over with people. Maggie reckoned there were more folks crammed into one place at the Rankins' than anywhere else in town.

Although Summer claimed to like visiting the MacAuleys'—where it was always "lots quieter"—Maggie also enjoyed her visits to Summer's house. The Rankin cabin was so noisy and crowded that the two of them could do mostly as they pleased without anyone taking notice. The grown-ups and young'uns were forever jawing at one another, and even though there was usually a baby crying somewhere, there was plenty of laughter as well. Often, there was also music, with Summer's da playing his harmonica and Mrs. Rankin singing.

At Summer's house, no one seemed to mind if they tracked in mud from the outdoors or if they left crumbs on the table and dirty dishes in the sink. Moreover, they could even drink Mrs. Rankin's strong black coffee instead of milk, and they were allowed to play hidey-go-seek indoors as well as out.

This afternoon, however, Maggie could tell as soon as she arrived that Summer didn't feel up for playing anything. She found her friend in the back bedroom that Summer shared with her three sisters—a small room separated from the kitchen by a faded blue drape. Summer was alone, already hunkered down under a pile of quilts, with nothing showing but her head.

Maggie took note of the fiery red stain mottling the other girl's face, a sure sign that the fever was on her again. Summer sat up, but the mere movement triggered a fit of coughing. Maggie perched on the side of the bed, waiting, trying not to notice the bright red splotches on the handkerchief when Summer took it away from her mouth.

"You're feeling bad again?" she said.

Summer nodded and then made a face. "Mama says it's because I played out in the rain. She threatened to switch me," she said with a weak grin, "but she didn't really mean it. I could tell."

To save her, Maggie couldn't imagine the good-humored Mrs. Rankin taking a switch to Summer—or to anyone else for that matter. Summer's mother never seemed to get overly cross with any of her young'uns, though she had been known to throw a frying pan at Summer's da now and again when he riled her.

They talked some about school, but Maggie did most of the talking. She could tell that her friend was feeling a lot more poorly than she let on.

She waited until last to tell Summer about the plight of Mrs. Hunnicutt and the Crawfords and the embarrassing attempt to take up a collection for them. Finally, she explained about the vote that was to be taken the next day. Even though it was plain that Summer wouldn't be back in school by then, Maggie asked her opinion on the matter.

"According to Kenny, we ought to 'vote our conscience,'" she said. "But I don't rightly know what my conscience is telling me to do. I feel real sorry for the Widow Hunnicutt. And even though it's kind of hard to feel sorry for Dinah and Duril, I wouldn't want the new Crawford baby to go hungry. But the whole purpose of the collection was to buy a flute for Mr. Stuart. And if we don't do it soon—"

She broke off. For the second time that day, she had caught herself thinking that Mr. Stuart's time might be limited. Maggie wasn't superstitious—her da said it was a sin to pay heed to such pagan notions—but still and all some things were probably best left unsaid.

Summer seemed to understand. She nodded, pushing herself up a little more on the pillows propped behind her.

"So, what do you think?" Maggie asked her directly. "If you were to vote tomorrow, what would you do, do you reckon?"

Summer looked at her and then glanced away, staring at something outside the window, her fingers plucking at some loose threads on the quilt in a kind of even rhythm, over and over again. Maggie shivered. Picking at the bedclothes was known to be a bad omen. Indeed, some of the old folks claimed it was a sign that a body's end was near.

Shaken, she forced herself to look away. "Well, what do you think?" she asked again, her tongue thick. "How would you vote?"

A thought struck her then, and without waiting for Summer's reply, Maggie brought up Mr. Stuart's suggestion about "giving something of themselves" instead of money.

"Now, it seems to me," Maggie said, more to herself at this point than to Summer, "that we could use the collection to buy a flute for Mr. Stuart and do something else—like some chores around the house—for Mrs. Hunnicutt and the Crawfords."

When Summer made no reply, she added, "After all, Mr. Stuart said that 'giving of yourself' can be just as good as giving money. Sometimes even better. He said it's like giving God a gift too."

The more Maggie thought about it, the more she believed she had found the perfect solution. It wasn't as if it was her idea, after all. Mr. Stuart was the one who had brought it up in the first place.

Summer turned to look at her. The flush to her skin had deepened, and the smudges below her eyes were so dark that she appeared to be bruised.

A peculiar feeling crept over Maggie. It was as if someone had poured an icy dipper of water down her back. Without knowing exactly why, she suddenly felt afraid. Afraid—and mortal foolish for giving in to the fear.

The feeling passed when Summer spoke. "I reckon if I was to vote tomorrow," she said, her voice so soft Maggie had to lean forward to hear her better, "I'd first try to figure out what Mr. Stuart would do."

Maggie stared at her. "What do you mean? Mr. Stuart doesn't even *know* about the collection."

"But if he did know, what do you think he would tell us to do?"

Maggie shrugged, impatient with a question that seemed to have nothing to do with their present predicament.

Again Summer turned to look out the window. The afternoon light was almost gone, and it had begun to snow, large heavy flakes that drifted down like a curtain falling over the gloom of evening.

"I recollect," Summer said in the same quiet voice, "Mr. Stuart teaching us that when we have a hard thing to decide we need to try and reason what Jesus would do. He says if we try to follow Jesus, we won't ever go wrong."

The brief speech seemed to have exhausted her, and she closed her eyes. Maggie could hear the wheeze and rattle coming from deep inside Summer's chest, and she worried that all the talking might bring on another bad coughing fit.

But after a moment, Summer opened her eyes and said, "I can't always think what Jesus would do. Sometimes I don't even know where to look in my Bible to find out. Those times, I just watch Mr. Stuart real close and try to imagine what *he* would do."

At Maggie's frown, Summer twisted onto her side toward her. "See, I think Mr. Stuart lives like Jesus wants *us* to live. Sometimes I almost think I can see Jesus...living...in Mr. Stuart and looking out from his eyes. So I reckon if *I* do what I think Mr. Stuart would do, then I'll most likely do the right thing."

Maggie's stomach knotted. Now it was *she* who was plucking at the bedclothes as she sat watching her friend.

"I expect," Summer went on, "that Mr. Stuart would give whatever he had to someone who needed help."

She appeared to be exceedingly tired and ill, and her voice had taken on a rasp. But she smiled, brightening a little, as if a thought had just occurred to her. "Why, even if we was to give him a brand-new flute, I wouldn't be at all surprised if he didn't just...sell it and put the money in the collection plate for the Widow Hunnicutt and the Crawfords."

As Maggie watched, Summer's smile broke apart and her eyes seemed to lose their focus. "That's what he would do, I expect. Feed the hungry...heal the sick...that's what Mr. Stuart would do...just like Jesus..."

She started coughing then, hard, and they both remained silent. For a long time after the coughing subsided, Summer seemed to doze, but Maggie didn't leave right away. Instead, she sat studying her friend's labored efforts to breathe, thinking about Summer's words. *"Feed the hungry...heal the sick...that's what Mr. Stuart would do...just like Jesus..."*

Maggie didn't doubt but what Summer was right. She knew her Bible well enough to know that Jesus did indeed feed the hungry and that He also healed the sick. But why, then, didn't He heal Summer... and Mr. Stuart?

Her mother said they ought not to question why the Lord healed some and not others, that He had His reasons and it wasn't for them to puzzle over His will. But it was hard—powerful hard—not to question why when two of the people who meant most to her were in such fierce need of healing.

And they were *good* people—people who always did what Summer called "the right thing." Mr. Stuart was kindness itself, and Summer—well, here she was, too sick to get out of bed and yet all she could think of was doing the right thing.

Guilt crept over Maggie at the thought of Summer's resolve to do what Jesus would do in any situation. The truth was that, unlike Summer, she sometimes just plunged straight in to doing a thing without considering whether it was right or wrong.

Sometimes she simply did what seemed easiest. For her.

Mr. Stuart had once told them that doing the right thing wasn't always easy. That it was sometimes very hard indeed, so hard it might make a body feel heavyhearted, even sorrowful. And heavyhearted was exactly how Maggie felt at that moment, sitting on the bed beside her sick friend, trying to digest Summer's words. The awareness of the "right thing" to do in the present situation slowly, reluctantly settled over her, and just the knowing made her feel as if one of the enormous old stones from the river bank had rolled over onto her heart.

This pressing burden, combined with the undeniable evidence of Summer's worsening condition, suddenly began to hammer at Maggie with a vengeance. Dizziness swept over her, and for an instant, she thought she'd be sick to her stomach.

Somehow she managed to say a proper goodbye to the drowsy Summer, but she fairly bolted out the kitchen door before Mrs. Rankin or one of the other children could delay her.

Outside the darkness was relieved only by the falling snow, heavier now, with the promise of several inches before morning. It was colder too, with icy patches forming on the path leading away from the Rankins'.

When she was almost home, she stopped, letting the damp cold and snow wash over her, cooling her skin as if to wash away the gnawing panic that had been building inside her throughout the evening.

From the direction of the mines on the Hill came the lonely sound of a dog howling, while the white pine trees bordering both sides of the road soughed in the wind. A tree branch snapped from the weight of the snow, and Maggie hugged her arms to herself, shivering, but not from the cold.

She felt the loneliness of the town and the night press in on her, stirring an old, familiar dread that hinted of bad things, sorrowful things...and setting off a near desperate longing to escape whatever was coming, perhaps to escape Skingle Creek itself.

Now she turned and ran, stumbling over the slippery stones, nearly falling in her haste to reach the faint light that seeped through the curtains of the front windows of home.

Nine

Maggie and the Angel Touch

More like the Master I would ever be…

Charles H. Gabriel

As it turned out, the vote planned for the next morning had to be postponed until later in the day. The snow of the night before had given way to a freezing rain, making for such a miserable morning that no one wanted to tarry outside.

The dark and dismal day fit Maggie's mood. She slugged through the early classes, attention lagging, her heart still heavy. She hadn't realized until today how much the collection and all the activity surrounding it had occupied her. In truth, it had kept the entire class humming while it lifted their spirits. The additional odd jobs to raise money, the stolen moments of whispered ideas and plans had given them all something to look forward to—a spark of excitement and warmth in the cold and dreary days. Now all that had changed, and Maggie knew only a leaden sense of defeat and disappointment, coupled with a vague feeling of dread for the days to come.

So morose had been her state of mind throughout the morning that she didn't notice anything different about Mr. Stuart until almost noon. The teacher was standing at the blackboard with his pointer, marking off decimal places for Maggie's arithmetic group. After a moment he reached for his pocket watch—and withdrew his hand—empty. He glanced down over his vest, his expression confused, but his gaze quickly cleared as he dropped his hand back to his side.

In that moment, Maggie knew what had escaped her until now: Mr. Stuart's gold pocket watch was gone! She had seen him make the same gesture two or three times throughout the morning, each time with the same reaction, but she'd been too absorbed in her own low spirits to register the significance of his actions.

Now it came to her all too clearly.

He sold his watch! Mr. Stuart has sold his fine gold watch!

The sudden realization brought Summer's words of the night before rushing in on Maggie: *"Why, even if we was to give him a brand-new flute, I wouldn't be at all surprised if he didn't just sell it and put the money in the collection plate for the Widow Hunnicutt and the Crawfords."*

Maggie stared at the teacher as if she had never seen him before. Summer had been right. She had known exactly what Mr. Stuart would do: *"Feed the hungry...heal the sick...that's what Mr. Stuart would do...just like Jesus..."*

Maggie continued to watch Mr. Stuart, and as she did, she was seized with an urgency she had never known before—an urgency to pray. Never mind that she wasn't on her knees and that her eyes were wide open. In fact, she squeezed them shut, right there in the middle of class, without caring whether anyone noticed or what they might think if they did.

Shut off from her surroundings in a way she could never understand, Maggie prayed. She prayed that somehow—though she didn't know how in the world such a thing could ever be—she, too, would be able to live like Mr. Stuart lived.

Like Jesus would want her to live.

I know what I'm supposed to do now, Lord—what I have *to do. And if anyone else is still on the fence about this collection, then give them a push too, like You just did me. We've all got to do the right thing here, but some of us find it harder than others, and I reckon I'm one of them. Just help me and all the rest of us do what we know we need to do, no matter how much it hurts. And it does, Lord. It* does *hurt. But probably nothing like it hurt Mr. Stuart to sell his good watch.*

❧

The vote was taken at noon, the weather having relented long enough that they could tolerate the outdoors for a brief time.

It went just as Maggie had known it would. Indeed, as soon as she called everyone's attention to Mr. Stuart's missing gold watch, they voted—to the last student—to turn the entire amount over to the Crawford family and Mrs. Hunnicutt.

There was no arguing, no fussing. Even Lily Woodbridge kept quiet—until Junior Tyree raised the question of who did they think might have purchased the teacher's watch.

For once, Lily spoke in a quiet voice instead of the smug, know-it-all tone Maggie disliked so much. "My father," she said. "Mr. Stuart came to our house last night, and my father bought his watch. I heard them talking."

Her gaze darted from one to the other. Maggie's mouth burned with the taste of bitterness, but Lily's uncharacteristic nervousness and total lack of gloating quickly squelched any antagonism. Selling the watch would have been Mr. Stuart's decision, after all. It wasn't as though Lily's father had had to twist his arm. Obviously, this was what Mr. Stuart wanted, and who else in Skingle Creek, other than Kenny Tallman's father, could have afforded to buy it? There was no point in holding bad feelings toward Lily.

The others in the group seemed to take their cue from Maggie, and as things turned out, they actually appointed Lily to present the money jar to Mr. Stuart on behalf of the entire class.

If Maggie had had any doubts beforehand, Mr. Stuart's response to the collection made it blazingly clear that they had made the right decision.

The instant Lily walked up and thumped the jar down on the teacher's desk—with considerable flourish, Maggie noted—Mr. Stuart's face brightened with the biggest smile they had seen from him in weeks.

Clearly taken aback, he studied Lily and then the money jar. "Lily? What is this?"

At her desk, Maggie held her breath, hoping Lily would manage to get through her speech before Mr. Stuart could ask too many questions.

She needn't have worried. Lily was beaming, and, just as she'd been instructed, proceeded to hurry through an explanation. One thing about Lily: She was a born speechmaker. "This is for the Widow Hunnicutt and the Crawford family," she announced. "It's not from the class alone, of course. We couldn't raise so much money on our own. Our parents helped too."

The teacher rose from his chair and, turning the jar around by its neck, stared at it as if he couldn't believe his eyes. "This...this is wonderful. Lily...class...I can't think how you managed it, but I am *very* proud of all of you."

He looked around the room, for a moment almost appearing his old self again. He actually seemed happy, Maggie thought—if a bit stunned.

The teacher lifted the jar then and held it up to the class. "I shall deliver this to Pastor Wallace this very evening," he said, still smiling broadly. "He and Father Maguire will be so pleased and grateful."

Carefully, he set the jar down, and then he came around to stand in front of his desk. "I can't begin to tell you," he said quietly, his gaze resting on each student for a second or two before going on, "what this will mean to Mrs. Hunnicutt and the Crawfords. I know it represents a great sacrifice for you and your families, but I hope you realize that you have brought much delight to God's heart today. And to mine."

He stopped to clear his throat, blinked, and then glanced around the room once more. "Well," he said with a small nod, "let's get back to work now, shall we?"

Was she imagining it, Maggie wondered, or did Mr. Stuart have a little more spring to his step when he returned to his desk and began to review the day's spelling words?

As she sat there, only vaguely aware of the teacher at the blackboard, Maggie was surprised at how good she felt about the way things had turned out. Despite the fact that they no longer had any hope of restoring the stolen flute, they had obviously made Mr. Stuart proud of them. And happy.

She supposed it was a mark of the kind of man the teacher was, that he could sacrifice something as valuable as his fine gold watch and still be happy, and happier still because his students had done something good for others.

With all her heart, Maggie wished there were a way to do something nice for *him.* If ever a man deserved a special gift, Mr. Stuart did.

If only there were a way to give him back his music.

They could at least give him a birthday party...

Whoa!

Maggie caught a breath. She didn't know where the thought had come from, but excitement suddenly swept over her like a waterfall. That's exactly what they could do all right: They could give their teacher the best birthday party anyone had ever had! They could make him a special card. Bake him a cake. And perhaps they could still come up with some sort of gift. A surprise.

She sat there, staring at but not seeing the spelling words on the blackboard. Instead she pondered what kind of a surprise they might concoct for Mr. Stuart's birthday. Again she recalled what he had said to them about giving something of themselves...and "giving it with love."

In that moment an idea came over her that made the hair at the back of her neck stand on end.

This occurrence was deemed the "angel touch" by Grandma Vinnie, who wasn't Maggie's *real* grandmother but was called so by most of the town because of her advanced age and wisdom. Maggie had learned from experience that when an idea merited the "angel touch," it was almost always a fine idea. A real dandy of an idea. On occasion, according to Grandma Vinnie, it might even be a *heaven-sent* idea.

She shook off the chill and started writing notes to herself, hoping Mr. Stuart wouldn't call on her just yet. She wanted to get her thoughts down immediately, while they were still foremost in her mind, so she could present them to the others after school.

Of course, she already knew they were going to go for it.

Ten

Predators

If you're the only one that knows you're afraid—you're brave.

Old Irish Saying

From the moment Maggie related her plan for Mr. Stuart's surprise birthday party, a wave of excitement swept the school yard. The fact that there was so much to do and so little time in which to do it only lent more enthusiasm to the undertaking.

As a group, everyone committed to lunch hour meetings, and, except for a few, each student agreed to try to enlist their family's help. In fact, those who thought they could get away with it went so far as to volunteer their houses for special meetings.

Fired by the exuberance of the others, Maggie could hardly wait to tell Summer the news. First, however, she needed to tell her parents. She could only hope her da would be more agreeable about this idea than he had been about the notion of the collection.

⁂

Maggie was only vaguely aware that she had reached the Hill and was about to turn onto the path leading upward to Summer's house. So pleased had she been by the reaction of her parents to her idea for Mr. Stuart's birthday party that she'd nearly lost track of time and place since leaving home.

Not only had her mother committed to do some of the baking for the occasion, but Da had actually offered to help set up the schoolroom and put together a makeshift table for the refreshments. This was more than she could have hoped for. She knew Summer would be excited too and anxious to hear all the details.

The unexpected sound of muffled laughter off to her right jerked her out of her thoughts. She stopped and looked in the direction of the railroad tracks across the road, but seeing nothing, she took up walking once more.

When she heard it again, she stopped short, straining to see where the sound was coming from. But the thick copse of trees and brush that followed the railway tracks revealed nothing.

She waited, and then she went on walking, this time picking up her pace, shivering a little even though her coat was buttoned tightly all the way up to her throat. Earlier the day had warmed, melting the snow and leaving puddles of slush and water that, as the night grew colder, began to freeze. Every now and then she skidded on a patch of ice or slick mud.

The laughter grew louder. Maggie kept going, picking her way carefully but walking faster as she started up the Hill.

She wasn't exactly afraid. Coming and going in the dark was nothing new to her. But it was a lonely kind of night, with nothing but the sough of the wind in the pines and the occasional crunch of ice under her feet to break the silence. The kind of night that made her feel as if no one else was outdoors except her.

Even though the low rumble of laughter and talk on the wind told her all too clearly that she wasn't alone.

She reassured herself with the thought that, most likely, some of the miners had stayed over to work on the track or the coal cars. Probably having themselves a drink over there in the trees where they couldn't be seen.

All the same, she took the path up the Hill as quickly as she could.

Suddenly, she realized that the laughter had shifted and was now coming from behind her. At the same time she heard the snap of dead branches and the sloshing sound of someone coming at a near run through half-frozen puddles.

Not someone...more than one...

She stopped and whirled around to look.

Her mouth went dry, and her heart took up a heavy pounding, the blood slamming hard in her ears.

Orrin Gaffney and Billy Macken were trotting up the hill, grinning at her.

Mustn't let them know I'm afraid...

None of the other boys at school worried her a bit. The worst they ever did was tease, and Maggie could give back as good as she got. Even Duril Crawford at his bossiest didn't scare her none.

But Orrin Gaffney and Billy Macken were different. Maggie had long had a sense that these two weren't like the other boys at school.

They were almost always together, and they seemed to delight in terrorizing the younger children. Her older sisters were leery of them, calling them "creepy," and even Mr. Stuart sometimes regarded them with a watchful kind of expression, as if he half expected them to stir up trouble at any moment. He didn't trust them, that much was clear, and his suspicion was enough to keep Maggie on point anytime they were around.

Billy and Orrin weren't merely ornery. They were mean. Just plain mean.

They were both big for their age. Billy was only fourteen, but he stood as tall as his father and was nearly as broad. Orrin wasn't as heavy, but he was tall too, and he had the hard, wiry look of a scrapper about him.

One of them alone was trouble. The two of them together made a train wreck.

Fear seized Maggie in earnest, but she stood her ground, unmoving, watching the two approach.

They didn't stop until they were directly in front of her.

"Hey, Carrottop," said Orrin, still grinning.

It was a name that unfailingly made Maggie grind her teeth and long to punch anyone who dared to use it within earshot. It wasn't a fair name either. Her hair was a full shade darker than carrots.

"What're you doin' out so late, Carrottop? Past your bedtime, isn't it?" asked Billy.

Maggie clenched her hands into fists at her sides, ready to fight if it came down to it, refusing to think about what kind of chance she would have against these two great lumps.

"I'm on my way to see Summer," she said evenly.

"The ghost," said Billy Macken, winking at Orrin.

The blood roared in Maggie's head. "Don't call her that!"

They both laughed. "Ghost," Billy said again. "That's what she looks like. Carrottop and the ghost. What a pair."

Orrin cackled and slapped Billy on the shoulder as if he were the cleverest thing ever.

Maggie swallowed hard, turned her back on them, and started up the Hill again.

She managed only two or three steps before Billy Macken's beefy hand caught her by the shoulder and stopped her.

"Hey—no one said you could go yet, Carrottop! Hold on."

He gave her a hard tug, forcing her around to face them. Shocked by this unexpected roughness, Maggie refused to look at either one of them. Instead, she stood staring at the ground. "Let me go, Billy Macken," she said, trying hard to keep her voice from quivering.

"Let me *go,*" Billy mimicked.

"I don't think she likes us very much," Orrin said.

"Maybe she's *afraid* of us." Billy ducked his head to make Maggie look at him.

Maybe she was, but she'd never let them see it. Maggie forced herself to laugh. Loud.

Orrin reared back and raised a hand as if to strike her, but Billy shook his head, holding on to Maggie even tighter. "Now she *is* scared. Just look at her face. It's as red as her hair."

Maggie somehow found her voice. "It would take more than the likes of you two to scare me." If she hadn't been a girl, she might have spit at him. As it was, she just glared at him as if she were *about* to spit.

Something changed in Billy's face. His eyes went cold as a snake's, and he leaned closer to Maggie with a look that was pure menace.

"Oh, is that so, Carrottop? Well, just what would it take to scare you, you bein' so tough and all?"

His voice was as hard as his eyes, and Maggie thought she might be foolish entirely to say another word. But she had seen these two in action at school, and she knew that if she let them intimidate her—or, worse, if she should start to cry, and she was all too close to doing just that—she would only encourage them.

"Oh, stop it, Billy Macken! Summer's folks know I'm on the way. They'll be out looking for me. You'd better stop with your tomfoolery."

"They know you're on the way," Billy taunted. "Then for sure we'd better not keep you." He stopped, his hateful eyes raking over her in a way that made Maggie feel as if something rotten had touched her.

"Tell you what, Carrottop. You give me and Orrin a squeeze and we'll let you go."

Maggie looked at Billy and then at Orrin. And in that moment she knew something had shifted. She wasn't sure what it was, but she recognized a different kind of threat, one more dangerous than the usual school yard bullying.

Maggie had any number of tricks at her disposal for dealing with smart-alecky boys. Her favorite, and the one that seemed to work nine times out of ten, was the poke-fun-at-them-and-make-them-feel-ignorant maneuver. She'd discovered that this one worked especially well on the older boys, who hated being thought dumb, even though some of them behaved as if they had no more sense than a worm on a hook. It usually did the job with the younger ones too, who tried to act older but ended up just looking stupid.

In truth, though, she'd never been sure just how to handle Billy Macken or his pal, Orrin. They were an odd pair and then some. In the first place, they were the oldest boys in school, past the age when most of the boys in town had already gone into the mines. Stranger still was that neither of them seemed to have any shame. Even when Mr. Stuart came down hard on them for misbehaving, Orrin and Billy would simply stare at him as if they hadn't heard, and then when the teacher's back was turned, grin at each other as though they thought it all a big joke.

They were grinning now, the two of them, smirking at Maggie. Orrin was dancing around behind and then in front of her while Billy held her fast.

Maggie was genuinely afraid now, and she knew she was that close to not being able to hide it any longer. Her mind raced, and though she looked wildly around for a way of escape, she already knew there was little if any hope that she could get away. Still, if she could break free of Billy's hold on her, she had a chance to outrun them. She was the fastest runner in school, never losing a race.

But Billy Macken was as strong as he was mean, and his peculiar, glazed stare made it clear he had no intention of letting her go.

She was trapped.

Eleven

An Unlikely Hero

That in my action I may soar as high
As I can now discern with this clear eye.
That my weak hand may equal my firm faith,
And my life practice more than my tongue saith.

Henry David Thoreau

Kenny heard them before he saw them. He was on his way home from exploring around the slack dump and the old abandoned hunter's shack in the woods. He could usually find some good stuff lying around if he took his time.

By now he had nearly all the wood he needed—a nice, solid block of pine and some hickory sticks, as well as some other stuff he planned to use. Tomorrow night after his chores and homework, he could start building. It wouldn't take him long because he already had the frame started.

He was almost to the railroad tracks but stopped at the sound of voices coming from partway up the Hill. With his canvas bag slung over his shoulder, he ducked into a stand of pine trees and stood staring at the scene across the tracks.

Although it was completely dark now, the sky was clear. But even if the moon hadn't cast enough light to reveal the figures on the hillside, he would have known them by their voices.

At first he was confused by the sight of Maggie with Billy Macken and Orrin Gaffney, but it didn't take him long to figure out what was going on. Billy had hold of Maggie while Orrin was circling around her, again and again, snorting that maddening horsey laugh of his.

Maggie was trying to get away from them, but he could tell even at this distance they had no intention of letting her go.

Carefully, he put his bag down on the ground. Then, with pine needles scraping his face as he went, he began to inch his way forward through the trees, moving as soundlessly as he could, actually going on tiptoe as if to muffle his steps.

Just before he reached the clearing, he stopped and parted the branches of one of the larger trees so he could see better.

Even in the dark, Kenny could tell that Maggie was plenty scared. Her voice was higher than usual and shaky, as if she were trembling.

Like him.

And why wouldn't she be scared? He was scared too. Billy Macken and Orrin Gaffney were the bane of the school yard, the terror of the younger students, and a constant reminder to Kenny of just how defenseless he was anytime they felt like picking on him. Which was often.

He was scared of them, all right.

But when he heard Maggie's shrill demand to let her go, heard the fear in her voice and their hateful, mocking laughter in response, the blood roared to Kenny's head in a fury.

He had to make a move now, before he lost his nerve. With a sharp pull of breath, he broke through the trees, stopping only long enough to bend over and scoop up the largest rock in sight. Then he took off barreling toward the Hill, yelling as he went.

Maggie had almost decided she would resort to biting if she must. As a rule, she held nothing but contempt for biters—it was such a babyish, cowardly way of fighting. But at the moment she wasn't past biting or anything else that would get her out of this fix.

This time when Orrin moved in on her, Maggie was ready for him. Drawing her leg up, she kicked him as hard as she could. She knew where to aim too. Da had taught her and her sisters how to protect themselves should any of the strangers that sometimes passed through a mining town try to bother them.

Her aim was right on target. Orrin went to his knees, grabbing himself and screaming like a girl.

Billy gave her arm a vicious yank, forcing it behind her as he called Maggie an awful name. The ugly name hurt nearly as much as his pressure on her arm. No one had ever used words like that in front of Maggie. Not ever.

"Stop!"

Reeling from pain and the shock of Billy's curse, Maggie looked around, confused, thinking it was Orrin yelling at them to stop. Only when she saw Kenny Tallman charging toward them did she realize it was Kenny shouting.

Billy was plainly caught off guard by Kenny's arrival, enough so that his grip on Maggie slackened—though not enough for her to break free.

"Let her go, Billy!"

Kenny stopped a few feet away. He was breathing so hard Maggie thought he might strangle, and as she took a closer look she realized that he was shaking from head to toe. But his eyes behind his spectacles were blazing, his mouth set in a hard line. He was clearly in a rage.

Maggie stared at him, scarcely able to recognize this wild-eyed youth who suddenly looked a lot older than the twelve-year-old boy she saw every day at school.

"I suppose you're gonna make me let her go, Four-eyes!" Billy taunted. "Go on home, you worthless little sis! Get outta here!"

"I said to let her go!" Kenny roared.

As Kenny stepped forward, his arm came round from behind him, and Maggie saw the large rock in his hand. She stared in amazement as he raised his arm and reared back.

"Duck, Maggie!"

Maggie ducked. And just in time. The rock split the air with a deadly aim that defied Kenny's delicate appearance and Maggie's once-held opinion that he might be a bit on the puny side.

The rock slammed into Billy's chin with a crack. He cried out, grabbing his chin and dropping his hold on Maggie. Blood was oozing from the corner of his mouth, and he covered the bottom of his face with both hands as if to hold it together.

"Maggie! Run!"

It took Maggie another second to realize she was free. She took off running down the Hill toward Kenny, who stood waiting for her.

Billy Macken was screaming, yelping in pain and letting go a stream of awful curses and threats. His chin must really hurt because his words sounded like corn being fed through a grinder. "You're gonna pay, Tallman! You just wait till I get my hands on you!"

When Kenny made no move to run, Maggie grabbed his hand and tugged at him. "Kenny, come *on!*"

"They're not going to come after us now," Kenny said, his voice strangely calm. "We took the wind out of their sails."

Maggie gaped at him. "*What?*"

"Besides," he went on, "we can outrun them."

Maggie knew *she* could, but she wasn't so sure about Kenny. But then she'd obviously misjudged him before. Maybe she ought not to doubt what he said from now on. Still—

To her amazement, he released her hand and started up the Hill.

"Kenny! What are you *doing?*"

He lifted a hand to indicate that she should wait, and then he turned back to the other boys.

Orrin Gaffney had finally got to his feet and was standing—

stooped over and moaning—next to Billy, who clutched his chin with one hand as he shook his other fist in the air. He shot Kenny a murderous look. But Kenny simply stood, both hands at his sides, as if waiting to have his say.

When he finally spoke, his voice was strong, again surprising Maggie, who would have expected him to be shaking too hard to say anything.

Shaking like *she* was shaking.

"Don't you even think about touching Maggie again, either one of you. Not ever."

"Don't *you* tell us what to do or what not to do!" Billy spluttered. "Just you wait! I'm gonna make you and your ugly little girlfriend *eat* that rock you threw at me!"

"No, you're not," Kenny said, his voice calm and steady. "And don't you ever call Maggie 'ugly' again."

Maggie stared. Kenny didn't sound one bit like a schoolboy anymore. He sounded like a man grown!

"You're not going to touch us," Kenny went on. "Because if you do, I'll tell my dad. And *your* dad—and Orrin's too—will be out of a job. Or did you forget that my dad is their boss?"

Maggie almost choked. But Billy and Orrin merely stood glaring at Kenny as if they wanted to murder him. Billy started to curse again, but Orrin grabbed at his arm and said something to him, under his breath, causing Billy to whip around and look at him before turning back to Kenny.

Kenny had clearly said all he meant to. He took his time returning to Maggie. He caught her by the hand and started walking. Walking quickly, but not running. "Come on," he said. "You'd best be getting home."

"I was going to Summer's—"

"I expect you'd better go on home instead, Maggie."

Maggie looked at him. "Okay," she finally said, for the first time feeling smaller than Kenny instead of a good inch taller. "I guess I can go tomorrow night."

After they'd gone far enough to make certain Orrin and Billy hadn't followed them, Kenny slowed his pace a little. "Doggone," he said, "I forgot my wood."

"Your wood?"

He nodded. "For my ship."

Maggie stopped, taking back her hand. "Your ship?"

Kenny went on, obviously expecting her to follow. "I build ships."

Maggie lifted a skeptical eyebrow but started after him.

"Model ships," Kenny said as she caught up to him. "You know—like real ones. Only smaller. Reproductions." He smiled a little as if the word pleased him.

"Oh." Maggie was relieved. "A *model* ship." For a minute there she'd thought he was funning her. And she had had just about all she could take of being laughed at for one night.

"I didn't know you liked ships," she said.

"I've built a bunch of models," he said. "Mostly clippers and sailboats. This one is going to be a four-master."

This was a revelation to Maggie. She had always pegged Kenny as the kind of boy who probably sat around with his nose in a book or worked himself into bone weariness with all the chores his da assigned him. Everyone talked about how mean his da was.

"Someday I'm going to build real ships," he said, glancing at her as if to see whether she believed him. "I'll have my own shipyard too."

Maggie darted another look at him, deciding there was a lot more to Kenny Tallman than she'd ever guessed. A *lot* more.

"That'll really be something, Kenny."

He nodded, and then he stopped and turned to look at her. "Are you all right now, Maggie?"

"I'm fine." She almost told him how scared she'd been but figured he didn't need to know that. "Do you honestly think they'll leave us alone now?" she asked.

"I'm pretty sure they will."

Maggie thought about it. "Was that the truth, what you told them? Would your da really fire their das from the mine?"

Kenny shot her a look. "Probably not," he said, his expression unreadable as he turned his gaze back to the road. "But they don't know that."

Maggie felt the beginning of a smile. Then, without looking at Kenny, she slipped her hand in his again as they started off toward home.

❧

Jonathan Stuart saw them pass. He'd drawn back a corner of the curtains at the window to look out on the night. Not so long ago, he, too, might have been out walking. But for weeks now he'd been fortunate just to walk around his own house, much less able to summon the strength needed for the long evening strolls he had once enjoyed.

He smiled at the sight of the somewhat precocious Maggie MacAuley and the quiet, intense Kenny Tallman. He couldn't be sure until they passed under the gaslight, but, yes, now he saw that they were holding hands.

He was a little surprised, given their young age, and he rather imagined that the MacAuleys might be less than thrilled at the sight of their twelve-year-old daughter out after dark, holding hands with the son of Matthew MacAuley's hard-edged employer.

Or perhaps not. Perhaps young Maggie's parents knew their daughter well enough to trust her behavior. Indeed, of all the students at the school, Jonathan could think of none he would trust as quickly and as completely as Maggie MacAuley and Kenny Tallman.

Besides, they were children. And apparently close friends. He smiled again.

Good for them, Lord!

Perhaps someday they would be more than friends, and what better foundation could be set in these early years for a lifelong love but that of a solid friendship, formed in their youth?

He had had a friend like that once. A childhood friend whom he had grown to love more than life. He knew what a precious gift such a friend could be.

He and Ainsley had grown up together, lived two doors down from each other in Lexington, gone to academy together, attended church together, played together. Their parents had been best friends as well, both families spending many of their holidays in each other's company at a private lodge in the Blue Ridge Mountains. From an early age, it was simply assumed that Jonathan and Ainsley would marry.

Certainly, Jonathan had assumed it.

He had been devastated when Ainsley, her discomfort obvious, came to him one summer afternoon when the sun was high and so bright it seemed evening would never come. Haltingly, tearfully, she tried to explain to him that she couldn't marry him, that it would be too much like "marrying her brother."

"Don't you see, Jonathan? I know you too well. Oh, my dear, I do love you—but as a friend. We're...family, Jonathan! You're my best friend, my...brother. I can't feel toward you as you do me. I've tried—I want to! But I simply can't."

Soon after, she left with her older sister for a "tour of Europe," not returning for several months. When she came home, she was accompanied by her British fiancé.

It wasn't that Jonathan had grieved himself into permanent bachelorhood. He had grieved, of course, had thought himself inconsolable for an entire year. But once he realized that Ainsley really was lost to him, he'd gone away to university and become involved in a new life, a life away from Lexington and Ainsley.

Even before graduation, he'd begun to sense God's call on his heart. At first he resisted any departure from the academic life he had envisioned for himself. He'd been offered a position on the faculty even before he graduated and had every intention of accepting it. But as the pressing of God's Spirit became more and more impossible to ignore, and the signs of his tenuous physical condition became more worrisome, he gave himself up to a lengthy season of prayer in search of God's directive.

In truth, nothing but the Divine will could have lured him away from his quiet, well-disciplined, and comfortable life to a seemingly ignoble and vastly underpaid position in a little mining town in the hills of Kentucky. Yet through a series of unimaginable circumstances—

and increasingly unavoidable signs that defied any practical explanation—he had finally resigned himself to the inevitable.

Over the years his students and their families had in a way become his family. Only rarely did he regret his single state and what he might have missed. This was his home, and he counted himself a man blessed by what he'd found here. Only on nights like these, when his strength was low and the night seemed to draw in upon him like a shroud—and the bittersweet scene of two of his favorite students holding hands tugged at his heart—did he allow himself a moment of regret for what he didn't have...for what he would never have.

At times like these, he realized he was dangerously close to indulging in the one thing that could destroy whatever strength and sense of purpose remained to him.

He had long known that self-pity was not only his enemy, but it could also prove to be the final hammer blow in his destruction. He was determined he would not strike that blow himself, but nights like this were inclined to test his resolve. It would be so easy to give in to feeling sorry for himself, to mourn what couldn't be his, to surrender to the fear that he might spend whatever time he had left as an invalid.

As he watched the children disappear from view, he gathered his strength. He even managed to smile and say a brief prayer for God's blessing upon their lives, with a silent plea in his heart that, whatever waited for the two of them in the future, it would not be loneliness.

Twelve

Two Are Better Than One

If one falls down,
his friend can help him up.

Ecclesiastes 4:10

As luck would have it, there had been no questions from Maggie's parents the night before. She'd gone inside to find her sisters at the kitchen table, doing their lessons, and her da working on a broken table leg. Her mother had gone to the O'Briens to help with the birthing of a new baby.

Maggie was relieved that she wouldn't need to fudge with them. She didn't want to lie, but she couldn't tell them about the incident with Billy Macken and Orrin Gaffney. Da's temper being what it was, there was no telling what he would do. If he were to go after the two boys, that would only put Maggie, and no doubt Kenny too at risk for more of their devilment. That being the case, both she and Kenny had committed to keep silent.

"For now," she'd agreed. "But if it happens again, we'll have to tell."

For more than one reason, Maggie could only hope Kenny was right in his belief that it wouldn't happen again.

⁂

The clouds had been heavy and dark all day, promising more snow or sleet before morning. By the time Maggie finished supper and started off for the Rankin place, night was gathering in. Da had allowed only an hour for her visit with Summer, so she took the road at a near run.

When she saw Kenny standing at the foot of the Hill as if he were waiting for her, uneasiness gripped her. Had he told his da about last night after all? Was Mr. Tallman going to make trouble?

His hands in his pockets, Kenny stood watching her approach. When Maggie was close enough to see that he didn't look particularly scared or worried—just serious and none too happy, which was normal for Kenny—she let out a breath.

"What are you doing?" she asked when she reached him.

"Waiting for you. You said you were going to Summer's tonight, so I figured I'd watch for you."

"Why?"

Kenny frowned at her as if he shouldn't have to explain. "Just…to make sure there's no trouble again."

"Didn't you say they'd probably not bother us from now on?"

He glanced away. "And I don't think they will. But I expect it's best not to take anything for granted."

Kenny was acting really strange. He just stood there, digging at the ground with his toe as if he'd lost something in the dirt and was trying to unearth it. His face was red, and he wouldn't look at her.

"Did they say anything to you at school today?" Maggie asked him.

"Billy and Orrin?" He shook his head. "They never came near."

"Then why did you think they might show up again tonight?"

"I didn't say I thought they would. I'm just keeping an eye out in case they do."

"Well, you don't have to do that."

He raised his head but still didn't make eye contact. "I know I don't *have* to."

"Then why are you?"

Now he looked at her, studying her as if he had something to say but didn't know whether he ought to say it.

"Because I like you! Okay? Because I don't want you getting hurt!"

His outburst caught Maggie completely off guard. She realized her mouth was open and snapped it shut.

As for Kenny, his face flamed and his eyeglasses slipped down his nose a little. When he moved to straighten them with one finger, he missed and poked himself in the forehead instead.

Maggie almost laughed but caught herself. In truth, she wondered if her face might not be red too. Her cheeks felt as if someone had singed them with a hot iron.

At the same time, she felt kind of...happy. Excited. It seemed that what the other girls had been telling her was true. Kenny liked her. He liked her, and now he had actually said so.

So what was she supposed to do? She reckoned she ought to say something, but for the life of her she couldn't think of a thing that wouldn't sound witless entirely.

Finally, she found her voice. "Well...okay, then. I'd best be getting on up to Summer's."

Kenny nodded. "I'll just watch you up the Hill. How long will you stay?"

"Da said no more than an hour."

He nodded. "I'll have to get home before then. You be careful. Ask Mr. Rankin to walk you partway, why don't you?"

Maggie had never asked Mr. Rankin anything of the kind and wasn't about to start tonight, but she didn't tell Kenny that. "I'll see you tomorrow, then."

At last they looked at each other straight on. Still red-faced, Kenny cracked a somewhat wobbly smile. Maggie grinned at him and quickly turned to go.

She was almost halfway up the Hill when he called out to her. "Maggie?"

Maggie stopped and turned. He hadn't moved but was standing straight as a post, his hands in his pockets.

"Do you like me back?"

Maggie hesitated and took a couple of steps backward, all the while looking everywhere but at Kenny.

At last she pulled in a deep breath and let it out. "I might," she shot back. "I'll have to think on it!"

Without another word she whipped around and took off at a run.

Kenny's stomach tightened, and he felt the fist in his chest as he always did at the rare times when his father actually gave him his full attention.

Judson Tallman was sitting at the kitchen table, papers strewn all over the place in front of him. The flame from the kerosene lamp flickered crazily in the draught as Kenny walked in.

Closing the door, he turned to find his father watching him, his heavy eyebrows knit in a frown, his expression impatient.

"Where have you been, boy?" His dark eyes bore into Kenny's.

"Just—out looking for some more wood, Daddy."

His father made a sound in his throat. "You'd be better advised to keep your nose in your books. Those toy boats of yours aren't going to get you out of this stink hole."

"I know, Daddy. I did my lessons before I went out."

Kenny stood with his hands behind his back, unsure of whether there was more to come. He thought not. His father was obviously involved in his work, as he almost always was. Still, he waited, watching the movement of his father's thick hands as he stacked a pile of papers neatly to one side.

"Why did you have your supper so early?"

"You said you'd be late, Daddy, so I went ahead. I wanted to go outside for a bit before dark."

His father was already back at his work, dark, shaggy head bent over a ledger, one hand rolling a pencil between his fingers. Kenny knew he'd been dismissed.

"I guess I'll go get ready for bed. Goodnight, Daddy."

His father gave a distracted wave in response.

In his bedroom Kenny went directly to the table he used as both desk and work site for his ship building. He picked up the paper on which he'd drawn the plans for the four-master, but his mind wasn't on the ship. Not tonight.

He knew he was a terrible disappointment to his father, and he wondered, not for the first time, if he'd been as much of a letdown to his mother, if that's why she had left them.

The first time he'd asked about her, he'd been maybe three or four years old. Having noticed that the other children he played with seemed to have a mother, he grew curious. His father had simply dismissed his questions with a curt, "I'll explain it to you when you're older."

The reply had been the same until the last time. He had been no more than seven or eight years old when he made the mistake of asking his father about her again, more specifically this time—where she had gone…and why she had gone.

Kenny hadn't realized that this time his questions would bring on a firestorm. He would never forget the terrible look that had come over his father that day.

Judson Tallman's always dour expression went livid. Kenny had actually jumped back, for fear of being struck.

His father hadn't touched him, but his words had hammered harder than any blow. "You won't speak of her in this house, boy! Not ever again. She's dead to us, do you understand?"

He took a step toward Kenny, who again stumbled backward to get out of his path.

"She was no good, that's what she was! A harlot and nothing more. She only married me in the first place to get away from the fists of her lunatic father. Don't you ever speak of her again, do you hear? She's gone, and good riddance to her."

At the time, Kenny hadn't known what a harlot was, but the venom in his father's voice left no doubt but what it was something terrible. Not long after, he looked up the word in the big dictionary Mr. Stuart kept at the front of the schoolroom. He had to track down several other words before he grasped its meaning, but what he discovered made him so sick to his stomach he'd had to go to the outhouse and throw up.

He never asked about his mother again.

But he still thought about her. He wondered if it was wicked of him to think about a woman his father had condemned as bad. A harlot. Even worse, he sometimes caught himself wondering if, even though she had been a bad woman, she had ever rocked him as a baby or sang to him or sat on the side of his bed and told him stories...or maybe kissed him goodnight. Had she smelled powdery and nice and worn a ribbon in her hair like Maggie's older sister Eva Grace?

What would it be like, Kenny wondered, to have a mother in the kitchen when he came home after school? A mother waiting for him, who would smile at him and ask him what he'd learned today and maybe even sit with him and help him do his lessons.

A mother who would *look* at him and really see him, not just glance at him and look away as if the sight of him brought a bad taste to her mouth.

That was how his father looked at him. *When* he looked at him, which was seldom indeed.

Although he scarcely remembered her, it seemed to Kenny that he resembled his mother. He had no recollection of her voice or her touch, but he had a partly faded photograph he'd found one day at the bottom of his father's storage trunk. He'd taken it and hidden it in his room, in the small Bible Mr. Stuart had given to each student.

He turned around to make sure his bedroom door was closed, and then he pulled the photograph from his Bible and studied it. He looked like her. His hair was light, like hers, only hers had been wavy, not straight like his. His face was thinner, and not so comely, of course, but there was a definite resemblance.

Certainly, he looked nothing like Daddy. His father was a storm cloud, a thickset, powerfully muscled bear of a man who seemed always in motion except when laboring over his paperwork. Even in his sleep, he tossed and thrashed and mumbled. Throughout the night, Kenny often heard the sound of his father's bed, thumping and creaking under his heavy movements.

The son of a Welsh miner and a British orphan girl, Judson Tallman seemed to care about nothing but work. He worked most of his waking hours. He had no interests other than his job as mine superintendent, no friends, no living relatives other than his son. His life consisted of working, eating, and sleeping.

Kenny thought his father a hard man and an unfeeling one, and judging from the way they acted in Judson Tallman's presence, others were of the same opinion. He had no memory whatsoever of his father ever touching him, except for one occasion when he had slapped him in the face hard enough to make his ears ring because Kenny had talked back.

He had never laid a hand on him again. Neither had he ever tucked Kenny into bed, read him a story, or taken him hunting or fishing. Kenny walked to church alone because his father refused to even discuss going with him. And on the one occasion when Kenny had tried to speak of God and faith, his father had given him such a withering look of contempt that Kenny would have cut out his tongue rather than raise the subject again.

As he grew older, he sought refuge from his father's remoteness in his books, his handmade ships, and the schoolhouse. He had few friends, his closest being Maggie MacAuley and Lester Monk.

He and Lester were opposites in how they spent their time and in all things related to learning, but they were much the same in their dislike of noise and crowds. Besides, Lester needed him, and Kenny was grateful to have someone who depended on him.

Lester wasn't exactly slow-witted, but learning came hard for him, and he also had trouble making decisions. Kenny helped him as best he could, and for his part, Lester regarded his friend with something akin to hero worship.

As for Maggie, he thought it likely he would court her when they were of an age and just as likely that he would marry her someday, even though her nature seemed to run contrary to his own.

Besides Maggie, the one person Kenny liked and admired more than anyone else he knew was Mr. Stuart. He was convinced that the schoolteacher was the smartest and kindest man in Skingle Creek, maybe in the whole state of Kentucky, and he trusted him more than he trusted his own father.

In truth, although the thought never came without a prickle of guilt, Kenny had often wished he had a father like Jonathan Stuart. He reckoned it a terrible shame that the teacher had no children of his own. Indeed, he could not imagine a finer thing in the world than to have a father like Mr. Stuart.

His gaze and his thoughts returned to the photograph in his hand, and he found himself wondering if his father would have been a different sort of man, had Kenny's mother not been a harlot and if she had not abandoned them.

Thirteen

Heartsong, Heartache

I go down from the hill in gladness,
and half with a pain I depart.

"A. E."

Maggie said nothing to Summer about what had transpired between her and Kenny earlier. She did, however, after swearing the younger girl to silence, tell her what had gone on with Billy Macken and Orrin Gaffney the night before.

Almost immediately she wished she had said nothing, for Summer was clearly upset when she learned what had happened.

"Don't worry," Maggie assured her. "Kenny says they won't bother us again. And besides, I have more important stuff to tell you."

Maggie proceeded then to tell her about the vote and about Mr. Stuart's surprised—and obviously pleased—reaction when they turned the money jar over to him. She also confided the fact that their teacher had sold his gold watch in order to make his own donation.

Summer smiled at this and gave a small nod, as if she weren't in the least bit surprised.

By the time Maggie completed a full account of her ideas for the birthday party, Summer looked to be weakening again. She leaned back against the pillows with her eyes closed, her thin hands clutching the quilt. A deep flush stained her hollow cheeks, and, even though the room seemed cold to Maggie, the other girl's hair was damp from perspiration.

Watching her, Maggie felt a sting of disappointment at Summer's tepid show of enthusiasm. But as she studied the other's frail, unhealthy appearance and the small body that was little more than an outline under the bedclothes, disappointment quickly turned to guilt for the pettiness of her thoughts. Clearly, Summer's quietness had nothing to do with a lack of interest. She simply hadn't the strength to express her feelings.

Uneasiness stole over Maggie, dulling the luster of her earlier excitement, but she made an effort to force a cheerful note into her voice. "Now then, Summer Rankin, you have to get well in a hurry. I'm going to need your help getting everything done proper."

Summer smiled but still didn't open her eyes.

"I mean it now," Maggie said, employing her seldom used I'm-older-than-you tone. "You absolutely *have* to be at the birthday party! It will spoil everything if you're not there, do you hear? And I will need your help. Lily is the only one who volunteered to help organize things, and you know how useless *she* is."

Maggie thought a moment, and then she added, "Well, Kenny offered to help too, but we both know how *boys* can be." She rolled her eyes, not wanting Summer to catch on to how things were with her and Kenny. In truth, she knew that Kenny was as good as his word. Mostly, she'd just wanted to say his name.

Summer opened her eyes, but a fierce coughing spasm seized her. When she was finally able to speak, her voice was faint, her words thick. "Kenny's nice," she said. "And smart too. He'll be a big help."

Maggie nodded, her mind now totally fixed on Summer.

She felt a little sick herself but didn't want her friend to see how worried she was. "What will you give Mr. Stuart for his birthday?"

Was the false brightness in her tone as obvious to Summer as it was to her own ear? She hoped not. She was convinced it would only make Summer feel worse if she knew how frightened she was for her.

"I don't know," Summer said with a shake of the head. "I reckon I'd like to give him something real special, but I can't think of anything just now."

There was a faint rasp to her voice, and her usual wheezing seemed to be more ragged, more labored.

Maggie's own chest felt heavy with the ache that had descended on it. "Never mind for now," she said briskly. "The first thing is for you to get well. We can decide on your present for Mr. Stuart later. Besides," she added, "I won't actually have anything special to give him either, though I surely wish I did."

Summer turned to look at her. "That's not true a bit," she said quietly. "You'll be giving the most special thing of all."

Maggie frowned. "How do you figure that?"

Summer lifted herself from the pillows a little and touched Maggie's arm. Her fingers felt scorching hot and dry as paper.

"Why, Maggie, you'll be giving the most important gift of anyone. You'll be the one who sees that things get done and everything turns out right. Just like you always do. You'll see to it that Mr. Stuart has the best party ever. That'll be your gift."

That said, she sank back against the pillows again. She had grown so slight, Maggie noticed again, that she scarcely made an impression in the bedding.

Maggie thought about her friend's words. It would be nice if Summer were right, but no doubt her sisters would have a good laugh over her estimation of Maggie. Especially Eva Grace. As the oldest, she seemed to fancy herself a beauty and the smartest member of the family, whereas Maggie might as well be a toad on a river rock, hopelessly awkward and dumb as a doorstop.

Of course, in all fairness, Maggie sometimes believed Eva Grace to have the smarts of a pump handle.

They were quiet for a time, each thinking her own thoughts, until Summer again pushed herself up and leaned toward Maggie. “What if we were to give Mr. Stuart a birthday present from the two of us?”

“Like what?” Maggie said, at this point skeptical as to what sort of gift they might be able to come up with, given so little time and even less money.

“I might have an idea.”

Maggie looked at her. Summer’s eyes were bright and glistening, and Maggie wondered if the fever was rising.

“Well, it couldn’t cost much, you know. I hardly have anything left after the collection.”

“Me too. But I bet Junior Tyree’s daddy would make it for us real cheap. He’s awful clever with his hands, and he doesn’t charge much for anything he makes. He fixed some new handles for Mama’s stove for practically nothing.”

Maggie studied her friend, saw the flicker of excitement glinting in her sunken eyes where there had been only a glaze of pain before, and suddenly she felt desperate to keep that flame glowing so brightly it would burn away the fever and the dread illness that was draining away the life of her best friend.

“Well?” she prompted, scooting up a little closer to the bed. “So tell me!”

Summer hesitated. “I’ll show you,” she said, and with obvious effort pushed herself up a little more. “Ask Mama for some paper, why don’t you?”

It was dark when Maggie started down the Hill for home, Summer’s drawing in hand. A light freezing rain was falling, glazing the deeply pitted path and slowing her progress considerably.

She didn’t feel nearly as lighthearted as she had on the way up the Hill. She wouldn’t allow herself to think about Kenny now. Her excitement about his declaration that he liked her had been little more than an hour ago, but it seemed far removed indeed. And with

Summer so weak and unable to fully share the enthusiasm about Mr. Stuart's birthday party, she found it difficult to recapture her earlier cheerfulness.

She was also finding it hard to match her friend's excitement about the gift for Mr. Stuart's birthday. The idea seemed so far-fetched, so impossible to imagine. She didn't understand why Summer was so convinced it would work.

But when she'd questioned her, Summer had insisted that "God will make it work if we ask Him to. We just...have to ask. And then believe. It will make Mr. Stuart happy, Maggie. I know it will."

Maggie didn't doubt God's power to make anything happen, not for a minute. But weren't they taking a risk that He would bother with something like this? It wasn't as if she and Summer were some kind of important people. People of *consequence,* Lily would say.

Yet since it was for Mr. Stuart—who was definitely important, at least to his students—and because she had given Summer her word, tomorrow after school she would go down to the junkyard with Junior and ask his da about making what Summer had drawn. Of course, there was no guarantee Ezra Tyree would even agree to work on such a project without getting paid for it. There was no reason he should, after all. The Tyree family needed a living just as much as anyone else in town.

Yet Maggie was pretty sure Junior's da would do it. He had made things free of charge for the school before, she was almost certain. Like the wall hanger that rolled the maps up and down. And the new frame and flower box for the building's only window. She knew Ezra Tyree had done the work, and it must have been for no pay, because Da was a member of the school board, and he said there was never any extra money in the budget for the school building.

Just like home. In fact, just like *everything* in Skingle Creek: There was never any money for "extras."

Maggie's mood darkened as she picked her way over the ice-coated ruts leading off Pine Street, away from the railroad tracks. A terrible ache closed in on her as she turned the corner toward home. She imagined this was what it felt like to be squeezed between the metal jaws Da used to clamp two pieces of wood together. Not even the confirmation that Kenny liked her or the plans for Mr. Stuart's party could make the ache go away.

She stopped and turned around once, looking up the Hill to Summer's house. The lights glowing in the windows made it appear friendly and cheerful, even in the dark. But then she thought of Summer, who, surrounded by all the clamor and commotion of her rowdy family, lay alone in the cold back bedroom, fevered and coughing and weak to the point of wasting away.

Her throat swelled until she could hardly swallow, could barely draw in a breath. She was almost home before she realized that the cold dampness she'd been wiping away from her eyes ever since she'd left Summer's house wasn't rain.

Fourteen

Pity the Children

O God! That bread should be so dear,
And flesh and blood so cheap!

Thomas Hood

Matthew MacAuley was just leaving No. 2 when Arthur Sheehan, one of the older breaker boys, came running up to him.

The boy gasped for a breath and then scooped off his cap. "Mr. Kelly said to come quick, sir! It's Benny Pippino. He's hurt bad!"

Matthew lifted a hand to shade his eyes. The daylight was painful after being in the tunnels most of the morning. "What happened?"

It was a bad sign for Sean Kelly, the breaker boss, to send for help. Never a man to panic, Kelly was used to injuries among the breaker boys and routinely handled most situations on his own—mostly small fingers caught in conveyors or wee lads falling down the chutes, where they could easily smother in the coal.

"Benny was oiling the shafting but got his hand caught in the gears.

Mr. Kelly pulled him free, but his hand—" Sheehan stopped, his face pinched as though he were about to be sick.

Matthew felt the bile rise in his own throat. More than one boy had lost a limb—or a life—in the machinery. "But he's alive, then?"

Sheehan nodded. "Aye, he is. But passed out, sir. And…bleedin' bad."

Matthew started to move but then stopped, catching the boy by the arm. "You go for Doc Woodbridge. I'll get on over to the breaker and see what I can do in the meantime."

Sheehan took off running while Matthew headed the other way. The little Pippino boy—"Pip," as he was called by most of the miners—was the youngest of four boys, all of whom worked below.

He shouldn't have been in the mines at all. Boys were supposed to be at least twelve, and Pip wasn't more than nine, if he was that. But because Maria Pippino had lost her immigrant husband in last year's cave-in and needed all her sons' wages just to survive, the inspector had looked the other way when the youngest child signed on.

It was a common practice in the coal fields, where even a child's wages could make the difference between life or death.

Matthew took the steep, narrow steps two at a time, ignoring the noise from the machinery.

At the top his eyes darted past the long chutes that extended from the roof of the breaker to the ground floor. Most of the boys were still at work, hunched on wooden boards, divided in rows, their clothing and faces black from the dust and smoke. As they worked, they lifted and lowered their feet to stop the coal pouring down the chutes just long enough to take out the culm—the pieces of slate and rock that needed to be separated from the coal itself—before letting the coal continue on to another boy. Their mouths were covered with handkerchiefs to block as much coal dust as possible, and most of them chewed tobacco in an effort to keep any escaping dust from going into their throats.

The sight of their dust-covered faces never failed to tug at Matthew's heart, even more so their bare hands, which were always red and often bleeding. No gloves were allowed so as not to interfere with their finger movements and sense of touch.

He spied a small group huddled together at the far side of the building, watching Sean Kelly. Kelly was on his knees, clearly intent on the small form in front of him. By the time Matthew threaded his way through the rows of boys at work, Kelly had seen him and got to his feet, waiting.

Matthew took in the situation with a glance. The Pippino boy was on his back, eyes closed, his right hand swathed in a cloth that was already blood-soaked. He showed no sign of movement, but Matthew could see that he was breathing.

"He's out cold," Kelly said. "Has been from the time we got his hand free o' the shafting."

Matthew went to one knee and ran a hand over the boy's forehead, and then he bent closer to check his heartbeat. His eyes went to the bloody cloth. They would have to get the bleeding stanched soon, or the lad wouldn't have a chance. Perhaps he didn't anyway, but they had to do their best for him.

"His hand?" Matthew said in a low voice, turning to look up at Kelly.

As if anticipating the question, the breaker boss shook his head. "Most of it's gone. He'll lose the rest."

Matthew shuddered and touched the boy's dusty cheek. "There, lad," he murmured as if Pip could hear him. "We'll get you fixed up, whatever it takes. Things will work out all right, you'll see."

He felt like a terrible liar the moment he uttered the words. There was little "fixing up" to be done for a small boy with a missing hand. And as for things working out all right—Maria Pippino and her brood would be fortunate indeed if they were not set out of their house onto the road, even in the dead of winter.

The company was not known for an abundance of mercy, nor for showing pity to a coal miner's widow with no man to earn their keep. Even with three sons still fit and able to go into the mines, they would be hard-pressed to stay in Skingle Creek at all, would find it harder still to maintain a decent way of life.

It was times like this that stirred an old rage in Matthew, making him painfully aware of his helplessness to improve the lot of his men, and dredging up the hateful reminder of just how subject he and his family were to the same ill fortunes as their neighbors. There were no labor unions in Skingle Creek. Indeed, the company had made it known in no uncertain terms that they would fire any man from his job for even raising the subject of a union and would not hesitate to shut down the mines if the issue were pressed.

Matthew had seen enough from men like Judson Tallman to deduce that if the mine owners themselves were as hard-hearted as their superintendent and his kind, threats of revenge from the bosses against union organizers were not merely idle words.

"The doc is here."

Sean Kelly's voice pulled Matthew back to his surroundings. He got to his feet to make room for Lebreen Woodbridge—for whom he had little use and, if truth were told, even less trust. Still, the injured boy desperately needed attention, and capable or not, Woodbridge was unquestionably the one man in town who stood any chance at all of helping him.

At supper that night, as Maggie listened to the exchange between her parents about the fate of the little Pippino boy, she could sense her da's frustration as keenly as her mother's distress. Where her mother could not seem to think of anything but the injured boy's condition, her father seemed fixated on the hopelessness of the town as a whole.

He scared her a little, talking as he did about there being no hope of improving the lot of the miners and their families, no possibility of things ever getting any better than they were today—indeed no future for the folks of Skingle Creek except more of the same. As the conversation went on, Maggie began to realize that her father's anger wasn't so much directed at the men who owned the mines as toward himself.

He seemed to be overwhelmed by a feeling of helplessness and even guilt.

Clearly, her mother had also picked up on Da's strange quarrel with himself, for at one point in his tirade she reached to cover his hand with her own. "Don't take on so, Matthew. Things can't be as bad as you're making them out to be, and even if they are, none of it is your fault."

Da pushed his plate away, even though he'd scarcely touched his meal. "The safety of the men—and the children—is my responsibility, Kate. A foreman ought to be able to keep a wee lad like Benny Pippino safe! He shouldn't be working in the mines to begin with! He's little more than a babe!"

"Matthew, you do your best. You do what you can."

"Small comfort, that, when I can't even protect a child! The boy lost his hand, Kate, and he may yet lose his life. It should never have happened at all, and I can't so much as get proper treatment for him."

"But you said the company will pay the hospital bill."

Da scowled, his face turning even redder. "Aye, they'll pay for the hospital all right, but if the boy isn't fit to work one-handed the day he comes home, then the bosses will throw him and the rest of his family out the door to make room for new renters who can pay!"

Maggie jumped, as did her sisters, when he scooted his chair back with a terrible screech. "I'm going for a walk." His words were clipped, his tone harsh as he tossed his napkin onto the table and crossed the room to yank his coat from its hook on the wall.

He was no more out the door than Maggie's mother stood and went to get her coat. "I'm going after your father," she said, tugging her collar snugly about her neck. "You girls mind the baby."

She glanced at Baby Ray, who sat in his high chair, stuffing potatoes in his mouth with his fingers. Then she hurried out the door, leaving Maggie and her sisters staring at each other and wondering what was happening with their parents.

Matthew was a good ways down the road before Kate managed to catch up with him. The cold wind stung her face and burned her eyes. By the time she reached him she was chilled through.

The hunched shoulders, the head tipped down instead of lifted high as it usually was, hands in his pockets—all spoke to her of his self-debasement and feelings of powerlessness.

"Matthew—"

She caught his arm. He stopped and turned to look at her. "Leave me be, Kate. I need to clear my head."

"You need to stop beating yourself up for something you can't help."

He shook his head. "That's not it, Kate."

"Then what, Matthew? What's eating at you so?"

His shoulders sagged still more as he turned to stare into the night. For the first time, Kate saw signs of aging upon the face she knew better than her own: the lines that webbed outward from his eyes, the even deeper lines that creased his forehead, the silver shot through his copper hair about the temples. She reached a hand to his bearded cheek, and he caught it and held it there.

"It's because no one can help," he said.

The ache of despair in his voice tore at Kate's heart like a knife slashing her skin.

"Oh, Matthew, you can't keep this up," she said, her own voice hoarse. "You can't go on trying to shoulder everyone else's troubles! You're only one man."

He took her hand and passed it over his eyes, and then he held it against his heart. "When a man cannot protect a helpless child, Kate, he is not much of a man."

Something turned in Kate, and her voice broke when she answered him. "You are the strongest—the finest man in this entire town, Matthew MacAuley. But you're not an army, and an army is what it would take to heal the troubles in Skingle Creek."

He let out a long breath, looking at her as if he knew she was merely trying to make him feel better. But Kate could see that he *wanted* her to make him feel better, and so she kept on.

"I know it's hard for you, Matthew. But it won't always be this way. One day we'll have our farm, and your only boss will be yourself. Things will be better for us then."

He gave her a lame smile and kissed the palm of her hand. "Ah, Kate, that dream is wearing thin, and you know it. Besides, I'd still have to work for the company, at least for the first few years. A farm alone wouldn't keep us without a second wage."

"Shush, Matthew," she said, growing impatient with his stubbornness. "If you'd spend as much time praying as you do worrying, you might just be surprised what would happen."

He looked indignant. "I *do* pray."

"Yes, but you worry more."

He caught her by the forearms and held her away from him as he studied her. "You can be a terrible scold sometimes, Kate MacAuley, for such a slip of a girl," he said, his Irish tongue thickening.

"Perhaps because I married such a hardheaded man."

"Oh, is that so?" He slung an arm around her and, turning her toward home, started walking.

"Indeed."

"Ah, Katie, Katie. You are a treasure, and that's the truth."

Kate dug in a bit closer against him, pleased to hear the smile in his voice. "The children will be wondering what's become of us. Let's go home."

He stopped, dipped his head, and kissed her lightly.

"Matthew, someone will see!"

Ignoring her protest, he kissed her again. When he lifted his face from hers, he searched her eyes for a long moment. "I can't think what I would ever do without you, Kate."

Kate didn't know if it was the events of the day or his earlier dark mood infecting her, but she felt a cold shadow pass over her heart. She had always known that, strong and capable as he was, Matthew would be all right without her. What chilled her soul was when she let herself consider what she would do without *him.*

Every time the question stole into her mind, she determined to pray just that much more faithfully for the farm he had dreamed of all these years. Wouldn't he be surprised if he should learn that she wanted that farm even more desperately than he did?

Kate wanted, more than anything else, whatever would get her husband out of the coal mines. And the sooner the better.

Fifteen

What Kind of Man?

I am only one,
But still I am one.
I cannot do everything,
But still I can do something.

Edward Everett Hale

Matthew saw it as nothing short of a miracle that the Pippino lad managed to survive. Though the boy lost his hand, he would live, and Matthew was determined that he would remain on the payroll. To ensure it, he meant to face Judson Tallman man to man.

He came up from below early Monday, washed up as best he could at the pump, and headed for the superintendent's office. By the time he reached the top of the steps, his hands were clammy, his heart beating way too fast. It grated on him that a man like Tallman could make him squirm, but then he doubted there was a miner among the lot of them whose insides didn't clench in the super's presence.

Judson Tallman was one of the oddest types Matthew had ever come up against. To the best of his recollection, Tallman had never shown a hint of interest in any man who worked under him nor a drop of compassion in the face of injury or death. He had never seen Tallman smile, had never caught a glimpse of emotion in the man. So cold, so unfeeling did he appear that he almost seemed more like one of the machines used in the mine than a human being with a soul.

Matthew couldn't help but wonder what sort of father Tallman was to his son, who must be the same age, or near to it, as his own Maggie. Sure, it would not be easy for a child to live in the shadow of such a stone.

It was widely known that Tallman's wife had run out on him. That no one seemed to know the truth surrounding the scandal only raised more questions and added fuel to the rumors that Tallman might have been violent with her.

It occurred to him as he knocked on the door of the superintendent's office that this probably wasn't the time to be puzzling over the super's personal life. As it was, there seemed little likelihood that he would gain a sympathetic audience from the man on the other side of the door; it wouldn't help his cause to go in predisposed against him.

Tallman acknowledged him with a curt nod and a cold stare. He sat at his desk, drumming the fingers of one hand on a stack of papers in front of him, a mannerism he quickly traded for rolling a pencil between the fingers of the same hand.

He offered no attempt whatsoever to put Matthew at ease, but then Matthew had not expected that he would.

"If I might have a word with you, sir?"

Cap in hand, Matthew managed not to cringe at the note of subservience in his voice. He straightened his shoulders, put his hands behind his back, and lifted his chin, adding, "It's about Benny Pippino."

"Who?"

Matthew found it discouraging to his purpose that the man didn't even recognize the boy's name. "The breaker boy who lost his hand last week."

Recognition seemed to dawn slowly, though Tallman gave nothing more than a slight turn of his head. "What about him?"

"I was hoping to keep him on the payroll. His father was killed in the cave-in last year, you see, and even with his three brothers working the mine, they barely manage to survive. The lad's wages are needed just to keep them from the road."

The other gave an impatient shrug. The thing about Tallman, Matthew realized, was that he *always* seemed impatient.

"If the boy can't work, he doesn't get paid."

Matthew swallowed. "But that's just it, sir. There must be something he can do, some way he can stay on."

"I hardly think so."

Clearly, Tallman was dismissing the idea without further thought—and dismissing Matthew at the same time. He turned his attention back to his desk, leaving Matthew to feel like a great fool.

Fool or not, he had no intention of giving up so easily. "Doc Woodbridge says the lad should be up and about again in a few days," he said. "Surely we could find something for him by then."

Tallman's head came up sharply, his expression one of contempt. "I said *no*, MacAuley. There will be no sympathy pay around here." A glacial finality laced his words.

As if you would know anything about sympathy, you cold, unfeeling—

Matthew flinched, for an instant thinking he had spoken aloud. Even if he had, Tallman probably wouldn't have heard. As if Matthew were no longer in the room, the superintendent had already returned to his work, his dark head lowered, his concentration fixed on the papers in front of him.

Matthew felt his blood heat. His grip on his cap tightened. He knew he must keep his temper in check lest he risk his own job, but even so, he would not be banished like a bumbling, disobedient child.

"If I may, sir—"

Tallman looked up, his mouth hard, his eyes going over Matthew with unmistakable irritation.

Stubbornly, Matthew plunged on. "Would you object to keeping the boy on the payroll if I can find a job that needs doing—one that he can handle in spite of his injury?"

He held his breath as Tallman glared at him, his fingers again tapping on the desk.

"And what sort of job do you think that might be, MacAuley?"

Matthew shook his head. "I don't know just yet, sir, but I'll wager something can be found, something the boy can handle. Pip is a hard worker, according to Sean Kelly. I'd like to keep him on and so would Kelly."

Tallman's eyes narrowed still more. Matthew had all he could do not to squirm under the intense scrutiny. Finally, though, the super curled his lip, gave a short wave, and said, "All right, then. But there'd better be no trickery. I'm not passing out any favors here."

Matthew caught a breath. "Aye, sir. It will be a job that needs doing. You have my word on it. And thank you, sir."

Matthew turned to go, but Tallman stopped him. "MacAuley?"

He turned back. "Sir?"

"If I find out that little *dago* isn't holding his own, I'll call *you* to account along with him, do you understand?"

The offensive word—heard all too often in the mines—made Matthew clench his teeth. He managed to keep the venom out of his voice only with the most deliberate effort. "I understand, sir."

I understand all right, you hardheaded Welsh bigot.

He took the steps away from Tallman's office two at a time, fuming in his rush to get home and rid himself of the foul taste in his mouth.

Maggie watched her sleeping sisters in the bed they shared beside her own. Nell Frances was snoring lightly, while Eva Grace slept on her side, one hand tucked daintily under her head as if to keep her long blond hair from getting tangled.

Eva Grace, of course, was far too refined to ever snore.

It was well after eleven. Maggie was always asleep long before this time, but Da's story at supper about his visit to Mr. Tallman kept running through her mind, making sleep impossible.

Even now she shivered at the account of Mr. Tallman's coldness and lack of sympathy. Was he that heartless where Kenny was concerned? She hated the thought of Kenny being hurt, especially by his own father. Her da could be a hard man, but she never had to question whether he cared about his family.

Her mother said that Da would lay his life down for any one of them, and Maggie never doubted but what it was true. Though Da might give her a thorough scolding one minute, in no time at all he would catch her up in one of his big old bear hugs and set her to squawking with laughter. And every once in a while would come that squeeze on the shoulder or tug on a lock of hair that let her know he was pleased with something she'd said or done—or maybe that he was just pleased with her for no special reason.

She couldn't imagine having a father who didn't love her. Even the thought of it made her eyes sting. She could only hope Mr. Tallman was nicer at home than he was at the mine.

Benny Pippino, who didn't have a father, came to mind again. Da said Mrs. Pippino depended on the wages of all her sons just to pay the rent and keep food on the table. What would she do without the extra pay?

There must be *some* kind of job for the boy. Da seemed to believe there was and clearly he was bent on finding that job.

But why was Mr. Tallman so dead set against the idea?

She supposed she ought to pray about the situation. But she was finally getting sleepy, and the room was so cold. Even with the rag rug beside the bed, she hated setting her bare feet on the floor. On nights like these, the cold would seep right through the thin material and shoot up her legs.

Still, didn't Mr. Stuart always say to pray if you have a problem, and pray even harder if someone else has one? She drew a long breath, delayed another moment or two, and then she threw the bedcovers off and slipped out of bed to her knees.

She was shivering, but she reckoned the Lord didn't mind that her teeth were chattering as she said a prayer for Benny Pippino and for Mr. Tallman's hard heart.

And for Kenny, just in case Mr. Tallman wasn't any nicer to his son than he'd been to her da today.

Sixteen

When Hope Falters

I falter where I firmly trod.

Alfred, Lord Tennyson

What was going on with Maggie MacAuley?

Jonathan Stuart studied the cloud of fiery red hair as the girl bent low over her desk. She was supposed to be copying her spelling words—five times each, as he had instructed the class—but for at least five minutes now she had been leaning on her elbow, her pencil poised in midair with no detectable movement from head or hand. Had it been any other student besides Maggie, Jonathan might have thought she was dozing.

Not that this was the first time he had caught the girl being idle. Indeed, over the past few days he'd frequently had to rouse her from these episodes. But today she had seemed particularly distracted. Several times he had caught her either staring out the window, seemingly oblivious to her surroundings, or else making a poor pretense of working at her studies when he could tell she wasn't concentrating at all.

Jonathan had been a teacher long enough to distinguish between the predictable and fairly common distractions that could steal a student's concentration and those that pointed to something more serious—problems at home, the onset of an illness, or spring fever.

He was almost certain there was no trouble at home of any serious nature. His impression of the MacAuleys over the years had been that of an extraordinarily close and devoted family. Matthew MacAuley was known and respected as an honest, hardworking mine foreman who was good to his family and his neighbors. As for illness, Mrs. MacAuley was the type of mother who kept a watchful eye on her brood and wouldn't think of sending one of them out of the house if there were any sign of sickness. Besides, Maggie certainly showed no hint of being unwell.

And the snow falling outside almost guaranteed this wasn't a case of spring fever.

It wasn't that Maggie's total attention was riveted on her studies a hundred percent of the time. She was an extremely bright girl, curious and eager to learn, but she possessed the sort of mental acuity that needed to be continually challenged lest she grow restless and bored.

Jonathan knew the girl had been troubled for a long time now over the ailing Summer Rankin—and well she might be. In truth, he feared there would be an even more bitter grief for Maggie in the not too distant future. It was possible that her behavior was due solely to Summer's illness, but somehow Jonathan thought not. So, although he disliked keeping such a good student after school because of any negative implication the other students were sometimes quick to attach, he thought he would at least let her know that he was concerned about her and give her an opportunity to explain.

The familiar lag in his heartbeat reminded him that what he should do was go home and rest. Not that he begrudged the extra time needed to speak with a student. It was just that any additional drain on his energy was nearly immobilizing. He was increasingly frustrated because there was so much he wanted to do for his students, yet so little he was able to do. Sometimes it seemed to tire him merely to think.

He could not help but wonder how his illness might be affecting the children. He would hate for them to believe he had lost interest in them, that he no longer cared about them.

Most of his students, like Maggie, had decent, caring parents who involved themselves in their children's lives. But there were others—Kenny Tallman came to mind—who often appeared, if not dejected or somewhat lost, at least lacking in some elemental, enabling sense of worth.

If God had gifted him in any way at all, Jonathan sensed it was to be a kind of shelter for his students. To his way of thinking, his responsibility wasn't only to teach, though certainly teaching was a high calling in itself. But he saw it as equally important to offer each child who entered his schoolroom a place of safety, where there was someone to trust, someone who would at least make an effort to understand that child's heart and needs. Someone who would recognize the spark of the Divine in each youthful spirit and nurture it.

It ate at him like a cancer that he could no longer provide what his students needed. Of late, he seemed to live under a cloying cloud of failure that thwarted his efforts and threatened to deny him in part the goals he had set for himself as a teacher.

The truth was that his students deserved better than he had been giving. He was determined that this downward spiral on his part would not continue.

Maggie felt strung as tight as a slingshot and slightly breathless as she stood waiting for Mr. Stuart to clean his eyeglasses.

She couldn't think of what she had done to bring on a talking-to, but she knew she must have done something. Mr. Stuart seldom kept a student after school, and when he did it was most usually for one of two reasons: that student had caused trouble and was up for a scolding, or else extra help was needed in a particular lesson.

To the best she knew, she hadn't done anything actually wrong—although Mr. Stuart had caught her woolgathering again. She knew she wasn't failing any of her subjects—her grades would have showed it before now. Well, she couldn't draw worth anything, and her grade showed *that* too, but that wasn't exactly anything new.

The thing was, Mr. Stuart had looked uncommonly serious when he asked her to stay after school, and her mind had been racing ever since to come up with a reason. Watching him slip his glasses on, Maggie figured she was about to learn that reason.

"I asked you to stay, Maggie, because I thought we might have a little talk."

Jonathan smiled to put the girl at ease and indicated that she should pull up a chair beside his desk. Once she was seated, he sat quietly and studied her for a moment. Then he decided to come right to the point.

"I've been wondering, Maggie, if everything is all right with you."

A pinched frown replaced her earlier expression of uneasiness. "All right? Ah...yes, sir." She paused. "Am I in some kind of trouble?"

Jonathan hurried to reassure her. "No, no. Not at all. It's just that you've seemed somewhat...distracted...lately, and I wanted to make sure there's nothing wrong." He waited. "Is there?"

As he watched, the girl's usually cheerful countenance underwent a series of changes. At first something like fear flickered in her eyes, almost instantly replaced by what could only be described as anger or resentment, followed by an expression that completely baffled him, for what he saw looking out at him appeared to be a plea for help.

Then it was gone, and she was again closed to him, her spirit shuttered by an adolescent wall of defense Jonathan recognized and knew from previous experience to be very nearly impenetrable, at least by an adult.

Had he heard about the incident with Billy and Orrin? Maggie shifted on the chair, tempted to spill the entire story, including her worry for Kenny.

She'd seen the two boys watching him during recess and after school, staring at him hard and then snickering to each other. No matter what Kenny said, she didn't believe for a minute those two were finished with their meanness. No way would their bullying cease just because Kenny had threatened to tell his father.

But as for telling Mr. Stuart, she couldn't. Both she and Kenny had agreed to keep silent. Besides, what could the teacher do? He was certainly no match for thugs like Billy and Orrin, especially with him being so poorly these days. Why, if those two set their minds to it, they could hurt Mr. Stuart—and hurt him bad.

Not that Mr. Stuart would ever believe anything of the sort. What with his being a teacher and all, and being the kindhearted man that he was, more than likely it would never occur to him that two of his students might actually hurt another student...or him.

She should have known he would notice that she wasn't exactly herself these days, though. Mr. Stuart was never the one to miss much, and Maggie knew her mind was jumping around in all directions lately, hardly ever landing where it belonged. She tried to concentrate on her schoolwork, but it seemed that when she wasn't thinking about Summer and wondering when she was going to get better...wondering *if* she was going to get better...then she was worrying about Kenny, about what Billy and Orrin might do to him. Or fretting about Mr. Stuart, which was most of the time. And if that wasn't enough, she also had poor Benny Pippino on her mind too.

Her mother always said that worrying didn't do a bit of good, that if, instead, they would spend their worry-time on praying, they'd see more results. Ma might be right, but what Maggie couldn't seem to figure out was how you stopped worrying, at least about the people who were important to you. How did you just stop being afraid for someone you cared about?

Of late, it almost seemed as if she was always afraid. She felt as if she spent most of the time holding her breath. In fact, how long had it been since she'd taken a really deep breath? When was the last time she hadn't felt fearful and twisted in knots inside?

Clearly, she needed to tell Mr. Stuart something. Otherwise, he'd think she was just another silly girl mooning about boys and clothes. Someone like Lily Woodbridge. She definitely did not want to be lumped in the same basket with Lily, especially by Mr. Stuart.

But she had already decided she couldn't tell him about Billy and Orrin. And she didn't feel like talking to anyone about Summer. Somehow it only seemed to make things worse to talk about her. It was almost as if she didn't dare say out loud what she was afraid of, that maybe, if she kept her fears to herself, what she dreaded wouldn't happen.

She could tell the teacher about Benny Pippino. Even though the boy wasn't one of his students, Mr. Stuart would care about him. In fact, maybe he could even think of something to help. What a grand surprise for Da *that* would be!

❧

Jonathan's spirit shrank like a child before a thrashing as he realized where Maggie's story was headed.

"And because he lost his hand, he can't be a breaker boy any longer, and Mr. Tallman—"

She stopped as if she couldn't decide whether to finish what she'd started.

"It's all right, Maggie. I'll keep your confidence."

She nodded then and continued. "Mr. Tallman wanted to put him out of the mines altogether. I reckon he figures Pip won't be able to do anything worthwhile now. But Da coaxed him into keeping him on, and he finally agreed. But only if Da can find him a job that truly needs doing. Otherwise, Da might be in trouble too."

Jonathan's heart hammered and then slowed. He felt as if he might strangle on the knot of resentment in his throat. But anger at Judson Tallman would accomplish nothing for the injured child. Like any other strong emotion it would only chip away at his own tenuous strength.

He took a deep breath, waiting for Maggie to go on. When she didn't, he said, "It's good of your father to try to help the boy."

Again Maggie nodded, but her expression sobered even more. "I don't think he has much hope of finding another job for Pip, though. Da says you mostly need two hands to work in the mines."

Something stirred at the back of Jonathan's mind. He tried to think, but he was fading quickly. He needed to rest, for a short while at least. Perhaps later he could come up with an idea. He might even speak with Matthew MacAuley. But he mustn't say anything to Maggie. Not just yet.

"I'm glad you told me about this, Maggie," he said. "I'll pray for—Pip, is it?" And of course he would. Even if he could do nothing else, he could pray for that unfortunate child.

Jonathan wanted to ask her about Summer, but he sensed that she had closed this part of herself to him, perhaps to anyone, at least for now. He also suspected that she was holding back something else, something she wanted to tell him but for whatever reason couldn't bring herself to divulge. And, disgusted with his own sorry weakness, he realized that at this moment he simply did not have the strength to encourage any further confidences.

"You should be starting for home now," he said. "Your mother will worry."

"Oh, I don't go straight home after school," she told him, getting up from her chair. "I work at the company store most days."

Jonathan watched her leave, a cloud of discouragement settling over him. He didn't like to think about the future that might await Maggie MacAuley.

The girl had the kind of intelligence that hungered for more and more knowledge, the sort of searching curiosity that would never be easily satisfied. But the wages of a miner were barely adequate to keep a family in food and shelter. There was little hope for any advanced education for the MacAuley children. Instead, it seemed all too likely that Maggie, like so many others before her, would end up cutting her schooling short to go to work in the company store or somewhere else until she married—most likely a coal miner—and brought children into the same world to live the same kind of life as her own: a life of hard work and narrow boundaries and little promise of anything better.

More than anything else, it was this lack of promise, this bleak absence of hope for children like Maggie—children he had come to love—and his utter helplessness to do anything about it that sometimes caused Jonathan to feel as if his own hope was bleeding to death, one drop at a time.

Seventeen

A Meeting of the School Board

I feel like one who treads alone...

Thomas Moore

On Thursday evening a special meeting of the school board was held at Jonathan Stuart's request.

Pastor Ben Wallace came early and had a fire blazing in the iron stove. When Jonathan arrived, the meeting room was already comfortably warm. Someone—most likely Regina Wallace, the pastor's wife—had thoughtfully set out an ample supply of coffee and cookies. All in all, the room was cozy, the setting friendly.

By the time the other members began to file in, however, Jonathan was struggling with a severe fit of nervousness, prompted, of course, by the proposal he was about to make. He knew these men, knew their hearts were good, and over the years they had seldom refused him anything they could manage. Even so, money was scarce in a mining town, and he was fairly certain that any extra funds came directly from the board members' pockets. That being the case, he had always tried to be rigorously conservative with his requests. In truth, he disliked asking for anything and routinely took care of many of the school's small expenses out of his own money.

What he intended to suggest during the next few moments wasn't exactly extravagant, yet there was no denying that it was out of the ordinary and could hardly be considered a critical need. Except, perhaps, to a widowed mother with four children and a little boy with a missing hand.

❧

He watched each man who entered, studying their faces as he laced his fingers together to still his unsteady hands. Ben Wallace, the pastor of Jonathan's congregation and his closest friend in Skingle Creek, was by nature generous to a fault and would do anything he could for the children. Charles Ferguson, the manager of the company store, was occasionally somewhat dour and took forever to make a decision, but in the end he almost always voted the same way as the others.

Lebreen Woodbridge, the town's one physician and a difficult man to predict, was wearing his usual mask of guarded cynicism as he walked in with Ernest Gibbon, president of the town's only bank. It was a bit of a push to call the small white dwelling with the stone front a "bank." Miners were paid mostly in scrip and, far from managing to put a little extra by, were usually in debt to the company store. But for the fortunate few who were able to maintain a small savings, as well as for the non-mining families in the community—also few—the bank existed under Gibbon's able management and the assistance of one clerk, Gibbon's son.

Not far behind the doctor and Gibbon came Henry Piper, an aging bachelor who lived just outside of town on a large piece of land his family had farmed for years. Henry was thought of as the town eccentric. Never seen in anything but a plaid flannel shirt and a pair of overalls that were a full size too large for his scrawny frame, he smoked some sort of offensive-smelling tobacco in his pipe, its odor accompanying him everywhere.

Word had it that Henry Piper was an educated man, a graduate of the state university who had in fact once studied for the law. But upon his father's death, Henry had come home to manage the farm and at the same time care for his mother and younger sister.

As it happened, his mother died within six months of Henry's father, and not long after the sister married a buggy salesman and went to live in Richmond. After losing his family, Henry apparently isolated himself more and more on the farm, his only involvement with the town being his place on the school board and his regular weekly attendance at the Baptist church.

Jonathan doubted that Henry was a true eccentric. More than likely, he was just another lonely man who needed companionship but was either too shy or too set in his ways to seek it out.

The last to enter was Maggie MacAuley's father. Matthew MacAuley was the only miner on the board—perhaps a sop to the "laborers" of the community—and as practical and levelheaded a man as Jonathan had ever known. Indeed, he had come to trust MacAuley's judgment and held him in high regard.

Having talked with MacAuley beforehand, he was assured of at least one member's full support. Well, he could probably count on the support of two members. Although Ben Wallace hadn't committed himself, Jonathan knew his friend well enough to be reasonably certain of what his decision would be.

As soon as all the pleasantries were exchanged and all the coffee mugs filled, Ben called the meeting to order, immediately deferring to Jonathan.

As he walked to the front of the room, Jonathan was keenly aware that all eyes were upon him. They were friendly gazes, and he reminded himself that he was among good people who truly cared about Skingle Creek and the town's children. For that matter, they had demonstrated more than once that they also cared about him.

Nevertheless, he was about to strip himself of his pride and lay bare the truth—more of the truth than what he would have chosen to tell under normal circumstances—about his medical condition. He could hardly impress upon them any existing need without being ruthlessly candid about why that need existed.

With his heart delivering a hammer blow to his chest, Jonathan clenched his hands behind his back, cleared his throat, and started in to explain just why he had reached the point of needing some assistance. Assistance of a physical nature, not in a teaching capacity.

The longer Jonathan Stuart spoke, the more Matthew MacAuley found himself struck anew by a genuine admiration for the man and a fresh realization as to why his Maggie and the other children were so devoted to their teacher.

For the first few months after Stuart had come to town, Matthew had thought him quite a puzzle: a good enough sort of fellow, but with his grand education and solitary ways, a bit difficult to warm up to. It had taken a year or more before he could manage to be reasonably at ease with the man.

Even now, he could not help but be sensitive to the differences between the schoolteacher and himself. Whereas Stuart was slight, albeit fairly tall, Matthew had the heavy shoulders and chest, the beefy arms and hands of the MacAuley tribe, causing him to feel something of a lout in comparison. Then too, while Stuart's grooming was that of a gentleman—never less than impeccable—Matthew could scrub for a month and still not completely rid himself of the black dust ground into his knuckles and under his fingernails from years in the mines.

It seemed that everything about the genteel Jonathan Stuart only served to remind Matthew of his own coarseness.

Over time, though, as he had come to know Stuart better, he often forgot to feel awkward in the schoolteacher's presence, forgot to be intimidated by his intelligence and fine manners. Instead, he became increasingly appreciative of the man's kindness and his unflagging efforts to benefit the children in his charge.

He had also come to believe, like Kate, that Jonathan Stuart was "a man owned by God." It did seem that Skingle Creek's only schoolteacher was that rarity known as a "good man."

Despite the respect Stuart had earned for himself, however, Matthew had taken care to warn him not to get his hopes up tonight, for the board members might view his plan as too far-fetched—and too expensive.

Not long into his delivery, though, Matthew realized that Jonathan Stuart apparently had anticipated any objections that might be raised. Watching Stuart, he was surprised at how nervous the teacher appeared to be. He was also gripped by a very real concern for the man as he noted the pallor of his skin, the severe leanness of his frame, and the unmistakable shortness of breath as he spoke.

Slowly, it dawned on Matthew how high a price this address was bound to exact from Jonathan Stuart. It was clear the man had no thought of sparing his pride in order to achieve his goal. Consequently, his respect for the schoolteacher rose another notch.

Only when Stuart was nearly finished with his discourse did Matthew realize that he had been silently but fervently praying for Jonathan Stuart with nearly every word he spoke.

When Matthew walked into the kitchen later that night, Kate was waiting for him, just as he'd expected.

He had told no one but Kate about Jonathan Stuart's plan. Maggie, especially, would have given him no peace at all if she'd known what was afoot. Even Kate had that impatient, gritty look in her eye, as if she would not wait long to hear all about the meeting. But Matthew signaled her that they would talk later, after the children were in bed.

Later, in their bedroom, she didn't waste a moment before starting in on him.

"Well? What did they say?"

Matthew shrugged, undoing his collar. "Nothing."

"What do you mean, 'nothing'? Sure, and they must have said something."

"Only that they would give it some thought and get back to him."

"That's all?"

Matthew dropped his suspenders and then realized he hadn't brought Sadie inside. "That's all. I expect they'll make up their minds in a few days."

"Well, what do you think they'll do, Matthew?"

"There's no telling," he said, sitting down beside her on the bed. "I can predict Ben Wallace's vote well enough, I expect. And perhaps Charley Ferguson's as well. But as for the rest of them..."

Again he shrugged. "The only thing I can tell you is that this could not have been an easy thing for Mr. Stuart to do. I expect it took a considerable notch out of his pride, and he had to know he was risking his job by admitting just how ill he really is."

"Oh, Matthew! You don't think they'll let him go?"

Matthew shook his head. "No. Some men might, but not these men. I'll wager that Mr. Stuart's job is safe as long as he's able to make it to the schoolhouse."

"Thanks be," Kate murmured.

"Aye," Matthew agreed. He stood and hiked up his suspenders. "Well, I'll just go and let the dog in."

"You'll tell me as soon as you hear anything?"

"You know I will, Kate."

When he reached the kitchen, he was surprised to find Maggie standing at the sink, draining the last of a jar of milk by the flickering light of a candle. Her eyes widened, as if she'd been caught at some mischief.

"Da," she said, quickly setting the milk in the sink. "I was just going to bed."

"Ah. And I thought you were just having yourself a drink of milk."

"I'm sorry, Da. I was being as quiet as I could."

"What are you doing still up at this hour, girl? You have school tomorrow, you know."

She nodded. "I couldn't get to sleep. I know how you always say a cup of milk helps you to sleep, so I thought I'd have one myself."

"*Warm* milk, lass. Did you warm it?"

She shook her head. "Maybe I should have some more and warm it this time?" she asked hopefully.

"I think not," said Matthew, feigning a sternness he didn't feel. "What is it that's keeping you awake, then?"

She shrugged, not looking at him. "I don't know. I just...I don't know."

Matthew was fairly sure she did know. He could tell by the way she was avoiding his eyes that something was eating at her. Now that he thought of it, the girl had not been herself lately. Too quiet. Too quiet altogether. And evasive. Was it her concern for Jonathan Stuart? Her wee friend Summer? What?

He knew from experience she wouldn't confide in him, even if he were to ask. Like her sisters, she took her secrets only to their mother. Kate had a good way with them. He always told her she was too soft with the children, but in truth, he was glad of it.

Girls needed a mother they could turn to, someone who could make them feel safe. He knew they considered him too hard, too set in his ways. Perhaps they were even a bit afraid of him, though he didn't like to think it.

He had been afraid of *his* father, he had—a man fond of beating on his two sons and even his wife when he was in his cups.

There had been a night just past his sixteenth year when Matthew stopped being afraid.

Even then, he had been big. No bigger than the old man, but not nearly so soft and flabby, either. His da had kicked their dog across the room and then gone after Matthew's mother with his belt because she'd given the hound—her pet, not his—a leftover biscuit and what was left of the gravy from supper.

Seeing his mother, crouched like a dog herself before her husband's rage, Matthew felt something snap inside him. The next thing he knew he'd ripped the belt away and turned it on his father, lashing him across the back with a furious threat that if he ever hurt his mother again, he would use an oak club on him instead of a belt.

There had been bad blood between him and his father from that night on, but it was the last time the old man had touched Matthew's mother in anger.

It was also the last time Matthew ever raised a hand to another soul. The fury that exploded out of control in him that night had actually frightened him. Never again would he risk turning into the wild thing he had become for those few deranged moments in his mother's kitchen.

His memories of his father gave him reason enough to hate the thought that his own children might fear him, yet he couldn't seem to find a way to be softer with them, to encourage their trust in him. So he fell into the practice of handling the practical side of their needs and applying any necessary discipline, while leaving to Kate their more personal matters and confidences.

Now, looking at this daughter of his with her mane of flaming hair and large, troubled eyes, he sensed a sudden, but not unfamiliar, desire to gather her in his arms and hold her and rock her to sleep as he had once done when she'd been but a babe.

Instead, he merely gave her a quick pat on the shoulder and told her to go on to bed.

After she left the kitchen, Matthew went to the door and let the dog in, stooping down to rub her cold ears and stroke her back, waiting until she plopped down on her rug behind the stove before going back to his own bed.

Kate was only half awake when he slipped in beside her, shivering from the cold, but she opened her arms to him, holding him until the chill had passed and he finally fell asleep.

Eighteen

An Exchange of Pain

Do you know that your strong heart,
so noble and true,
strengthens all those who stand
in the shadow of you?

Anonymous

Maggie had been told she was a lot like her grandmother on her mother's side.

She didn't remember her Grandma Min, who had died only a year or so after Maggie was born, but she had heard plenty about the old lady she was said to resemble.

In truth, she would eavesdrop on as many hushed conversations as possible between her mother and Aunt Vivienne, Ma's sister who came to visit them from Frankfort every few months. It seemed that Grandma Min had been "strange." Not strange in that her mind was unhinged or that she did bad things, but more that she was different from their other relatives. Different from just about everybody, from the sound of it.

Fascinated by the stories she'd heard, Maggie was pretty sure that if she were to take after one of her grandparents, Grandma Min most likely would have been her choice.

Except on days like today.

It seemed that Grandma Min got "feelings." Maggie had heard her mother, who was older than Aunt Vivienne, say that Grandma Min had always seemed to know when something bad was going to happen. Aunt Vivienne seemed fixed on the idea that it was "an Irish thing."

Maggie thought that sometimes she got "feelings" too. Not strong ones like Grandma Min, but more a kind of nudge that something was wrong, or something was about to happen.

She still remembered the first time she'd experienced such a feeling. One of the Twomey twins, who lived across the road a few houses down, was teasing an old hound dog with a stick, chasing it up the road a few feet at a time. Maggie had been standing at the gate, watching, when all of a sudden she felt a strong sense that the ornery little Twomey boy should hotfoot it back to his house and get inside as fast as he could.

She shouted at him, but as all the Twomey young'uns were wont to do—there were at least seven or eight of them—he ignored her and went right on deviling that old hound dog. Suddenly, the dog turned on the boy—who couldn't have been more than three years, if that—and went after him with a bloodcurdling growl, his teeth bared and his ears standing straight up in points.

The little one was so surprised he couldn't seem to move his feet, but just stood shrieking, water running down his legs from under his short pants from where he'd wet himself. The dog chomped down on his foot, and the boy let go a terrible scream.

Maggie snatched up a rock and charged out the gate, screeching at the dog and hurling the rock as she ran. She missed the dog, but it bolted, leaving Maggie to tend to the Twomey boy, who was still squawking as though he were being murdered.

By that time Maggie's mother, who had been around back of the house hanging up the wash, came tearing across the road, her apron flapping in the breeze. At the same time, Mrs. Twomey came running out of the house, followed by two or three of the other young'uns.

The Twomey twin came through just fine, with only a small gash where he was bit, but when Maggie, still excited and running loose at the mouth, tried to tell her mother about her "feeling," she received not only a fierce scolding for "taking on so," but was also banished to the bedroom.

By the time Da came home and was told about the incident, it seemed that the old hound dog had become a wild dog and Maggie's attempt to rescue the little Twomey boy might as well have been a jump into a fiery pit. Moreover, when she tried to explain to Da about her "feeling"—her mother having already raised the subject—her father's face turned so red Maggie looked for him to start foaming at the mouth at any minute.

She was sure she was in for it, but all he did was send her to the bedroom. Again.

For some reason, her parents seemed to think that being sent to the bedroom was punishment, but Maggie never quite saw it that way. For one thing, it meant she could have the bedroom all to herself because neither Eva Grace nor Nell Frances was allowed to share it during the time of her punishment. She actually *liked* being confined to the bedroom because she relished the peace and quiet.

So even though she didn't see her punishment of that day as anything more than an inconvenience, she picked up on the fact that her folks didn't care for her having "feelings." In fact, they seemed to find it downright worrisome.

Only once after that did she ever forget herself and again mention a "feeling"; this time was when she got it in her head that something bad was going to happen at the mines. To her enormous relief, nothing did happen, but the very mention of a feeling that something might happen was enough to bring her da to his feet with a terrible scowl and a direful warning that he'd not have "that old country superstition" in the house.

It hardly ever happened after that, and even if it had, Maggie wouldn't have mentioned it. But two or three times since, she had caught an inkling of something about to occur or change.

It never seemed to her a bad thing. Nor was she convinced, like her Aunt Vivienne, that it was "an Irish thing." Indeed, it seemed such a simple thing that she was surprised when she realized that not everyone could feel the "difference" as she did. In truth, she expected they could, if only they weren't always so busy, going here and there and doing this or that. More than anything else, it was like the sudden change that could be felt when the weather was about to turn—like on a summer day when the wind was getting ready to stir up a rainstorm.

Like today.

⁂

The feeling struck her the instant she saw Orrin Gaffney and Billy Macken sneaking around the corner of the schoolhouse after dismissal, hitting each other on the back and laughing like a couple of rowdy six-year-olds.

They didn't see her, and Maggie waited until they were a good piece down the road before coming out from behind the privy. She very nearly left the school yard then and started for the company store. She actually did hike her knapsack up a little higher and head toward the road, but something made her stop and turn back.

As she neared the building, she heard something. Something that sounded like coughing or gagging.

Or maybe even someone crying.

It was coming from around the side of the building.

The side of the building where Kenny dumped the ashes from the stove into an iron drum, a chore Mr. Stuart had assigned to him when the weather turned cold.

In that instant, fear snaked down her back like an icy trickle of water.

⁂

She crept around the corner, careful to wedge herself close to the building so as not to be seen. But the thin layer of ice beneath her feet crunched and gave her away.

Kenny looked up as soon as she came into view, immediately throwing his hands up over his face and turning away from her. But not before she had seen.

He was on his knees by the drum. His face was nearly black, covered with ashes, except for where tears had tracked down the sides of his face. Even his hair and his hands had been dusted.

He was coughing and sniffling, and Maggie instinctively started toward him.

But before she could reach him, he thrust his arms out in front of himself, shaking his head as if to warn her off.

She hesitated and then stopped. "What happened?" Her voice sounded high and strained. "Kenny?"

But Maggie already knew what had happened. "I'll go and get Mr. Stuart!"

Kenny was on his feet in a shake, his eyes huge and blazing at her from his blackened face. *"No!"*

Maggie stared at him. "But you've got to tell him, Kenny! You can't let them get away with this. I'll go—"

"I said *no,* Maggie!"

Again he covered his face with his hands and turned away from her.

Maggie didn't know what to do. She just stood there watching him, aching for him.

She wanted to go after that awful Billy and Orrin. She wanted to make them sorry. She wanted to hurt them.

She had to do something. Someone had to know.

"Kenny—"

He whipped around so fast Maggie caught her breath.

"You've got to promise me you won't tell Mr. Stuart, Maggie! You can't tell anyone!"

"But why not?"

His expression turned hard. "Because if Mr. Stuart finds out, he'll go to my dad. And I don't want my dad to know."

She stared at him. "But your dad *has* to know. You can't—"

"Maggie!"

Kenny didn't sound like Kenny. The way her name ripped from him was ugly, like he was mad at her.

"You have to promise me you won't tell. My dad already thinks I'm a-a coward."

"But that's so wrong!"

"You'd have to know him." Kenny's face looked about to shatter. "He-he just doesn't have much use for me. If he finds out about this, he won't let it rest. He'll nag me to death about being too much of a coward to take up for myself." He stopped. "And besides—he really might fire Billy and Orrin's fathers from the mine. What do you think will happen to me then?"

Maggie stood transfixed. She couldn't fathom what he was saying. How could a father torment his own son so? And how could Mr. Tallman think for a minute that Kenny was a coward? Kenny was anything but a coward! But was he right? It would only go worse for him if Mr. Tallman fired Billy's and Orrin's fathers from the mine.

She thought she knew the answer. She found she couldn't swallow for the numbness that had seized her.

"Promise you won't tell?" Kenny asked, now sounding exceedingly tired.

Maggie couldn't seem to get a deep breath. "I promise...I won't tell for now," she finally said. "But I won't promise for good, because I think you're wrong. They'll do this again if they think they can get away with it. They might even do worse."

Only then did she note the thin trickle of blood at his temple. She reached a hand toward him, but he jerked away.

"Kenny, you're bleeding! They hurt you bad!"

He touched his face, brought his hand away, and looked at the blood on his finger. "I'm all right," he said shortly. "It's just a scratch."

"This is my fault," Maggie said, her voice low, suddenly consumed with guilt. It *was* her fault. They were punishing Kenny because of her.

"No, it's not!" he countered. "It's not your fault they're ignorant. They're dumb bullies, that's all. Besides, they didn't hurt me all that much. I told you, I'm all right."

"It's not fair," Maggie said woodenly. "They hurt you because you took up for me the other night. It's me they should be attacking, not you."

At last he met her gaze straight on. "No, Maggie," he said, sounding more like himself now. "It would have only hurt me worse if they'd done this to you."

Maggie stared at him, not knowing how to answer. She bit her lip, hard. Hard enough to make her eyes burn with unshed tears.

She felt as if she was going to be sick. She tried not to give in to it, not to think about it. "You can't go home like that," she said lamely. "Not if you don't want your daddy to find out."

He looked at her, and then he lifted a hand to his face as if he'd forgotten. "I'll go down to the creek and clean up," he said.

"That creek water will be freezing," she said. A meaningless remark, but she could think of nothing else to offer.

"It won't be that bad." He began to brush off his coat. "We'd better go now. I don't want to be here when Mr. Stuart comes out."

Maggie was reluctant to leave, but he stood looking at her as if he were waiting for her to make the first move.

"You're sure you'll be okay?" she asked him.

He nodded. "I'm sure."

Maggie nodded too and gave a weak little wave. Then, out of habit, she said, "See you."

And just as if nothing had happened, he replied, "See you."

When Maggie got partway up the road from the school, she turned to look back, but he had already gone beyond the bend, on his way to the creek.

She stopped by the side of the road, darted in behind some bushes, and finally allowed herself to be sick.

Nineteen

Kenny's Quandary

Faint not nor fear, His arms are near,
He changeth not and thou art dear.

John S.B. Monsell

On Monday Kenny came to school with a cold. Maggie figured it was because he'd washed up in the ice-cold creek water. Fearing another episode like Friday's, she hung around the outside of the building after school until he emptied the ashes. Billy and Orrin were nowhere to be seen, however, and Kenny let her know in no uncertain terms that he could take care of himself, that she wasn't to "follow him around."

Maggie just glared at him. Then she turned and flounced down the path from the schoolhouse without looking back.

At least she hoped she was flouncing. She had read a book not long ago in which the heroine flounced, and she liked the image the word conjured up.

She hoped she didn't just look knock-kneed.

On Tuesday, Kenny didn't come to school, and Maggie figured his cold had turned worse, so she didn't worry. But when he wasn't at his desk on Wednesday morning either, she grew uneasy.

At lunchtime, she decided to ask about him and went inside before the bell rang. "Is Kenny still sick, Mr. Stuart?"

He was writing the spelling words on the blackboard but stopped to answer her. "I expect so, Maggie," he said. "He seemed to have quite a bad cold Monday. I imagine his father is keeping him in an extra day or two before sending him back."

Maggie nodded but wondered. Somehow the idea of Mr. Tallman being extra careful of Kenny's health didn't fit with what Kenny had told her.

"Don't worry," Mr. Stuart said, smiling at her. "I'm sure Kenny is fine. He'll probably be back in school tomorrow."

Maggie brooded the rest of the afternoon. Every time she happened to glance at the vacant desks that belonged to Summer and Kenny, a painful gnawing in her stomach started up. The absence of her two best friends was like a raw sore deep inside her, and the more she worried about them, the more the sore seemed to lay itself open. Then she would look up and see Mr. Stuart, how pale and thin he looked, and the sore would open still more.

Sometimes lately Maggie would get a sudden, overwhelming urge to leave school and never come back. There was so much hurt now where once there had seemed to be nothing but good. The three people she loved best in all the world—in addition to her own family, of course—were hurting, and in terrible ways. Kenny, living with a father who thought he was a coward. Summer, so ill and so weak she could no longer leave her bed. And Mr. Stuart, the best man—the most kindhearted man—in the whole town, was fading even as she watched.

Nell Frances had once accused her of being in love with Mr. Stuart. It had made Maggie angry and set off a quarrel between them, not that that was anything new.

"I'm twelve, Nell Frances," she'd shot back with as much sarcasm as she could muster in an effort to hide her real feelings. "Twelve-year-old girls don't fall in love with their teacher. Only silly, cow-eyed, thirteen-year-olds like you."

In truth, most of the girls at school were probably in love with Mr. Stuart, at least a little bit. How could they not be, when the love just poured out of him to all his students? The older girls were the very worst, of course. They sometimes acted just plain stupid around him, but in her heart of hearts Maggie knew that if she were older, she might be no better than the others.

As it was, she *did* love Mr. Stuart in a special way, but it was a love shaped by respect and admiration and gratitude. In fact, when she said her prayers, she never failed to say thanks for Mr. Stuart. She might not often stop and think what their school would be like without him—what life would be like without him, for that matter—but when she did think about it, she was aware that the children of Skingle Creek had every reason to be grateful.

Indeed, more than any Sunday school lesson she had sat through and more than any sermon she had ever heard, Mr. Stuart had taught her what it meant to be blessed.

He had blessed an entire schoolroom of young people like herself. They were blessed because of his teaching and his life and his love for his students.

That's why it hurt beyond all endurance to think of life without him.

On Monday night, Billy Macken and Orrin Gaffney had cornered Kenny again, this time at the railroad tracks. They'd given him a beating and another warning about keeping his mouth shut before letting him go.

Kenny had been able to avoid his father that night by going to bed before Mr. Tallman came home from the mines, and he didn't go to school the next day, supposedly because of his cold. In truth, yesterday morning he'd been hurting all over with a black eye, a sore arm, and a wrenched back. When Kenny's father cracked the bedroom door open early in the morning, Kenny asked if he could stay home. For once there hadn't been a tongue-lashing for being a "baby," and with great relief he'd hunkered down under the covers, actually managing to sleep a few more hours.

The two of them hadn't crossed paths since then. Kenny had gone to bed early last night, leaving a note that he was going to stay in again today.

Now he sat at the kitchen table with part of a jelly sandwich, his stomach threatening to reject the little he'd eaten as he continued to worry over what would happen if his father found out about the beating. He couldn't hide the black eye or the broken glasses much longer.

If his father were to learn about Monday night, he might do something really awful. Kenny had thought his threat to the two boys about getting their fathers fired from the mines to be just that: a threat. But what if they *were* to lose their jobs? Or what if his father showed up at school and made a scene in front of Mr. Stuart and the entire class?

Judson Tallman was more than capable of being downright mean if someone went against him. He might not take any notice of his son except for the rare occasion when he remembered that he actually *had* a son, Kenny told himself bitterly. But his father's pride would never stand for someone else laying a hand on what was his.

Kenny's stomach clenched. Suddenly, he thought of Maggie. She could easily be as much of a problem as his father! Once she found out about this second incident, he would never convince her to keep it to herself.

And she *would* find out. He might be able to fool his father somehow, but he would never be able to keep the truth from Maggie.

She would spot the black eye the minute he walked into the classroom—and the cracked lens in his glasses as well. That's all it would take before she flew at him with a dozen or more questions.

Maggie already knew too much to put her off with anything less than the truth. Not to mention the fact that she seemed to have made it her mission to protect him.

He pushed the rest of his sandwich away. He would have to worry about Maggie later. Right now he needed to figure out a convincing story for his father.

Kenny hated to lie—it was a sin, and he knew it—but he didn't see that he any other choice. He didn't dare tell his father the truth.

If only he had the kind of father he *could* confide in. A father to whom he could admit just how afraid he'd been Monday night, how afraid he still was. Try as he would, he couldn't forget the terror that had gripped him when he realized what was about to happen.

At first they had only shoved and punched him. But then they threatened him, warning him that if he told anyone, it would be Maggie they went after next time.

And then Billy had said some things he would do to her—awful things—that sent Kenny into a rage. That's when Orrin grabbed his arm and yanked it behind him while Billy tossed his glasses on the ground and punched him in the eye, punched him so hard Kenny thought he would pass out.

He jumped at the unexpected sound of his father's footsteps on the porch. Just his luck. Daddy *never* came home early.

He quickly took his glasses off and covered them with his hand. He realized too late that without them the black eye would only be that much more obvious.

Of course, his father scarcely looked his way when he walked into the kitchen, but after he fixed himself a cup of coffee he sat down at the table across from Kenny. His heavy dark eyebrows met in a frown when he noticed the eye.

Kenny felt his face grow hot under his father's scrutiny. His hand trembled as he clutched his glasses.

His father was ominously quiet, but Kenny wasn't fooled. He was primed for an explosion.

"What is *that?*"

Kenny lifted his fingers to his eye, unable to keep from wincing when he touched it.

His father's voice was altogether too quiet as he set his coffee cup to the table. "Who did that, boy?"

"Nobody, Daddy. I mean, *I* did it."

Even though Kenny had thought he had his story ready, with those hard, dark eyes turned upon him, he found himself stammering as he fumbled for words. "I…felt better today and went out, just for a little while, to look for wood. I tripped on one of those old logs on the ground and came down on top of it."

His father's eyes narrowed. "You fell."

Kenny nodded.

It was all he could do to meet his father's eyes, but he knew he had to if he was going to get away with his story. "It hurt too," he added. "A lot. It's still sore." He paused. "And...Daddy?"

His father picked up his coffee cup, watching him.

"I-I broke my glasses when I fell."

His father's face turned to a thundercloud, and for a moment Kenny thought he would smash his coffee cup in the white-knuckle grip of his hand.

"Just one lens," Kenny hurried to say, holding up the glasses for his father to see. "I can still wear them. At least for now. I glued both pieces of the lens together, see. They'll probably hold for a while."

Still scowling, his father let out an impatient breath. "As if I don't have anything else to do but take you to Lexington for new glasses. And we're not rich, boy, do you know that?"

Kenny put the glasses back on the table, keeping his gaze locked on them. "I know, Daddy," he said softly.

Again his father set the cup to the table. "Well, you'll just have to make do for now. Maybe it will teach you to be more careful."

"Yes, sir."

His father studied him for another long moment. Then he gave a shake of his head and went back to his coffee. He might just as well have accused Kenny of being stupid and clumsy. His look of contempt could not have been any clearer.

"That's what you get for stumbling around in the woods," he muttered. "Foolishness."

Kenny said nothing, but simply continued to shrink inside himself.

"If you went out, then your cold is better. You'll go back to school tomorrow."

"Yes, Daddy."

Kenny let out the breath he'd been holding, for once not minding so much that his father thought him clumsy and useless. At least he had believed his story.

Twenty

A Reluctant Lie

I must be measured by my soul.

Isaac Watts

Jonathan Stuart took one look at Kenny Tallman Thursday morning and felt an alarm go off inside him.

Every rumor he'd ever heard about Judson Tallman mistreating his wife rushed in on him. Was it possible the man had done this to his own son? The very thought made Jonathan feel ill.

He watched the boy closely the rest of the morning. By the noon hour, he was convinced that, in addition to the black eye, Kenny was favoring his left arm and seemed to have some difficulty leaning over his desk.

As soon as he sent the class outside for a brief recess, Jonathan took the boy aside. "Kenny, when I dismiss the class this afternoon, I'd like you to stay, please."

The boy's startled expression instantly changed to a guarded stare.

Up close, the black eye appeared even uglier, and Jonathan saw now that one of the lens in the youth's eyeglasses had been cracked.

"It's all right, Kenny," he said, hoping to reassure the boy. "I just want to talk with you for a few minutes. I'll not keep you long."

The boy's only response was an evasive nod.

Later, during the same recess, Jonathan looked out and saw that Maggie MacAuley had Kenny cornered by the gnarled old maple tree at the south end of the school yard. Watching them, he decided that having to stay after school might be the least of Kenny's problems.

He had seen the shocked expression on Maggie's face once she got a good look at the black eye earlier that morning. It was obvious that she hadn't known about it until today.

Now, with her hands on her hips and her face flushed, she appeared to be in the process of giving her friend a thorough scolding.

Or could it be that she was demanding an explanation for his appearance?

If he hadn't been so troubled about the boy, Jonathan might have found the scene almost amusing.

As it was, however, there was nothing even remotely amusing about the situation.

Kenny couldn't help himself. If Maggie speared him with one more quarrelsome word, the tears that had been threatening to break free all morning would spill over and embarrass him to death.

She had already caught him weeping like a girl once. He had no intention of letting it happen again.

It didn't help that he felt purely miserable. His eye throbbed, his shoulder ached, and he was as sore all over as he imagined he would be if he'd been keelhauled. Billy and Orrin had been sneering at him all morning, every time the teacher's back was turned. Lester Monk had embarrassed him to death by slapping a hand over his mouth and running up to Kenny to see if he could "do anything to help." And

Lily—did she have to stare at him all boggle-eyed like she'd seen something crawling out of his forehead? Not to mention that the world looked like a broken egg, thanks to his cracked lens.

Now Mr. Stuart had asked him to stay after school.

And it was only noon.

He didn't need Maggie pestering him on top of everything else. If she was going to carry on like a harpy over something like this, something he couldn't help, he wasn't so sure he would marry her after all.

"I told you, they didn't hurt me that bad. And it'll only make things worse if I tell Mr. Stuart."

"They didn't hurt you that *bad?* Have you looked at yourself in the mirror, Kenny Tallman? And don't think I haven't seen the way you're walking around like a stoved-up old man! Don't you tell *me* you're not hurt that bad!"

"Let it go, Maggie," Kenny muttered. "Just...let it go. I'll handle it."

"But you *can't* handle it, Kenny. Don't you see that?"

All of a sudden, she didn't look angry anymore. She looked scared. Her voice trembled as she went on, and she kept glancing around as if to make sure no one was within earshot. "What if they don't stop, Kenny? What if they just keep beating on you and hurting you worse every time? Aren't you afraid?"

Kenny opened his mouth to say yes, he was afraid. He was more afraid than he was willing to admit, even to himself, much less to Maggie.

He changed his mind, though, and merely gave a shrug. Only then did he remember that the slightest movement hurt.

He took off his glasses and squeezed the bridge of his nose. He couldn't tell her what else Billy had threatened—what he'd threatened to do to *her*. He would never tell her, especially now that he knew she was really frightened.

The fear was there, in her eyes, looking out at him. If she knew the rest of it, she might not be able to keep it to herself. She might even tell her father. Mr. MacAuley looked to be a man who could take care of the biggest and meanest of bullies—but what would happen to Maggie afterward? Her father couldn't stand guard over her all the time.

But what if he kept his silence and Billy and Orrin got tired of picking on him and went after Maggie anyway? What if not telling on them turned out to make things worse when maybe he could have kept her safe if he'd only done what she'd been begging him to do: tell Mr. Stuart?

His mind slammed a door on the thought, but not before a cold dread settled over him.

"Kenny?"

Maggie was watching him with a pleading expression in her eyes. "Please, Kenny. Please tell Mr. Stuart. Tell someone."

The bell rang just then, calling them back to class. Kenny looked at her and then toward the building. "We'd better go in," he said, adding, "I have to stay after school, so I won't be able to walk to the company store with you."

Her eyes grew wide. "So you *are* going to tell Mr. Stuart?"

He shook his head. "He asked me to stay. He's probably going to question me about the black eye."

"What are you going to tell him?"

"I don't know yet."

"But you'll have to lie if you don't tell him what happened."

"Then I'll lie!" Kenny shot back. "Now will you just leave me alone?"

He could have clubbed himself the instant the words were out. Her face fell, and she jerked as if he'd slapped her.

"I'm sorry," he mumbled. "I didn't mean—we'd better go in."

Apparently, he needn't have worried overmuch about her feelings. The fire was already back in her eyes. Another second, and she whipped around and marched back into the schoolhouse, leaving him to follow.

One thing about Maggie: She had her pride.

He wondered if there would be anything left of his own pride when all this was over.

If it ever *was* over.

⁂

The boy was lying. Jonathan knew it as surely as if somebody had blared it out with a megaphone. He had been a teacher too many years not to know a youthful lie when he heard one, had come up against that evasive, trapped look in the eye too many times to dismiss it.

He sighed. This wasn't going to be easy.

"I see," he said when Kenny finished his tale about the fall in the woods. "Well, I expect you were fortunate that you didn't break a bone."

The boy nodded, seeming to relax a little. "Yes, sir."

"But you most likely did take some lumps, didn't you?" Jonathan pressed. "I noticed that you seemed to be favoring your left arm earlier."

Kenny blinked, and again came the shifting glance, the anxious note in his voice. "I...yes, sir. I guess I bruised it some."

"Did your father have Dr. Woodbridge take a look at you? Just in case something is broken?"

"No! No, he...didn't think it was necessary."

"Really?" Jonathan smiled at him. "My father always overreacted when I got hurt. He'd drag me to the doctor for the least little thing."

The boy managed a lame smile but said nothing.

Jonathan could almost feel the youth's growing discomfort, but he couldn't bring himself to let go of this quite yet. Frustrated with his own failure to break down the boy's wall, he decided to be blunt. "Kenny, whatever you say to me is in confidence. Please tell me if someone did this to you. Did someone hurt you?"

The boy gave Jonathan a startled look, as if trying to gauge what he might know and how he knew it.

Oh, yes. He is definitely lying.

Jonathan kept his gaze steady, his voice low. "Kenny? You can tell me the truth."

"No! I told you, I fell. That's all that happened. It was nighttime, and I don't see so good anyway after dark. I just...fell."

Jonathan studied him. A chilling awareness that something was terribly wrong seized him, but he hadn't a thought as to what he could do about it.

The boy was frightened, that much was evident. Again came the thought of Judson Tallman and the rumors that had never quite died about him and his wife. If this was a case of a father mistreating his son, then something had to be done. No child should have to live in fear of his own parent.

No child should have to live in fear of anything.

But if the boy wouldn't talk to him, what could he do?

Jonathan sensed he would accomplish nothing by pressing further. Young as he was, something about Kenny Tallman made it clear that he wasn't one to succumb to pressure. There was a strength there, a kind of steely self-containment, that belied the boy's age and almost fragile appearance.

It seemed that all he could do for now was to make certain Kenny knew he had a place to come to, a place of safety, should he ever need it. That wasn't enough, of course. It wouldn't be nearly enough if the situation turned out to be as vile as Jonathan feared it might be. But for now there seemed to be nothing else to do.

"All right, Kenny. You may go now."

The boy was off the chair before Jonathan finished.

"You may go, but I want you to promise me that if you need help—any kind of help, for any reason, at any time—you'll come to me."

Kenny wouldn't look at him, and his voice was so low as to be almost inaudible when he answered. "Yes, sir. Thank you, Mr. Stuart."

Jonathan got to his feet. "I mean it, son. There are things we're simply not meant to handle alone, things we *can't* handle alone. God puts other people in our lives so we won't have to handle those things by ourselves. Remember that there's always help." He paused. "You have only to ask, Kenny. Don't ever forget that."

Kenny looked up, and in that instant Jonathan knew the boy was struggling *not* to confide in him. He looked for all the world as if any second the words would come spilling out of him in spite of his best efforts to hold them back.

But the moment passed, and Jonathan was left to watch the thin, seemingly forlorn youth make his way down the aisle for the door.

He watched until the door closed. Then he sank back down onto his chair and prayed.

Twenty-One

Maggie in Charge

I have dreamed,
I have planned,
I have prayed—
I will do.

Anonymous

It was Thursday evening, and Matthew still hadn't heard a word from the other school board members. By now he was impatient with the lot of them and irritable with just about everyone else. After finishing his supper, he scraped his chair back from the table and announced that he was going for a walk.

"Matthew, it's sleeting," said Kate.

So it was, but he was tired of sitting around in the evening wondering what the other men on the board were going to do. He had already had his say, and there was nothing more he could do except to wait for the vote. But so far Pastor Wallace hadn't called for a meeting.

For his part, he thought it was past time. Just how much longer were they going to wait, after all?

As if she had read his mind—and sometimes Matthew suspected she could do just that—Kate said, "I'm sure you'll be called to a meeting soon."

"What in the world is taking them so long? They could have elected a governor in this length of time."

"It's only been a week, Matthew."

" *Only* a week? Kate, this is important. We need to take care of this now, not next month!"

"Who are they voting for, Da?" asked Maggie.

Matthew looked at her. "We're not voting for anyone. We're just trying to reach a decision."

"About what?"

"It's grown-up business," Matthew said.

The girl looked miffed, but her expression cleared after a second or two. "If you go for a walk, can I go partway with you, Da? I want to visit Summer."

Matthew looked at Kate, who shook her head slightly. "Not this time," he told Maggie.

"But why, Da? I haven't seen her since last week, and tomorrow evening I have to work at the store until seven, so I can't go then, and—"

"Maggie," Kate broke in quietly, "I'm afraid this just isn't a good time to see Summer."

Something in Kate's low tone seemed to have set off a warning. The girl turned to look at her mother. "Why?"

"Maggie, Summer isn't—"

Kate stopped, glanced at Matthew, and then went on. "I ran into Mrs. Rankin at the company store yesterday. She said that Summer's having a hard time of it right now. It seems...she doesn't have the strength to visit with anyone." She paused. "I'm sorry, Maggie, but you might as well know that Summer is in a bad way."

Matthew found it hard to swallow. The pain in his daughter's eyes was so raw, so intense, he felt as if he'd been struck with the same blow.

Silence hung over the table. Nell Frances and Eva Grace, usually chattering or arguing, now sat darting glances back and forth from their mother to their younger sister. Even Baby Ray had ceased fidgeting in his chair, his smile uncertain as he sensed the tension around the table.

Maggie's gaze locked on her plate, which still held most of her supper. "Summer is going to die, isn't she?"

It was the hard, thin voice of an older woman, not that of his twelve-year-old, lively natured Maggie. Maggie, the one whose spirits were usually inexhaustible, her faith in all that was good in life seemingly unshakable. The sound of that pronouncement and the defeated set of her shoulders chilled Matthew's very soul.

"Summer is going to die," she said again in that awful voice. "And so is Mr. Stuart."

"Somehow things will come out all right, Maggie," Kate said, her tone gentle. "God knows what He's doing."

The girl didn't so much as look at her mother. "Nothing is ever going to be all right again. And I can't see that God is doing anything."

"Maggie, no—" Kate reached across the table toward her, but Maggie was already on her feet, the back of her hand against her mouth as if she were struggling not to be sick.

When Kate rose as if to follow her, Matthew caught her arm and shook his head. "Best give her some time," he said. "She needs to come to grips with the truth."

"That's asking a lot of a twelve-year-old," said Kate.

"That's asking a lot of any one of us, man or woman grown," said Matthew, the taste of bitterness burning his mouth. "Nevertheless, it's how things are."

Maggie headed straight for the washroom. It was the only place where she could be alone, the only room with a door she could close to shut out the rest of the household.

Sadie had followed her, whimpering a little at the closed door until Maggie opened it and let her in.

For a time Maggie paced, wave after wave of anger and helplessness churning up in her and clamoring for release. As she crossed the room again and again, she pressed her hands against her ears, as if to deafen herself to the pounding of her own blood and the world outside.

If she could have screamed without somebody running to rescue her, she would have. From time to time she struck the palms of her hands together, hard, as hard as she could bear. Then she began to yank at her hair, wanting to hurt herself, needing to make the pain inside of her accessible, something she could physically reach.

Finally exhausted and shivering in the cold, she slid down the rough-hewn, unpainted wall and sat huddled on the floor, her legs propped up, her head resting on her knees. Sadie came and squeezed her head onto her lap, and Maggie mindlessly began to stroke the dog's spotted fur. Like warm silk beneath her hand, it was unexpectedly comforting.

Eventually her heartbeat slowed, the rage quieted, and the sharpness of her pain grew dull and numb. The dog's even breathing seemed to fall in with her own, and this, too, was somehow calming.

She tried not to think, but there was too much clutter in her mind to avoid wading through it. She ought to pray, she supposed. Ma was forever saying that prayer had a way of turning burdens into blessings, but she wasn't sure she believed that anymore. Maybe that worked when you were little with small problems, but she was no longer a little girl, and her troubles seemed to grow bigger and heavier all the time.

In truth, she didn't really know how to pray about the things that were happening. She felt as if something had given her world a hard shove, and now it was tilted, with the things of life falling every which way and craziness and ugliness replacing all she had once trusted and depended on.

If this was growing up, she wished she could stay a child forever

She remembered Mr. Stuart telling them that the Savior knew everything that happened to them and cared about it all, that there was nothing too small or unimportant for His attention. Over the years of Mr. Stuart's teaching, Maggie had come to see God not as she once had—as a feeble old man who spent His days sitting on some kind of a throne and giving orders to the angels—but more as the quiet-voiced, gentle-natured Son who smiled a lot and loved children and music and everything about the beautiful world He had made. Although it was hard to imagine how He could see a place like Skingle Creek as something beautiful, Mr. Stuart said He did.

But if that was so, why would He let a little girl who had never done anything bad in her whole life get so sick she might die? And why would He let no-accounts like Billy Macken and Orrin Gaffney beat up on someone like Kenny Tallman, who was the nicest boy in school, no exception? Kenny, who was always doing helpful things for the younger students or sticking up for the slow ones, like Lester Monk and others. What about Benny Pippino—Pip—who had lost his hand? And poor old Mrs. Hunnicutt, who could have starved to death or died of the cold and nobody would have even known. And the Crawford twins' da, injured in the mines, leaving his entire family at the mercy of whatever the town could scrape together to keep them going.

And Mr. Stuart. Especially Mr. Stuart. If God really knew everything and cared about even the smallest things, then what was He thinking, to allow a good man like Mr. Stuart to keep growing weaker and sicker when the children needed him and loved him and depended on him more than any grown-up in town could ever understand?

Why?

Her head hurt from holding back all the tears that had been building up, and she finally had to let them go. They were so hot as they streamed down her face they seemed to scald her skin, and when she tried to wipe them away she tasted the warm, bitter salt on her hand.

Why? she asked again. *If You really know everything like Ma and Mr.*

Stuart claim, and if You really do care about everything that happens to us, then why don't You do something? It's not enough to just care *about bad things happening to folks if You don't care enough to* do *something about it!*

Maggie tried to recapture the picture of Mr. Stuart, standing at the front of the class, his smile somehow taking them all in at once, as he told them about "A Love So Great."

"A love so great it held the Son of God on the cross when He could have freed himself with a word...One plea to His Father, and the cross would have crumbled into splinters, and He would have escaped into heaven...But instead He bore the unbearable and died an ugly and horrible death so that we wouldn't live only a few years, but instead would live forever, with Him, in His kingdom.

That's how big God's love is. That's how much He loves us, every one of us. There isn't any part of our lives that He doesn't know about or care about. If you're ever tempted to think God has forgotten you or simply does not care, remember the cross. That's how much He cares. How much more proof of His love do you need?"

Maggie leaned her head back against the wall and closed her eyes, still smoothing Sadie's fur with one hand. She walked through the chaos in her mind, and with each step she tried to face every bad thing, every fear she encountered, as if somehow simply confronting what she dreaded most would make her strong enough to endure it. But when she tried to meet head-on the awful truth, the dread reality of what was going to happen to Summer and Mr. Stuart, she stopped, unable to go any further.

She wanted Mr. Stuart to be right. She *needed* him to be right. She needed to believe "without a doubt."

He had told them there would be times when their faith would be tested, when they might have doubts and questions about what God was doing and why He was doing it. And when that happened, Mr. Stuart said the thing to do was to just to "keep on plowing through the doubts and the questions...live as though your faith is as strong as ever, as though you *have* no doubts or questions...and sooner or later you *won't.* You'll believe 'without a doubt.'"

With her mind still locked on the teacher's words, but exhausted now from the riot of her feelings, Maggie began to feel sleepy and almost dozed off. Suddenly, she opened her eyes with a start, as if someone had tugged at her. There was something she had to do, something that in the midst of the past few fragmented, frenzied days she had set aside and nearly forgotten.

Mr. Stuart's gift. The gift for his birthday party. She'd followed through almost by rote the plans and preparations for the party itself, mustering the help of the other students and parents—her own included—and she'd seen to the countless details that needed to be resolved to make the event a success.

But in the process, she had neglected her gift for the teacher. Hers and Summer's gift. She had made a promise to Summer, had set the plan in motion, and then she had forgotten it.

That last night they had been together, the night they planned their special gift for Mr. Stuart, Summer had seemed almost fierce in her insistence that Maggie take care of everything. Indeed, she had shown more interest, more energy, than Maggie had seen in her for weeks.

Maggie had tried to hide her skepticism about the idea, though she suspected Summer knew she had her doubts. But Summer had persisted in her notion that it would work, that it would be "the perfect gift."

"You'll see, Maggie. It will be the best gift ever! You'll take care of it, won't you? You'll take care of things just like you always do..."

When she saw how important it was to her friend, Maggie had pretended to be convinced and agreed to do everything Summer suggested. Including the part about praying.

"I can't do anything about the rest of it except to pray, Maggie. And you have to pray too. Promise you will...promise you'll pray...that's the most important part of all..."

Maggie had promised. And she *had* prayed. At first. But not lately.

How could she have forgotten something so important—so important to Summer?

Angry with herself and impatient to use the little time left, she scrambled to her feet, startling the dog and gasping at the cramps that shot down her legs from sitting in the same place so long.

She could still do this. She *would* do it.

She started to leave the room but then stopped, squeezing her eyes shut.

Help me do this. Please. Help me do it for Summer. And for Mr. Stuart. And please, somehow let Summer know *I'm doing it. Let her know I'm keeping my promise, that I'm taking care of everything, just the way she asked. The way she trusted me to do. Summer believes in her idea, in this special gift for Mr. Stuart. And...she believes in me. Most of all, she believes in You.*

Help me to believe that way—Summer's way. Help me to believe...without a doubt.

Twenty-Two

Secret Threats

Alas! It is a fearful thing
To feel another's guilt!

Oscar Wilde

For two days Jonathan Stuart kept a close watch on Kenny Tallman and Maggie MacAuley.

He saw nothing out of the ordinary from the boy, except that at times he obviously still favored his left arm—and the nasty black eye was by now a palette of different colors. As for Maggie, she seemed unusually quiet and occasionally secretive.

Jonathan didn't miss the frequent glances she darted at Kenny throughout the day. There was nothing strange about that, except that he seemed to be making a concentrated effort to avoid looking back at her.

Jonathan might have assumed there had been an argument, had Maggie's eyes held even a hint of anger or resentment. Instead, her expression appeared to be more a look of concern or else a vague, distracted stare. And, more unsettling still, Jonathan thought he also detected a glint of fear lurking when her attention was on Kenny.

One thing was obvious: Both of them seemed to have their attention focused anywhere but on their schoolwork.

Although Kenny had always seemed a solemn youth, exhibiting signs of melancholy rare in one so young, his studies had never suffered. Not until now. As for Maggie, she typically sailed through her lessons with time to spare and a willingness to help the younger children who struggled with their work. Lately, however, she sometimes came to class unprepared and then scrambled throughout the day to catch up.

What was going on with those two?

By Tuesday Jonathan was almost certain that whatever was responsible for Kenny Tallman's black eye and apparent physical discomfort—and for Maggie's peculiar behavior—might be more serious than he had initially suspected.

He was also beginning to wonder if Billy Macken and Orrin Gaffney might not somehow be involved. He hadn't missed the sly looks, the whispers, and the snickering that frequently passed between the two troublemakers when either Maggie or Kenny happened to walk by their desks. When he called them to order, they obeyed with sly smiles, only to repeat their behavior again later.

That afternoon, he happened to catch the Macken boy watching Maggie from across the room. The girl was bent over little Ira Turner's desk, helping him clean up a glue spill. Something in Billy Macken's expression set off a clutch of uneasiness in Jonathan. He had seen that kind of look before, but never in the eyes of one so young.

He reminded himself that the Macken boy was fourteen years old, and given his size and jaded attitude, far from being a child.

After that, Jonathan had trouble concentrating. Indeed, it seemed that every time he looked at the Macken boy, the tightness in his chest and the ache at the base of his skull intensified.

Maggie was eating her lunch at her desk, trying not to mind the loud whispers behind her.

Mr. Stuart gave them leave to talk during their lunch hour if they kept their voices down. But Billy Macken and Orrin Gaffney weren't even trying to be quiet. It was clear they didn't care that someone might overhear their nastiness; instead, they seemed to flaunt their hatefulness and off-color talk as if they dared anyone to try to stop them.

These days just seeing the two together made Maggie's stomach knot. She couldn't help but wonder if they were plotting more meanness against Kenny and, if so, what they might try next.

If only he would *tell* someone. Or let her tell. What she wouldn't give to confide in Mr. Stuart. She just knew he would handle it somehow, that he'd know what to do.

But Kenny insisted there was nothing the teacher could do. "*Look* at him, for goodness' sake, Maggie! It's all he can manage just to make it through the day! What do you think he's going to do with two bullies like Billy and Orrin? They're not the least bit afraid of him. And why should they be?"

Always, he came back to the same thing. "I told you. I can't let my father find out about this. He'll only make things worse. Not because he'd be worried for me," he said bitterly, "but because no one can go against Judson Tallman or anything that belongs to him without bringing bad trouble down on themselves."

Maggie couldn't help but wonder if Kenny's father was as cold-hearted as Kenny believed him to be. On the other hand, her father plainly disliked Mr. Tallman, and Da wasn't quick to take a dislike to someone without good reason.

Still, they obviously weren't helping matters by keeping silent. If anything, the situation was getting worse.

She tried not to think about what might happen to Kenny if Orrin and Billy jumped him again. They seemed to be getting meaner and rougher with each attack. She kept an eye on him as best she could, but she couldn't very well follow him around all the time—especially after school.

Certainly not if Kenny had *his* say.

If only Billy would quit school. Maybe Orrin by himself wouldn't be such a devil. But everyone knew that Billy's mother had made it her business to keep him in school in order to keep him out of the mines.

More the pity.

As for Orrin, no one seemed to know why he'd stayed in school, whether it was by his own choice or that of his parents. According to Maggie's sisters, he had told some of the older students that he'd be quitting at the end of this term.

Maggie, for one, would not miss him.

Without warning, something came flying over her head. It was a partly eaten apple, and it hit Lily Woodbridge on the shoulder. Lily yelped and jumped out of her seat. A loud explosion of laughter sounded from Billy Macken, with an echoing roar from Orrin.

Maggie looked at Mr. Stuart. He had been leafing through some papers at his desk but was now standing, his hands braced on top of his desk as if to steady himself.

"Mr. Macken," he said, sounding exasperated entirely. "Come up here, please."

It seemed a long time before Billy scuffled out from behind his desk and sauntered toward the front of the room. Maggie shot a glance at Kenny, who sat across the aisle from her, one seat back. He looked at her and rolled his eyes.

Maggie couldn't hear what the teacher was saying to Billy, but she watched as he used his pointer to direct him to the empty desk right across from his own. She held her breath when Billy didn't move right away, but instead merely stood there, red-faced and scowling. He was nearly as tall as Mr. Stuart and a big hulk of a boy, whereas the teacher was slender-built and of late appeared even thinner than ever.

In that instant, Maggie sensed that Billy was deliberately baiting the teacher, meaning to insult him. Mr. Stuart didn't so much as blink, though, and after a moment, Billy sat down. But not without first turning and shooting an impudent grin at Orrin.

She jumped when Mr. Stuart cracked his pointer on top of Billy's new desk, leaned over, and spoke, this time loudly enough for the entire class to hear and in a voice harder and colder than Maggie had ever heard him use before. "One more word out of you today, Mr. Macken—one more incident—and I will be at your house tonight to speak with your father about the possibility of a suspension. Do you understand me?"

Billy's face flamed. He gave a sullen nod, folded his arms across his chest, and sat staring directly at Mr. Stuart without saying a word.

The room had gone so quiet that even Maggie's breathing sounded loud to her.

She felt as though something else had now been added to her growing heap of worries. For whether Mr. Stuart knew it or not, he had just been added to Billy Macken's hate list. And although it wasn't the normal way of things—a student threatening a teacher—that's exactly what had just happened.

It was a silent threat, but a threat all the same.

That being the case, she reckoned that from now on she'd have more to worry about where Mr. Stuart was concerned than his failing health.

As if that in itself wasn't enough.

Jonathan was straightening up the clutter from the day, at the same time keeping an eye on the two boys he'd delayed after school. He had set Billy Macken to cleaning the chalkboard while Orrin Gaffney swept the floor. Now that they'd finished, he looked around for something else that needed to be done, reasoning that they might just as well be at something useful for a change instead of causing trouble.

"The coal bin needs to be filled, boys. If each of you will make a couple of trips with a bucket, that should do it."

The Macken boy shot him a resentful glare, but they both grabbed a bucket from behind the stove. As Jonathan watched, they hurried out the door, leaving it open behind them for a raw December wind to blow inside.

With a sigh, he started down the aisle. He had his hand on the door, ready to close it, only to have his curiosity sparked by the sound of Maggie MacAuley's name, followed by a spurt of laughter.

His normal aversion to eavesdropping didn't stop him from cracking the door slightly and listening.

"Yeah. Makes you wonder if one of them told old man Stuart anything." This from Orrin. "He sure don't have much use for us anymore."

"Nah. Neither one of them's going to talk. They're too scared. And when did Stuart *ever* have any use for us?"

"I don't know, Billy. That Maggie can be a real wildcat sometimes. She don't seem scared of much of anything, if you ask me."

"Except me." More laughter, though Orrin's sounded somewhat tentative.

"You sure Tallman won't tell his old man?"

"Are you kidding? You heard what I told him we'd do to his smart-alecky girlfriend if he blabbed! You think he's goin' to take a chance on her getting hurt? Or getting himself beat up again? He knows if it's not him, then it's gonna be her."

Silence for a moment. Then, "'Course, at some point she's goin' to get what's coming to her anyway. And I plan to enjoy it."

"What're you going to do, Billy?"

"I figure you and me can have some real fun after the Christmas Exchange."

"We're gonna go to that? I thought you said it was just for the little squirts."

"No, we're not goin' to it! But Tallman and the girl will go. When do they ever miss out on a chance to toady up to old Stuart?"

"Yeah, but if we're not going—"

"Think, dumbhead! We're goin' to meet up with them after the exchange. On their way home. Say, down near the tipple? They won't have any idea we're around since we won't be at the schoolhouse. This way we can work on both of them for a change."

"Oh."

"Yeah. Oh!"

There was more snickering, and then words spoken too low for

Jonathan to hear. But he'd heard enough. Enough to be so alarmed—and so furious—that he had all he could do not to rush outside and throttle the both of them.

As if he could.

With a shaky hand, he closed the door and went back to his desk. When the boys returned, he pretended to be occupied with grading papers and gave no indication of their presence. After they completed their second trip and the bin was full, he issued them a curt dismissal.

For a long time, Jonathan sat staring at the top of his desk without really seeing it. It was sickeningly obvious what was going on. Those two were routinely harassing the Tallman boy, even beating on him, while threatening that if he told anyone what they were up to, Maggie would also suffer.

It didn't take much to figure out why Kenny had kept his silence. The boy was no coward, of that Jonathan was certain, but he wasn't about to risk harm coming to Maggie.

And what about Maggie? Did she realize that Kenny was enduring their cruelty to protect her? That he was suffering so she wouldn't?

Apparently no one—except himself, as of now—had any idea what these children were going through.

And what was he going to do about it?

What *could* he do?

He had never felt so humiliated, so helpless, as he did at this moment. That he was powerless against the brutality of two fourteen-year-old boys was a devastating admission, a huge blow to his pride, to his manhood. And yet there was no denying the truth of it.

How could he possibly stop this madness without making things worse for Kenny and Maggie?

Clearly, he couldn't stand up to Billy and Orrin physically if they decided to defy him. And that they would defy him, Jonathan had no doubt.

What if he went to the Mackens and the Gaffneys? Would they control their sons?

More to the point, *could* they control them?

They might well take them out of school, and as much of a relief as that would be to Jonathan—though he felt ashamed to admit it—he would find it all but impossible to live with the thought that he was responsible for sending two fourteen-year-old boys into the coal mines. That was a hard enough life for grown men, but for mere boys?

Boys who were beating up other boys and planning unspeakable acts toward an unsuspecting girl.

What if he were to go to Matthew MacAuley? The man didn't strike him as one who would tolerate any sort of treachery toward one of his children, not for a minute—and certainly not the kind of danger this situation could breed. No, he thought certain Maggie's father would not hesitate to go after her tormentors himself.

But what would that mean to Maggie and Kenny?

And what about Judson Tallman? He couldn't very well tell one parent without going to the other.

The thought numbed him. What would Tallman do? He had the power to fire the fathers of both boys from the mines, if he so chose. And as much as Jonathan feared what the ultimate outcome might be if Billy and Orrin weren't stopped, did he really want to see their fathers lose their jobs?

In Skingle Creek, unemployed miners lost their homes, went hungry, ended up living in poverty. Was he willing to bring that kind of tragedy down on the heads of anyone, no matter what their sons had done?

On the other hand, would Judson Tallman take such drastic action? Did he even care enough to revenge his son?

Jonathan slumped over his desk, his head in his hands. Merciful Lord, what a mess this was! It seemed that no matter what he did, he might bring harm on another or even destroy lives in the process.

But knowing what he knew, he couldn't simply ignore the situation and hope it would pass. It wouldn't pass.

If ever a spirit of evil was at work, it was working here. He could not simply sit by and do nothing. Two children could be badly hurt and damaged in unimaginable ways.

He had to do *something.*

He looked down to find his hands trembling. His forehead was wreathed in clammy perspiration. His heart lagged, then raced, and he squeezed his eyes shut for a moment to try to dispel a wave of lightheadedness.

He was pathetic. A straw man. A joke. He didn't have the strength to turn a hand, couldn't even help his own students. Mere children, and he was useless to them.

It was all he could do to make it home in his buggy at the end of a school day. And even that exhausted him.

But he must think of something. No one else was going to help Maggie and Kenny unless *he* helped them.

He propped his head on his hands again, doing his best to ignore the self-disgust slamming through him. This wasn't the time for feeling sorry for himself. He had to think.

At the moment he could think of nothing except to pray for their protection. And he did that. But at the same time he sensed a mounting pressure building in him, an urgency suggesting that he himself was intended to be a part of that protection. So, in spite of the demoralizing awareness that he could be of little or no help in any sort of confrontation, he also sought the strength to at least try to be of some use, should a Divine plan be at work for the safekeeping...and rescue...of those two children.

Twenty-Three

Going On

Living and Dying,
Thou art near!
Oliver Wendell Holmes

Summer Rankin died ten days before Mr. Stuart's birthday party. She never saw the birthday gift she had conceived for their teacher, nor the scarlet hair ribbon that Maggie meant to give her as a Christmas present.

Maggie visited her friend for the last time two days before she died. Mrs. Rankin, her eyes sunken and red-rimmed, had kindly allowed her to stop by in the evening, though she cautioned that Summer would more than likely sleep the entire time.

Only once did the younger girl rouse, and although she seemed to smile, Maggie wasn't at all certain she recognized her. But she stayed a full hour, sitting on the side of the bed, holding Summer's frail hand and talking to her just as if she were wide awake.

Maggie couldn't tell if the younger girl heard anything she said, but she chose to believe she did. She spoke of inconsequential events at school and within her own family, updated her on how plans were progressing for Mr. Stuart's birthday party, and gossiped a little about her sister Eva Grace's latest admirer, Russell Gibbon, who worked at the bank with his father—and who was, according to their da, "about six long years too old for Eva Grace."

Before she left, Maggie did something she had never done before. Summer seemed to be sleeping deeply, even peacefully, her breath still labored and phlegmy, but without the terrible cough that had plagued her for so long. Maggie stood watching her for a moment, and then she bent, brushed a strand of silver-blond hair away from Summer's face, and kissed her lightly on the forehead.

"Well...goodnight for now, Summer," she said, her voice wavering. "You have a good rest."

She left in a hurry, slipping out the back door without stopping to talk with any of the family.

Two days later she came home from school to find her mother sitting at the kitchen table. When Maggie walked in, she looked up, as if she'd been waiting for her.

Supper was on the stove, but the table hadn't been set. There was no sign of Da, her sisters, or Baby Ray. From the look of her mother's eyes and the handkerchief in her hand, Maggie knew that her mother had been weeping.

And immediately she knew why.

"Maggie..." her mother said, rising part way from her chair, but Maggie stopped her.

"No," she said sharply, lifting a hand as if to shield herself. "Don't! Just don't...I don't want to hear..."

She turned and stumbled outside. Then she started to run. With the raw, cutting wind slapping her in the face and the freezing rain slashing her skin, she ran down the road away from home, away from what she couldn't bring herself to hear, as if shutting it out would somehow keep it from being real. Her lungs felt as if they would ignite and explode, and her face stung beneath the icy rain. She ran until her breath was gone and her legs were numb, and she began to stagger like an injured animal. Finally, she collapsed, drenched and shivering, beneath the mammoth old willow tree on the bank of Skingle Creek, where she and Summer had sometimes spent long, hot afternoons wading or splashing their bare feet in the water. She stayed there, rocking on her knees in the ice-glazed mud, shaking, not so much from the cold rain and wind but more from the wall of pain slamming at her heart.

Memories came roaring in on her like a flood...*Summer, before she took so sick, pelting her with snowballs, giggling and ducking her head as Maggie hurled them right back at her...she and Summer riding double on Mr. Dunbar's old chestnut mare, swatting the flies and gnats away from the horse's mane and each other's hair...she and Summer chasing fireflies after dark at the Rankins', who were never strict about bedtimes like Maggie's folks were...Summer, just this past October, growing so tired and weak after collecting colored leaves for her scrapbook that Maggie carried her piggyback the rest of the way home...*

Summer. How could she really be gone? And where was she now? In heaven, yes, but *where* in heaven? What was she doing? Would she be sleeping, resting, and getting healed by Jesus? Did she know how much Maggie would miss her, how much she was missing her right now, at this minute?

Maggie didn't know much about heaven. She reckoned no one did. And it had never bothered her, the not knowing, not until Summer got so sick. Even then, she'd not found it to her liking to think much about it, knowing Summer would be there and she'd be here and there would be no time together anymore. Truth to tell, she deliberately didn't think about it.

Now she wondered what it was like and wished she knew more about it. It was God's place, and Pastor Wallace talked a lot about it being a better place—a beautiful and happy, peaceful place. That being the case, she supposed Summer was a lot better off there than she had been here. But why did she have to go *now?*

Nine years wasn't very long to live. It was hardly time enough to even *start* living. And part of that time she'd been too sick to do much of anything.

She thought of the Christmas cards they'd been making for their families and Mr. Stuart, still at home in the bedroom, waiting to be finished. Now they never would be finished.

For some reason, that was the thought that undid Maggie and sent her tumbling over the edge from her pain and anger and bewilderment into the dark, bottomless pool of the hopelessness of it all. She choked on a sob trapped in her throat and, unable to contain the river of her grief any longer, she gave way. She wept until her heart grew so sore and wrung dry that she couldn't get a breath without pain slicing through her.

Later—she couldn't have said how much later—when she finally got to her feet and started for home, she was soaked through and engulfed by a fog so heavy she could barely find her way back to the road.

She had gone only a few feet, slipping with almost every step on the icy pools of water, when she saw her da walking out of the fog, coming toward her. Without a word, he took the coat off his back and wrapped her in it, then he picked her up in his arms and carried her home.

Maggie saw that his face, still black with the dust of the mine, was tracked with thin streams of water. From the rain, she reckoned, for Da would never, ever be caught weeping.

Over the next few days, Maggie seemed to live in a cave. She got up, did her chores, went to school, then the company store, and came home. She was scarcely aware of anyone or anything around her. She seldom talked with anyone, not even with Kenny. Her sole purpose was simply to get through the day so she could go to bed at night and sleep. When she was awake, she couldn't stop thinking about Summer, and when she thought of her, it seemed as though the ache in her heart would crush her entirely.

She took no comfort in the fact that Summer had at least known about the birthday party, had known as well that the gift she was so set on giving Mr. Stuart was being made according to her wishes. In truth, Maggie could find no comfort in anything. Summer's death seemed to be the final page of a story in which neither comfort nor hope played a part.

She hadn't realized until now that losing someone she loved would make her feel as though a part of herself had died too. And in a way she couldn't begin to understand, right alongside the cleaving pain that never quite left her, day or night, there was also a terrible, aching emptiness within her.

It was the same feeling that had seized her the day of Summer's funeral, when the lid to the coffin had been closed for the last time. She'd suddenly felt as though a piece of her own self had been locked inside that small wooden box and would be buried in the ground with her friend.

Her first thought every morning before she set her feet to the floor was that Summer was gone. Gone forever. Yet at night, when she tried to say her prayers, she still caught herself asking God to make Summer well.

Then she would remember again and either sob the rest of the way through her prayer time or just crawl back into bed, unable to voice another word.

At school the vacant desk across from her own was like a knife, twisting deeper and deeper, cutting away some secret part of herself that she had shared only with Summer.

Somehow she went on seeing to the details of the birthday party because she didn't know how *not* to go on. But all the plans and preparations, the mounting excitement as the time drew near, seemed to be taking place at a distance and held no reality, no real pleasure or sense of anticipation.

Without Summer, Maggie lived in a shadow world, where all the lights were dim and all the rooms were cold and there was nowhere she could run to get away from the pain. So she carried it with her.

Wherever she went, whatever she did, the pain was her constant companion.

She reckoned this was what grown-ups meant when they talked about grieving. Although she had never heard anyone say so, Maggie wondered if it wasn't a little bit...or maybe a lot...like dying.

The child was inconsolable.

It had been only a few days, of course, too soon for healing. But Jonathan saw no sign that Maggie MacAuley's grief might be easing, not even a little. The girl was a shadow of herself, pale and drawn, her eyes so solemn, so stricken, it wounded him simply to look at her.

He had asked her to stay after school in hopes of finding a way to encourage her, perhaps prompt her to talk about her feelings. Her father had mentioned that Maggie seemed locked inside herself and scarcely spoke unless absolutely necessary.

"Her mother has tried to talk with her, and before, Maggie would usually confide in Kate, but not this time. Not at all. We don't quite know what to do..."

He shook his head, his words falling away. After a moment, he added, "I'll admit that I'm not much good at this sort of thing, Mr. Stuart. Not even with one of my own. Maggie's mother and I, we were wondering if perhaps you could have a word with the girl?"

His question had been so like a plea that Jonathan couldn't say no.

But now, with Maggie sitting in wooden silence beside his desk, he found himself at a loss as to how to begin. He cleared his throat, attempted a bolstering smile, and felt it break and fall apart.

"Maggie...I've been wondering...how are you doing by now? I know you must miss Summer terribly."

She didn't look at him but simply gave a small nod, and then she continued to sit motionless, staring at her hands, which she had clenched into tight fists on her lap.

Jonathan groped for the right words, at the same time recognizing that any words that came to mind would be woefully inadequate. So he simply said what was in his heart. "I miss her too, Maggie."

Finally she looked at him. Her eyes were always smudged and red-rimmed these days, as if she cried herself to sleep every night.

"Would it help to talk about it?" he said gently.

She shook her head. "I don't reckon anything will help."

The voice that usually held such a lilting confidence was now dull and thin. Jonathan drew a long breath, wishing for some insight, some shred of wisdom with which to comfort her. But his own heart was so tired and heavy at the moment, his own hope so precarious, he hesitated to even speak.

Still, he had promised Matthew MacAuley he would try.

"Maggie," he said, again fumbling for words, "we'll always miss Summer. But everything she was, everything that made her so very, very special will always be with us. In our memories. We never completely lose someone we love, you know."

Abruptly he stopped, realizing how trite his words must sound to this heartbroken young girl. The usual bromides would do nothing but insult a child like Maggie. She was too astute by far, too sensitive of spirit, for such banality.

"Maggie, are you angry?"

Her head came up, and although the green eyes remained guarded, Jonathan thought he detected a spark of something else, a kind of recognition.

"Angry?" she repeated.

Jonathan nodded. "Angry with God because He didn't heal Summer? I'm sure you asked Him to. I know I did."

Her gaze was unnervingly intense. "Why didn't He, do you think? Why didn't He heal Summer?"

Behind that bluntly posed question, Jonathan thought he could hear the cry of the ages. A cry he himself had uttered, and not so long ago.

He attempted to give her the only answer—the only honest answer—he was capable of. "I don't know why, Maggie. I honestly don't know. But I wish with all my heart that He had."

He saw tears well up in her eyes and thought she might break into a fit of weeping. Instead, she looked at him straight on, her chin slightly lifted. "So do I, Mr. Stuart. I wish that more than anything. But since He didn't, I reckon what I have to do now is figure a way to just…be going on. That's what Summer always said after she had a bad sick spell. She'd say she reckoned she'd be going on, now that she was feeling better." She paused. "I expect if she could, that's what she'd tell me to do."

She paused, and again Jonathan saw her control falter as she blinked and looked away. "Summer said I was good at getting things done and making sure everything turns out proper."

It occurred to Jonathan that Summer had known her friend very well. Very well indeed. He said nothing, sensing that his own control was none too reliable at the moment.

Maggie turned back to him, and now Jonathan did see anger in those grief-darkened eyes. "I reckon she was wrong," she said, her voice edged with bitterness. "I wasn't able to do a thing for her. Nothing at all."

Her voice broke.

Jonathan studied the damp eyes and the taut, strained features that were so strong and yet so vulnerable. "There are some things only God can make right, Maggie," he said quietly. "He expects us to do the best we can, and nothing more. He doesn't ask us to do what only He can do."

She wiped a hand over her eyes, roughly, as if to banish any sign of emotion, and then abruptly rose to her feet. "I'd best be getting on to the company store," she said.

Reluctant to let her go like this, feeling that his awkward attempt to comfort her had failed miserably, Jonathan stood, saying, "Maggie, is there anything I can do to help? Anything else…you'd like to talk about?"

An entire parade of emotions seemed to scurry across her face—surprise, alarm, a hint of hopefulness—all of which quickly faded. "No, sir," she said, her voice so low he could scarcely hear her words. "There's nothing else."

Jonathan hesitated, and then he said, "Maggie, you can trust me. If there's anything troubling you—besides Summer, I mean—I wish you'd tell me and let me try to help." He wanted to tell her that he knew. He wanted to assure her that he would take care of everything: her grief, her fear, her sense of hopelessness. He wanted to somehow make everything right for her, and for Kenny too.

As for the grief, only time—time, and God's love and comfort—would heal the pain. And the other? There was still the unanswered question: What could he do that wouldn't make things worse?

She looked at him, and again Jonathan saw a kind of longing in her expression. But in an instant it returned to the same shadowed mask of restraint. "No. No, there isn't anything."

Jonathan swallowed down his disappointment. "I see. Well...all right, then. You go along. I'll see you in class tomorrow."

She turned to go, but then she stopped and faced him again. "Mr. Stuart?"

Jonathan waited.

"I-I like to think that Summer probably isn't coughing anymore. More than likely, she's completely well now, don't you think?"

Jonathan swallowed against the knot in his throat. "Oh, yes, Maggie, I do! I believe that with all my heart. And I'm glad you believe it too. Summer is well and strong now. She won't be coughing anymore. No doubt she's *singing*. Singing with God's angels."

He could sense the girl measuring his words. At last she nodded, apparently satisfied with his reply. "That's what I think too," she said solemnly.

"Maggie—" On impulse Jonathan again delayed her. "There's something I want you to remember. When you're missing Summer most—when you're feeling lonely without her—think about this. One day the two of you will be together again. You'll be reunited. And all the things Summer wasn't able to do while she was here because of her illness? Well, she'll be able to do them in heaven. You'll do them together. Summer will be healthy and whole and happy. You won't be separated from each other forever, Maggie. Only for now. And in heaven, I expect we'll finally realize that all this, this life and all it holds today, was only a brief moment in time. But heaven...heaven is forever."

Help me to remember this too, Lord...I need this assurance just as much as Maggie does...oh, how I need this engraved upon my heart.

As he watched, something flickered in her eyes, the eyes still damp with unshed tears. And then, for the first time in days, Jonathan saw just the faintest trace of a smile. It disappeared as quickly as it came, but it was something.

"Thank you, Mr. Stuart," she said. "Thank you for talking to me."

Jonathan watched her slender, straight-backed figure as she walked down the aisle, stepped outside, and closed the door behind her.

A cold silence fell over the room as he returned to his chair. After a moment he removed his glasses and folded his hands on top of the desk.

Somehow, he had to help that child. The weight of trouble coming against Maggie MacAuley was too much for one so young. It must seem to her that nothing in her world was right or good anymore. He couldn't stand the thought that her heart...or her faith...might be bruised, or even broken, under the burden of pain she was carrying.

How can I help her, Lord? There must be something I can do to lessen her pain and restore her hope. Give me the wisdom to know what it is...and the grace and the strength to do whatever I can. If nothing else, give me at least a part of her pain. It's too much for a child to carry alone. It's just too much...

Twenty-Four

In Praise of Good Men

And if my heart and flesh are weak
To bear an untried pain,
The bruised reed He will not break,
But strengthen and sustain.

John Greenleaf Whittier

When Pastor Ben Wallace walked into the schoolroom on Wednesday, Maggie's stomach clenched.

Something must be wrong. Pastor Wallace almost never came to the school except when there had been a bad accident in the mines or when somebody's mother or father had taken real sick or maybe even died.

She liked Pastor Wallace a lot, but just the sight of him today was enough to strike fear in Maggie. All she could think was *now what? What has happened?*

She was puzzled when the preacher remained near the door, even more curious when Mr. Stuart went to meet him, spoke a few words with him, and then stood waiting while Pastor Wallace went back outside.

Maggie turned to exchange looks with Kenny. She could tell from his expression that he was thinking the same thing she was: Something must be wrong.

Other students were whispering and looking around, too, making enough of a disturbance that Mr. Stuart cleared his throat and lifted his eyebrows. Everyone shushed but continued to watch the door.

After a moment, Pastor Wallace returned with a small, dark-haired boy in tow.

Only when Mr. Stuart took the boy by the hand did Maggie realize that he had but one hand. There was nothing where his other hand should have been but a piece of white bandage showing below his sleeve.

Benny Pippino.

The boy darted an occasional glance from side to side as Mr. Stuart led him forward. Maggie immediately felt sorry for him, coming into a room filled with strange faces so soon after his harrowing accident. But why was he coming to school now? According to Da, none of the Pippino boys had ever gone to school.

The entire schoolroom had gone totally still, but it was the kind of quiet stretched tight by the tension of waiting. They didn't have to wait long before Mr. Stuart stopped just in front of his desk, put a hand on the small boy's shoulder, and faced the students.

"Class," he said, "I want you to welcome our newest student. This is Benny Pippino, and he's going to be studying with us from now on."

The school in Skingle Creek rarely took in a new student. Maybe one or two a year. Nevertheless, Mr. Stuart had taught his class the proper way to welcome a newcomer.

"Welcome, Benny!" they said in unison.

"I know you'll all help to make Benny feel at home with us." Mr. Stuart looked as if he were about to say more, but the boy at his side murmured something so low the teacher had to bend over to hear.

Mr. Stuart straightened, smiling at the other students as he turned toward them again. "I stand corrected. Benny says everyone calls him 'Pip.'"

From behind her, Maggie heard Billy Macken mutter something that triggered a laugh from Orrin. She saw Junior Tyree shake his head in obvious disgust. To Maggie's surprise, Lily Woodbridge whipped around and gave Billy and Orrin one of her meanest looks along with a loud "Shush!"

Mr. Stuart's face tightened, but he said nothing. Instead, he went on with his introduction.

"In addition to being a student, Pip will also be working here at the school part-time," he said. "He's going to be doing some of the extra tasks that always need attention, but which I...never find time to do."

Maggie could hardly wait to get home to tell her parents. Da would no longer need to fret about finding a different job at the mines for Pip because Pip wouldn't need a job there anymore!

Mr. Stuart led Pip to a desk among some of the younger, beginning students, waited until he was settled, and then came to the front again. "By the way, class, I need at least two volunteers to stay after the Christmas Exchange to help clean up. Pip will be staying too, but we can use some extra help."

Without hesitating, Maggie raised her hand, and after a quick glance at Kenny, his hand went up too. Lily, never one to be left out, immediately started waving her hand in the air, but Mr. Stuart had already singled out Maggie and Kenny with a nod of his head. Lily wasted no time in yanking her hand down and giving an exaggerated shrug.

The Christmas Exchange was an event that Mr. Stuart had originated not long after he came to Skingle Creek, and something the class looked forward to every year. Instead of the students exchanging new and expensive gifts at Christmas—since none of the mining families had any money to spare for such extravagances—each student would wrap and give a homemade item. Names had already been drawn, and after school this Friday, they would exchange their gifts.

To make it even more special, Mr. Stuart always brought the refreshments: popcorn balls which he made himself and sweet cider from the Allen farm.

As she watched the teacher take some books and paper over to Pip, it occurred to Maggie that for the first time in a long time something good had actually happened. The way things had worked out for Pip made her feel a little better. And with the Christmas Exchange, there was actually something to look forward to.

She recalled that her entire family, herself included, had prayed for a solution to Pip's problem. Was it safe to think that what had happened was answered prayer?

She was almost afraid to take any pleasure in the moment for fear that she might somehow tempt something dark and wicked to purposely strike back in mockery at this rare and unexpected stroke of good fortune. She had heard too many of the older Irish women in town claim that laughter in the morning meant tears by night.

Even though her da said that was nothing but foolish superstition, Maggie wasn't willing to take a chance. She would be sparing with her happiness.

Especially since these days there seemed little enough of it to go around in Skingle Creek.

Maggie tensed when Mr. Stuart stopped her and Kenny as they were about to go out the door for afternoon recess. It didn't help when she saw Billy Macken watching them with narrow eyes, as if he were trying to hear the conversation.

She immediately started worrying that the teacher might somehow have learned about the situation with Billy and Orrin. She had seen the way his eyes sometimes followed the two boys, almost as if he was expecting trouble from them. And when he happened to look at her or Kenny these days, his expression was often peculiar, as if he was puzzling over something.

Maggie didn't see how he could know anything for certain, but that didn't mean he wasn't suspicious. Everybody knew you couldn't put much over Mr. Stuart, not for long.

Apparently, though, he meant only to talk about Pip.

"I'm hoping you and Kenny will keep an eye on the boy," he said. "This is all very new to him. He's never gone to school before, so he's going to need a lot of help. I'd like to know I can count on the two of you."

Maggie looked at Kenny, and both of them nodded.

"Good. Some things we can start right away. Although his mother has taught him to read a little, Pip's probably going to be somewhat behind the other children his age. Not only in reading, but in penmanship and arithmetic as well. I'm going to work with him as much as I can, but I can't give him all my attention during class. Since both of you often finish your work early, I'd like to call on you now and then to provide some extra coaching for Pip. Are you willing to do that?"

Again they nodded.

"I was sure I could depend on you. Now, there's also the matter of helping him to fit in with the other children. I realize that he's younger than both of you, but you can still be of help in making sure he's not left to himself too much during recess and lunch.

"You know, Pip has had rather a hard life so far, young as he is," said Mr. Stuart. "His father died last year in the mine cave-in, and now, having lost his hand, he's at a disadvantage, or he will be until he learns to adapt. His family is large, and he very much needs this job in order to earn a wage, but also to get whatever education he can. I was thinking that perhaps you could walk at least part of the way home with him after school for a few days, just until he makes some new friends his own age?"

"Sure thing," said Kenny, and Maggie agreed.

"I want to make certain he doesn't become the target of any mischief or roughness by some of our more...difficult...students." He looked first at one, then the other. "I believe you know the ones I mean."

Maggie tried not to look at Kenny. Neither of them said anything.

After a long silence, the teacher continued. "One more thing. You should know, Maggie, that your father was instrumental in working this out."

"Da already knows about Pip?"

"Oh, yes. In fact, your father is the one who set everything in motion."

He paused and then went on. "No doubt you've noticed that I'm not...as well as I'd like to be. With the help of your father, I was able to convince the board to give Pip a part-time job here at the school. His wage will be almost as much as what he was making as a breaker boy, and at the same time, he'll be able to get an education. This will help him, and it will help me. It's not likely, though, that any of this would have happened had your father not taken an interest in Pip and resolved to help him. He's a very caring man, your father. I must say I've come to admire him a great deal."

Maggie stared at the teacher. Mr. Stuart admired her da?

Her mind raced. In truth, she'd always thought of Da as a somewhat hard man, not a caring one. She seldom knew what he was thinking, and he was never one for explaining himself. In fact, her mother was forever explaining things *for* him: trying to soften some hard way or sharp word of his, always insisting he meant only to do what was best for them, taking up for him when he refused them some request or other.

What Mr. Stuart was saying would definitely take some thought.

The warmth that stole over her at the teacher's praise took Maggie by surprise, but it was a good feeling all the same.

At home that night, Maggie could scarcely wait until her da came out of the washroom and sat down at the table for supper. She started right in, as soon as he said grace and reached for the potatoes.

"Da, Pip came to school today!"

"Did he now?" He went on dishing up his potatoes.

"And Mr. Stuart introduced him and asked Kenny and me to keep an eye on him. And we're to help him some with his schoolwork as well."

"That'll be good. Just don't let your own work suffer."

"I won't. And guess what else Mr. Stuart said, Da?"

"Maggie, let your daddy eat before his supper is cold entirely," said Ma.

"It's all right, Kate. I can eat while she talks."

"He said that you played an important part in working things out to help Pip."

Da shook his head. "I did no such thing. I merely cast my vote with the rest of the board."

"No, Da. Mr. Stuart said none of this would have happened without your help. And you know what else?"

He sighed. "I don't, as a matter of fact. But I expect you're going to tell me, are you not?"

"Mr. Stuart said that he admires you, Da—a lot!"

His face reddened. "Now, Maggie."

"He did, Da! Indeed, he did."

Maggie noticed that she had her mother's full attention now as well. Even Nell Frances and Eva Grace were taking in her words.

Da had paused his eating. Slowly, he placed his fork on his plate. "Let me tell you something, lass," he said, leaving Maggie to marvel at this unusual event. Rare was the occasion when Da interrupted his meal to say anything at all other than to ask for seconds.

"I want you to know something about your Mr. Stuart. Seldom have I met a man with a heart so humble he'd be willing to bare it before other men, and for the sole purpose of helping a child. But that's exactly what your teacher did when he came before the school board to ask for help for that poor boy."

Her father leaned back in his chair a little, as if he were in no hurry at all and meant to tell this tale as it deserved to be told.

Maggie's astonishment grew.

"You know the teacher is ailing."

Maggie nodded, reluctant to talk about Mr. Stuart's illness. Apparently, though, that was just what Da intended.

"Well, now, in order to get the board members' attention, the man had to be more forthright than a man likes to be, especially in the presence of other men. Not only that, he risked his own job by admitting how ill he is to the very men who have the power to terminate his position. But your Mr. Stuart is a man who clearly prizes the good of others—especially that of the children in his school—above his own well-being."

Da folded his arms over his chest, but then, as if he'd just remembered his food, proceeded to take a bite of potatoes and a sip of coffee. Maggie feared that he might stop and tell them nothing more, but he went on.

"Mr. Stuart, he stood there in that room and stripped himself of every shred of dignity, never making the effort to save face at all. For the sake of wee Pip, he made his condition known to every man in the room. He spared himself nothing."

He stopped and then quietly added, "But in the process, didn't he gain the respect of us all?"

Ma made a soft click of her tongue.

The long and short of it, Da said, was that Mr. Stuart apparently knew he had to make the board aware of just how badly he needed help. He had to make them see the need for an extra pair of hands...or in this case, only *one* hand...if he were to keep going on as their teacher. "The man had to know he was taking a risk that they might simply dismiss him and look for someone more fit—more able-bodied."

Now Ma spoke up. "They might find a more able-bodied man, but not a better one, I'll warrant."

Da nodded. "Make no mistake about it. Mr. Stuart is the one who brought this about, not I. And it took a great deal of honesty and courage to do what he did."

Maggie was fighting back tears by the time her da finished his tale—tears of pride, for hadn't she known that Mr. Stuart was a special kind of man?—but tears of sadness as well, not only because he *was* so terribly ill, but because he had admitted his weakness to other men stronger and more fit than himself. That must have been a brutally hard thing to do.

How Summer would have loved hearing this, Maggie thought sadly. *How proud of Mr. Stuart she would have been.* The two of them would have chewed over every word her da said and taken some satisfaction in knowing that others—grown-ups at that—recognized what a fine man their teacher really was...and that Mr. Stuart admired Maggie's da!

Indeed, the only thing that diminished Maggie's pride and pleasure was the bitter fact that she could not run immediately to Summer and share everything with her.

Jonathan Stuart spent a long time on his knees that night. When he finally rose to get ready for bed, he was weak to the point of collapse—emotionally drained and physically exhausted as well.

But he thought he finally knew what he had to do, and he was convinced he could wait no longer.

There simply was no way to avoid going to Matthew MacAuley and Judson Tallman. Jonathan no longer believed he had a choice. The parents had to be told. Otherwise, he could see nothing but disaster on the horizon for Maggie and Kenny.

He hoped those two would forgive him for what he was going to do. He supposed he could rationalize his actions, since neither had actually divulged the situation directly to him. Still, he felt a sense of guilt, as if he were about to betray them, especially Kenny, who was being so brave and trying so hard to keep his silence and protect a friend.

On the other hand, his guilt would be greater if something terrible happened to either one of those children when he might have done something to prevent it.

Bringing this ugliness to an end was going to take more than talk, but his own failing health and weakness could no longer be an issue. He would simply have to trust that for the sake of those two children God would give him whatever strength was needed to carry out his plan.

Or else that He would appoint someone in his place, should he not live to go the distance.

Twenty-Five

The Beginning of a Plan

O use me, Lord, use even me,
Just as Thou wilt, and when and where...

Frances Havergal

Jonathan was dreading this evening like nothing else he could remember. But if he were to accomplish anything for Kenny and Maggie, he must first speak with their fathers.

It would be no easy task, however, to meet with both men without their children being present. Obviously, he couldn't visit their homes. At the time he would find them there, the children would also be at home. And although Judson Tallman had an office, Matthew MacAuley did not; he would be deep in the mine during the day.

He finally decided that his best chance would be to go to the mine at the end of the workday. So on Thursday evening, just before the whistle blew, he stationed himself at the pithead, waiting for the miners to emerge from below.

It was a wretched day, gray and raw, with the kind of rainy cold that knifed right through one's outerwear and bored into the bones. He was almost certain to take cold after standing out in this misery.

He felt more than a little out of sorts, wished he were anywhere but here, and at one point considered leaving. Fatigue was partly to blame for his petulance, no doubt, as was his aversion to what he was about to do. After only a brief time, however, of watching the cages unload their weary miners, he grew ashamed of his bad mood and resolved to stick it out.

He studied the miners as they passed by him a few at a time, stopping only long enough to leave their tools before heading for home or the local tavern. Seeing their fatigue, their faces and hands black with coal dust, many of their backs bent, Jonathan reminded himself that these brave men daily risked their lives working in bitter cold conditions, many standing in water, hunched over and cramped for hours in the dark space in which they worked. In the face of their grueling way of life and sacrifice for their families, surely he could withstand a few minutes of discomfort without complaint.

He nearly missed Matthew MacAuley, crowded as he was among the other blackened faces. As it happened, MacAuley saw him first.

"Mr. Stuart? Whatever are you doing out in this evil weather? Is something wrong? Has something happened to one of the girls?"

Jonathan wasn't a short man himself, but he still had to look up at Matthew MacAuley. It was a strange sensation, those piercing eyes staring out from the blackened face—a face that scarcely resembled the man Jonathan had seen at the last school board meeting.

He realized then that he had alarmed this man by coming here, that MacAuley was frightened for his children.

"The girls are fine," Jonathan assured him. "But I need to talk with you."

"Now?"

MacAuley's expression was skeptical, as though he thought Jonathan was either not telling the truth about his daughters or was at the very least acting suspiciously.

"Yes, I'm afraid we need to talk right away. It's important."

The big miner frowned in renewed concern. "Well, you're welcome to come home with me—"

"No, I'm afraid that won't do. I need to talk with you alone. My buggy's close by. We can get out of the worst of this and talk there."

MacAuley lifted his miner's cap, pushed a shock of dust-streaked red hair away from his forehead, and then set his cap back in place. "Ah, you don't want me in your buggy, Mr. Stuart," he said roughly, running a hand down over the front of his dusty jacket. "You'd be cleanin' it for a week. Besides, it'll be a bit warmer in the toolshed. Over here."

Jonathan followed him to a narrow, unpainted shack a few feet away. Some of the miners just coming out glanced at them curiously, spoke, and then went on.

Inside, it was dark and damp, the floor and shelves littered with what looked to be mostly broken tools in a state of disrepair. On one entire wall, though, hung rows of shovels and picks and axes, along with assorted tools with tags suspended below each.

"This will at least keep the rain and wind off us," said MacAuley.

He looked around, grabbed a piece of tarp, and spread it over a stool. "There you go."

Jonathan eyed the rickety piece of wood before lowering himself onto it.

MacAuley leaned back against a workbench, watching him. "If you don't mind, Mr. Stuart, you've got me worried some. What's this about?"

"I really wish you'd call me Jonathan. I'm sorry to worry you, but there's something you need to know. I fear I've already let it go too long."

MacAuley crossed his brawny arms over his chest, his gaze steady and relentless.

I would not want a man like this, Jonathan thought, *as an enemy.*

"Then you'd better not wait any longer to be telling me, I expect," said MacAuley.

So Jonathan began his story.

"And you believe the boy is keeping his silence for fear of what they might do to my Maggie?"

Jonathan had heard the term "red rage" before today, but this was the first time he'd ever seen it for himself. MacAuley was pacing the narrow expanse of the toolshed like a caged tiger. A moment ago he had thrown his miner's cap onto the workbench and was now raking a hand through his hair, layering it with the same black powder as his face and beard. Jonathan was certain that underneath the coal dust veneer the man's skin was flushed with fury.

"From what I overheard," he said, "they're keeping Kenny in tow by threatening to harm Maggie. And as I told you, I'm convinced they've already harassed her at least once."

MacAuley finally stopped pacing. "And now they intend to attack Maggie as well as the boy," he said, his voice a low rumble in the drafty shed.

"Yes," Jonathan said, nearly choking on the memory of what he'd overheard. His heart was hammering, and he was finding it difficult to get his breath, but he didn't want MacAuley to notice. "I asked Maggie and Kenny to stay and help clean up after the Christmas Exchange tomorrow evening. Now I don't know that I should have. It will only mean their leaving the building later than the other children."

MacAuley squeezed his eyes shut and again balled his hands into fists. The very thought that his daughter might be victimized by these two bullies had to be in itself unbearable to a father. But to his credit, Matthew MacAuley seemed as concerned for Kenny Tallman as for his own child.

"You actually heard them say they had attacked the Tallman lad?"

"Oh, yes. More than once. There was no mistaking what they were talking about. And I've seen the evidence of it myself. The boy has a black eye, a broken lens in his glasses, and a sore arm. I'm ashamed to admit that my first thought was of his father, that he might have—"

Jonathan didn't finish, but MacAuley clearly understood what he was getting at.

With a short nod, he again raked a hand through his hair. "Why didn't you come to me sooner, man? Why did you wait until now?"

"Mr. MacAuley—"

"'Matthew,'" the other interrupted.

"Matthew, I didn't know what to do. It's clear that both the boy and Maggie have been threatened. I believe Kenny took the beatings and kept quiet about it to prevent Maggie from being hurt, though I wonder if Maggie knows that. In any event, I'm fairly certain he swore her to silence too. It seems to me that each was set on protecting the other." Jonathan paused. "They're great friends, you know."

MacAuley scowled. "Well, the lass needs a friend with the wee Rankin child gone. But I'd just as soon she wouldn't have chosen the super's son."

"They've been friends for a long time," Jonathan said quietly. "Long before Summer died. And, Matthew, you can surely see what the Tallman boy is made of. I suppose we ought to be grateful he *is* such a good friend to Maggie."

The miner studied him for a moment, his eyes still burning. Then he expelled a long breath, saying, "Aye, I expect that's true."

He shook his head as if to clear it. "Well, we'd best go to Tallman and get it over with. He has to know."

Jonathan's heart lunged. In spite of the cold, a band of clammy perspiration broke out on his forehead, and his hands had begun to shake. He was growing weaker by the minute. "How well do you know Mr. Tallman?"

MacAuley made a dismissive wave. "Nobody knows that one well. He's the coldest devil I ever did meet, and that's the truth!"

"But surely he cares about his own son?"

MacAuley's answer didn't come right away. He shook his head slowly, obviously thinking about Jonathan's question. "It's a terrible thing, but I'm not so sure. You've heard the tales about why his wife ran off?"

Jonathan nodded. "I've heard the rumors, of course, but I'd rather not believe them. I can't bear the thought of that fine boy living with such a man."

"Well, whether Tallman is as bad as he's been made out to be or not, I doubt he'd tolerate any ill-treatment of his son or anything else that belongs to him," said MacAuley, his tone cynical. "He's a proud sort."

He stopped. "It's not that I need the likes of Tallman to help me put an end to this, mind. I expect I could handle those two no-accounts and not break a sweat, no matter how tough they think they are. But this involves Tallman's son, not just my girl, and by all that's right, he needs to know what's going on. So no matter how he takes it, we'll need to tell him the whole story."

MacAuley scooped up his cap from the workbench and set it back on his head.

"You don't have to involve yourself with Tallman, Matthew," said Jonathan. "I'm quite capable of dealing with him by myself. Besides, if there's any chance it could affect your job—"

MacAuley's mouth turned down at the corners. "With all due respect, Mr. Stuart—Jonathan—I don't believe you ought to face Tallman alone with this. I doubt you're accustomed to dealing with his kind. As for my job, that's not your worry. My Maggie is what's important here."

Jonathan knew himself to be put in his place, kindly but firmly. Besides, he wasn't about to argue. As long as he was going into the lion's den, it couldn't hurt to have a gladiator at his side.

Judson Tallman's initial calm had been almost maddening.

Jonathan thought he actually preferred the mine superintendent's expression of the moment—an unmistakable tight-lipped, white-knuckled fury.

He had met this man only a few times. Tallman wasn't one to attend school functions or drop in every now and then to check on his son's progress. The few times they'd met had been by accident—a chance encounter in town or at the company store.

Jonathan was accustomed to two fairly common types of behavior where he was concerned: either an awkward deference—which he disliked and lamented—on the part of those with little or no education who seemed to view him as some sort of an oddity; or a far more agreeable cordiality from most of the parents and townsfolk, those who actually seemed to appreciate his interest in and efforts on behalf of their children.

Tallman had never exhibited either mode of conduct. Instead, he commonly eyed Jonathan much as he might have a piece of furniture—as a purely functional object and thereby of no real interest.

At the moment, however, the mine superintendent looked for all the world as if he would like to hurl the massive iron paperweight from his desk at either Jonathan or Matthew MacAuley.

MacAuley's composure was plainly disintegrating by the second. Jonathan could actually hear the big miner's knuckles cracking as he clenched and unclenched his fists.

Presumably so he wouldn't be tempted to leap across the desk and trounce his employer.

Tallman's next statement very nearly broke Jonathan's control.

"So what you're saying is that my boy has been allowing himself to be beaten up rather than fighting back."

The Welsh accent was even thicker as Tallman shrugged and added, "No surprise, that. I've done my best with him, but he's weak. Always has been."

Anger flared in Jonathan like a straw fire. He let out a sharp breath, ready to defend Kenny, but MacAuley put a hand to his arm and spoke before Jonathan could.

"Did you not hear anything Mr. Stuart here has said, man?" His voice was rough as gravel. "Your boy is anything but weak!"

"My boy is none of your business, MacAuley," he said tersely.

"That's true enough, Tallman, but my daughter *is* my business, and they're both at risk if we don't do something. I mean to put a stop to this before either of them gets hurt—*again*—and I'm thinking you might be wanting to come along since your son is in just as much danger as my daughter."

The man actually shrugged. "The boy has to learn sooner or later to take his punishment if he won't fight his own battles. He can't stay a weak sister all his life."

Jonathan had never in his life been close to striking another human being until this moment. "Good heavens, man, can you really be that foolish?" he blurted out. "That heartless?"

Tallman went pale, his eyes like two dark marbles against his ashen skin. MacAuley again spoke before Jonathan could. "Don't you understand, Tallman? Your son *is* taking his punishment! And he's been taking my Maggie's punishment as well! He's anything but a 'weak sister'! He's the bravest lad in that entire school! Let me tell you something. Being a man isn't about fighting. It's about character. You obviously don't know your own son at all or you'd have realized long before now that he has the kind of character—the kind of courage—most grown men would envy." MacAuley stopped only long enough to get a breath. "Open your eyes, man. You have a son to be proud of!"

Tallman's heavy eyebrows knit together as he stared at Matthew MacAuley. "What do you mean, he's been taking the girl's punishment?"

"Just what Mr. Stuart has been trying to *tell* you!" MacAuley shot back. "Those two—bounders—they've been threatening your boy all along that if he rats on them about the beatings, they'll take it out on my Maggie. And now it seems they intend to go after her *and* your boy. *Tomorrow night!*"

MacAuley leaned forward and splayed his hands on Tallman's desk. The mine superintendent braced himself against the back of his chair as if he feared he was about to be struck.

"Your son is no weakling, Tallman," said MacAuley, his voice low but hard as stone. "He's as brave as any man working your mine, and then some. You must be blind not to see it!"

Tallman went white-lipped with anger. "You forget yourself, MacAuley."

The big Irishman pointed a finger at the mine superintendent. "Not for a heartbeat. But don't you threaten me, or I just *might* forget myself."

Silence hung heavy in the room. MacAuley's breathing was loud and ragged. The pain in Jonathan's chest threatened to topple him, and his own breath was coming in quick, sharp gasps.

Suddenly, Matthew MacAuley let out a sound of disgust and, whipping around with his back to Tallman, grated out, "Ah, let's get out of here, Mr. Stuart! I'll handle this on my own."

Jonathan didn't quite know what to do. He glanced back at Judson Tallman and saw with surprise that the man's features had gone slack, the anger in his eyes of only a moment before now giving way to a look of confusion.

"I only mean to raise him to be a man, to be strong," Tallman said vaguely, as if no one else were in the room and he was speaking to himself. "A weak man will be destroyed. Either by himself or by someone else."

He seemed to rouse then, sitting up a little straighter. "You think I don't care about my son?"

"Well, that's how it would seem," said MacAuley, his eyes flashing, his tone laced with acid. "And that's exactly what you have the whole town thinking."

The other stirred in his chair. "Things aren't always as they appear," he said bitterly. "You think I don't know what they say about me? About my wife? You think I haven't heard their stories?"

MacAuley broke in. "Not everyone believes what they hear, man. But right now I don't give a whit about your wife or the stories or anything else except my daughter and your son. They need help. They need *our* help! Now, are you *going* to help or not? That's all I want to know."

Tallman stared at Matthew MacAuley, and for the first time Jonathan saw a look of regret, perhaps even shame, come over the man. At one point he lowered his gaze as if unable to meet the other's.

Jonathan held his breath. But when Tallman again looked up, he slowly nodded, passed a hand over his eyes, and said, "Of course I'll help. Tell me what you think we should do."

MacAuley looked at Jonathan, who quickly deferred to him with a turn of his hand.

"All right, then," MacAuley said. "We can stop this, but not without a price. And before we go any further, I want your word that the fathers of these two boys won't be penalized for their sons' behavior."

Tallman bristled. "They have to pay—"

"The boys have to pay," MacAuley broke in. "Not their fathers. No matter what they've done or not done to raise such no-accounts, those men need their jobs. They have wives and other children to take care of."

Finally, Tallman inclined his head in agreement.

MacAuley then turned to Jonathan. "Mr. Stuart, I know that you're not well. You don't need to be a part of this. If you'd like to go on home now, that's fine. We'll work it out from here."

For just an instant, Jonathan was tempted. But only for an instant.

"Thank you, Matthew," he said. "And you're right, of course, about my not being well. Nevertheless, I'm going with you. I have to be there."

MacAuley studied him for another second or two and then nodded. "I understand."

Jonathan knew he did.

Twenty-Six

Night Wind

I hear all night as through a storm
Hoarse voices calling, calling
My name upon the wind...
James Clarence Mangan

Jonathan kept the children as long as he could after the gift exchange on Friday. It was imperative that he allow enough time for the miners on the evening shift to clear out—and for Matthew MacAuley and Judson Tallman to get to the tipple afterward.

Knowing it would be dark by the time the students finished exchanging their gifts and had their refreshments, he had made sure everyone whose parents couldn't come after them had a friend to walk home with. But one of the Pippino's boy's responsibilities was to stay later and help clean up, so by the time he was ready to leave, everyone else was gone.

Maggie and Kenny volunteered to see Pip home, but Jonathan

didn't quite know what to do. He hadn't planned for Pip. Although the boy was probably used to getting around on his own at night, he wasn't about to send him off in the dark alone. Skingle Creek had always been a safe little town, but it was still a mining town, with the occasional stranger passing through in search of work or a handout. It didn't pay to take chances.

On the other hand, if he sent him with Kenny and Maggie, he was placing the boy in known jeopardy. In the end, it seemed he had no choice. He tried to tell himself Pip would be safe enough; the plan was for the men to be in place long before the children drew anywhere near the tipple. Even so, uneasiness plagued him the rest of the evening.

When the time came to leave, Jonathan issued a stern warning to be careful, and then he sent the three of them off with their items from the gift exchange, as well as a small sack he'd prepared for each student with some rock candy and apples. In addition, his mother had supplied an embroidered handkerchief for each girl, and his father had sent some shiny new marbles for the boys.

He was taken completely off guard when Pip turned back at the door and threw his arms around Jonathan's middle in a warm hug. "Thank you, Mr. Stuart!" he blurted out in his broken English. "My mama and me, we pray and ask blessings for you every night for your kindness!"

Warmth flooded Jonathan as he hugged the boy back. "Thank you, Pip. And please tell your mother I'm very grateful for her prayers. Very grateful indeed."

Jonathan stepped outside to watch them off, but only for a moment. As soon as they reached the end of the school yard, he went back inside the building just long enough to get his coat, extinguish the lamps, and lock up. Then, moving as quickly as he could, he started for the buggy.

Matthew had cautioned him to give the children at least a ten-minute lead before he left the school, to make sure he didn't meet up with them on the way. But Jonathan didn't wait. He felt an almost desperate urgency to be in place before the three arrived at the tipple, and if he left now, he easily could be. He'd make certain their paths didn't cross.

He had never been this frightened before in his life. All he could think of as he climbed into the buggy was what would happen if Matthew and Tallman didn't get there in time, if they were late. *Too* late. What could he possibly do without them?

His hands felt boneless. He was shaking so badly by the time he took the reins he could scarcely hold onto them.

It was a clear night but bitter cold with a sharp wind. Their breath steamed as they headed for home, and no matter how tightly she burrowed into her coat, Maggie couldn't seem to get warm.

Ever since the night Billy and Orrin had jumped her on the way to Summer's, she didn't like being out after dark. At least not alone. Tonight wasn't so bad, though, with Kenny and Pip on either side of her. Not that Pip would be much protection in a pickle, but his chatter helped to dispel her jitters.

Kenny didn't have much to say for several minutes, but when Pip started trotting quite a ways ahead of them, he finally spoke up. "It's a nice thing Mr. Stuart does, isn't it? Making popcorn balls and all, and sending a gift bag home with us."

Maggie nodded. "Seems like it would be a lot of work, though. Especially with him being so poorly."

"Yeah," Kenny said quietly. "It was a lot better, all of us being together without Gaffney or Macken there for a change. Don't you think?"

"I sure didn't miss them." Probably her attitude was neither Christian nor charitable, but as far as Maggie was concerned, school in general would be a lot better without Billy or Orrin.

Pip had found a fallen branch and was now pretending it was a sword as he jabbed it toward the trees and barbed wire fence along the road.

"Hey, Pip—slow down a little," Kenny warned him. "You're getting too far ahead."

The boy glanced around with an ornery grin. "Let's go this way," he said, pointing to the dirt run veering off from the road. "It's shorter."

Kenny looked at Maggie. She was cold and getting colder. Cutting through the Tapscott farm would save them at least ten minutes, though the path was rougher that way. "I guess that'd be okay," she said.

Seeing that they were going to follow, Pip took off again.

"Do you think Christmas vacation will make a difference with Billy and Orrin?" Maggie said.

"What do you mean?"

"I was thinking that maybe after a few days of being out of school, they'll forget about us and lose interest. Then when we go back, they might leave us alone."

"Maybe," he said, not sounding in the least convinced.

"Do you ever wonder," Maggie said, as much to herself as to him, "what makes some people so mean and others so good?"

"Not really."

"I do. I mean, think about the difference in someone like Billy Macken compared to Mr. Stuart. What do you think accounts for Mr. Stuart being as good a man as he is and Billy being so completely different?"

"My dad would say 'bad blood.'"

"What's that mean?"

Kenny shrugged. "He says some people are just born bad."

"Do you believe that?"

"I don't know. I guess it's possible. But I'm more inclined to believe they have a choice in how they turn out."

"According to Mr. Stuart, there's a choice in just about everything."

Maggie noticed Pip had taken to running again, and he'd gone a considerable distance ahead of them. "Pip! You wait for us. Mr. Stuart said you're to stay with Kenny and me."

But Pip didn't wait. As if he hadn't heard Maggie, the boy kept going, still brandishing his tree branch and conquering imaginary enemies.

They ducked under the fence that outlined Samuel Tapscott's farm and then picked up their pace. After a couple of minutes more, they came out near the place where the road narrowed and branched off, with the left fork going toward the railroad tracks and the right, which they would follow home, leading to the tipple and running the rest of the way through town.

Suddenly, an owl hooted. It sounded close by. Maggie stopped to look, as did Kenny. It was perched on the branch of a tree right beside the road, looking down at them with a bored stare.

It hooted again, and Maggie laughed. "I think he's telling us to go away and let him sleep."

"Nah. They mostly sleep through the day," said Kenny. "He's probably just waiting for supper to come along. A nice fat mouse or a rat, maybe."

Maggie pulled a face. "Eww. That's disgusting, Kenny!"

"Not if you're an owl."

As they left the path and turned onto the road, Maggie suddenly realized that Pip was nowhere to be seen.

"Pip! Come back here with me and Kenny!" she called out.

There was no reply, but Maggie wasn't alarmed. Not until she called twice more, still with no response. This time Kenny yelled for him too, but the only reply was silence.

They had reached the fork in the road and stood looking around. Both of them gave a shout and then another.

Nothing. No answer. No Pip.

Maggie's insides began to tremble. "How did he disappear so fast?"

Kenny looked, first toward the left branch of the road, into the dark trees that ran the entire length of the railroad tracks, and then to the right, where the tipple rose above the road.

"Pip!" he shouted again. "Where are you?"

"I don't understand how he got so far ahead," Maggie said, her voice breaking.

Kenny didn't answer, but stood listening, so still he looked to be holding his breath.

Maggie felt sick. Pip was just a little kid. A little kid with one hand.

"Kenny—" she looked toward the tracks. "Do you suppose it's true, that there are bears in the woods?"

"I've been back there plenty of times," he said, not looking at her, "and I've never yet seen a bear. Besides, he probably didn't even go that way."

"But he might have," Maggie said. "We have to find him, Kenny!"

"He'll come back in a minute. He probably just saw a dog or something and chased after it. He'll be all right."

But Maggie could tell by the look on his face that he didn't believe what he said.

"Besides," he added, "we don't know which way he went."

Maggie frowned. "We should have been watching. We shouldn't have let him run off that way. If he's over there—" she motioned toward the trees —"he might get lost."

After a moment they continued up the road a short ways, stopping beneath the tipple where its track and dump shafts crossed the road overhead. The aging structure butted right into the side of the hill, its slightly crooked hoist leaning toward town.

In front of the slag pile nearby squatted an old abandoned coal car. In the shadows of the hulking tipple and tramway, it looked like an enormous ugly bug.

They stood looking all around, seeing nothing. The night was darker than before, a cloud having pocketed the thin slice of moon. More clouds were gathering too, swallowing up the stars a few at a time. The wind had picked up even more and seemed to whip right through Maggie's coat.

"What are we going to do?" she said. "We have to find him. We can't go any farther without him."

"We'll find him," said Kenny.

"How?" Maggie was close to panic now. "We don't know where to look. Maybe we'd best split up. One of us can go over by the tracks—" she swallowed at the thought— "and the other look around the rail yard."

"No!" Kenny shook his head. "We stay together."

Relieved to hear him say it but ashamed of her own cowardice, Maggie protested. "He can't be very far off. We'd better split up."

"No, I said. We'll look over here first. Start yelling for him again."

They circled the rail yard and checked behind the tipple and the toolshed and other buildings, all the while calling out Pip's name. Finally, they started across the road toward the trees.

As they went, Maggie saw Kenny pull something from his pocket and close his hand over it.

"What's that?"

Not looking at her, he said, "Watch your step here. There's a bunch of rocks and broken track."

"Kenny? What is that?"

Still keeping his gaze straight ahead, he finally answered her. "A pocketknife."

Maggie stumbled, and he caught her hand. "I told you to watch out."

"Why do you have a knife?"

"I just do," he said. "Let's call him again."

They stopped, both of them shouting Pip's name as loud as they could, over and over again.

Maggie felt lightheaded with fear. "Where could he be, Kenny?"

"Don't worry. Just keep calling him. Once he hears us, he'll come."

Pip didn't come.

But someone else did.

Twenty-Seven

The Cabin

The bravest heart no more is brave.

William James Linton

From his hiding place among the big pine trees, Pip watched the two boys coming across the road from the tipple. They were headed right for him, but he knew they couldn't see him.

Not yet.

These were the bad boys who didn't like him. They made fun of him when they thought Mr. Stuart wasn't looking, making faces and pulling their sleeves down over their hands. They didn't like Mr. Stuart, either. When his back was turned, they made fun of him too. Other times they looked at him as if they'd like to hurt him real bad.

He didn't know what to do. He'd gotten off the path somewhere when he ran ahead of Maggie and Kenny, and instead of coming out on the road to the tipple, he'd ended up in the woods on the other side. Now he knew where he was, but he wasn't about to come out where those two boys could see him.

Maggie and Kenny had come into the woods too, calling for him, and they didn't sound very far away. He was afraid to answer, though, for fear the bad boys would find him first. But if he didn't answer, they would hear Maggie and Kenny and probably find all of them.

He would have to move deeper into the trees. They were coming his way, whispering behind cupped hands, stopping every few steps and standing really still, as if listening, trying to tell which direction Maggie and Kenny's voices were coming from.

He glanced behind him, and then he began to snake backward on his belly, watching the boys as he moved. A branch snapped from somewhere nearby, and Pip stopped, not breathing, waiting…

They stopped, turned, and looked his way.

Oh, no, no, no, don't let them see me… please, no…

Just then the wind carried Maggie's voice, and then Kenny's, through the trees. They were close, real close! Pip wanted to stay where he was so they'd find him, but feared the other two would find him first.

The boys started in walking again. Fear pounded at Pip's heart, and his breath stuck in his throat. He scrambled to his knees, clamping a fist against his mouth to keep from crying out.

Then he saw them. Kenny and Maggie, heading directly toward him, though he knew they didn't see him. From the corner of his eye, he glimpsed movement from the bad boys. In that instant, they began to run, fast, their feet pounding the ground as they crashed through the trees toward Maggie and Kenny, tackling them and throwing them to the ground.

Maggie screamed and Kenny yelled. Pip bit down on his knuckles to keep from crying out. Again he flattened himself on his stomach, fighting to silence his ragged breathing.

If they heard him, they would see him, for he was no more than a few feet away from where they stood. He mustn't be captured! If they caught him too, he wouldn't be able to get help for Maggie and Kenny—and the gooseflesh rising on his arms told him they were going to need help and need it soon.

Pip fought to swallow the thick taste of terror rising up from his throat, struggled against giving in to the wave of panic slamming through him. Shame scalded his skin and squeezed his chest. Should he break free of his hiding place and try to fight them? But he was only nine and puny. And he had only one hand. How much help would he be?

Something held him back, warning him to wait, to watch and remain silent until he could get away and go for help. He huddled against the ground, feeling as if the quiet of the night would surely give up the sound of his breathing and make known his presence.

In the spiny shadows of the pine trees, with only the faintest strands of light filtering through the branches, the two big boys looked like dark phantoms as they wrestled Maggie and Kenny to their feet and then began to drag them over the forest floor.

Maggie screamed, and then again, and they stopped. One of the boys pulled a cloth of some kind from his pocket and tied it over her mouth. Kenny was yelling at them, and the bigger of the two hit him, hard, with the back of his hand, telling him to shut up or they would beat him "to a pulp" and his "girlfriend with him."

Pip's stomach cramped. He inhaled the spicy odor of pine, moistened his lips, and tasted the soil dusted upon them from the ground. He had to sneeze but pinched his nose to stop it. Carefully, he craned his neck, trying to see where they were taking Maggie and Kenny.

But the trees were too dense, the night too dark to see anything other than what was right in front of him. He would have to follow them.

He stayed low, going at a crouch so they wouldn't spot him if they looked back. The ground was hard and littered with rocks and fallen branches. Once he stumbled and smashed his toe against a rock. He had to bite his tongue to keep from crying out.

They were moving fast, stamping through the woods, whipping the branches out of their way. A darkened shape suddenly came into view, and Pip saw now where they were headed. About halfway down a slope of knobby ground he could make out a darkened shape that looked like a cabin of some sort.

When they reached it, the boys stopped. Pip ducked down just in time as they stood looking all around. Then one elbowed the door open, and the other shoved Kenny and Maggie inside.

Pip crept as close as he dared, but he couldn't see anything. The cabin was as dark as the night, and now that they were inside, he had no way of knowing what they were doing. Still crouching, he moved in a little closer, then stopped behind a large shrub.

He could see that the front window was broken, with only a piece or two of glass left hanging on the frame.

He heard a sound like an animal in pain, and then he realized it was Maggie.

Pip stared at the cabin, shaking with fear, his heart drumming against his chest.

He knew now that whatever those boys were up to with Maggie and Kenny, it was something wicked, something dangerous.

A feeling like something crawling along his spine froze him in place. Whatever evil was creeping about the woods had now found the darkened cabin and forced its way inside.

Twenty-Eight

In the Woods

I see black dragons mount the sky,
I see earth yawn beneath my feet.

James Clarence Mangan

They had gagged her, silencing her ability to scream, hindering her breathing. But once she realized where they were, Maggie made an effort to call for help anyway.

Nothing came out except a guttural cry, like that of an animal.

Fear, and the effort to make a sound, plus the tightness of the gag, made her feel as if she would faint at any moment. *No! Can't pass out...have to fight...have to fight as hard as we can...have to get away from them...*

Once inside, Billy shoved her so hard she hit the wall and then fell to the floor. Again she tried to cry out, but she could manage no sound except a strangled noise in her throat.

They hadn't gagged Kenny, and he warned them now, in a choked, enraged voice that didn't sound like him, "You're crazy! You're both crazy! Don't you know you can go to jail for this?"

There was a thud and then something cracked. Kenny bellowed in pain.

"You broke my arm! You maniac! You broke my arm!"

He moaned, and Maggie saw him, little more than a dark shape, slide down the wall and collapse into a heap beside her. On instinct, she reached to touch his arm, and he yelled.

She pulled her hand back, unable to tell him she was sorry, unable to help him. She couldn't help it; she started to cry. Her shoulder still hurt from where Billy had yanked her arm behind her. She was terrified, for herself and for Kenny. They were trapped. And where was Pip? Was he lost somewhere, unable to find his way home? How had they ended up in this nightmare?

Lord, I can't see anything in here. It's too dark…I can't even see Kenny's face…but You can see us, I know You can…help us, Lord…get us out of here, get us away from them…Kenny's right, they're crazy…they're crazy-mean, and we don't have a chance against them, whatever they're plotting to do…help us…please help us!

She could feel herself falling into panic, tumbling down into a pit of terror where she wouldn't be able to think clearly or help herself… or Kenny.

She mustn't lose control, she mustn't…she had a sense that they would hurt Kenny even worse if she made them mad…whatever happened, she mustn't make them mad…

Kenny knew he was close to passing out from the pain. Nothing had ever hurt this bad before. His arm was on fire. It felt as if someone had rammed an iron rod down through it and then twisted it in the wrong direction.

He couldn't black out—he couldn't. He had to stay conscious for Maggie. He had to try to keep them from hurting her. Maybe if he could keep their attention on him they'd leave her alone.

He was lying to himself, and he knew it. They wanted to hurt Maggie in a different way, especially Billy. He'd seen it in his eyes. Billy was the worst. Orrin was just another bully, but Billy Macken was something else. If there was such a thing as evil on foot, Billy was it.

He hadn't been all that afraid of them until tonight. He always knew when they came after him that he was going to get hurt, but he still hadn't been afraid. He just braced himself against the pain until it was over. He was more afraid of the pain than of *them.*

But this was different. Tonight he was afraid of what they were going to do, because tonight wasn't the same. He'd seen something when they were still outside, when there had been enough light from the moon to see their faces. He'd looked into Billy's eyes and had to fight not to shrivel up inside at what he saw there.

He'd told them they were crazy, but what he'd seen hadn't been lunacy. It was something worse. Maybe it wasn't what he saw at all. Maybe it was what he *hadn't* seen. Because there was something missing in Billy's eyes. Something that should have been there just...wasn't.

It was so hard to see in here. Even if there had been light, he could not have seen all that well, because his glasses had gone flying off his nose outside, when they'd grabbed him and Maggie.

His head was swimming from the pain. He felt off balance, as if the room were leaning.

Something scurried across the floor, and a sound tore from Maggie's throat.

Kenny turned toward her. "It's all right," he said, his words coming out thick and slurred. "Don't be scared."

She was crying. He hated that. Maggie never cried. Almost never, anyway. She was the bravest girl in school, braver than most of the boys. But now she was crying, and it made him hurt even more.

Billy moved, coming toward them. Kenny knew it was Billy because he had legs like tree trunks.

"Brave guy," Kenny muttered. "Making girls cry."

"Shut up, Four-eyes!" The words were accompanied by a kick in the head.

Now the room did tilt, and Kenny went sideways, against Maggie, who reached to steady him.

"Leave him alone," Billy snapped. "Put him in the corner over there," he said to Orrin. "Get him out of the way. If he gives you any trouble, slug him again."

"What are you gonna do, Billy?"

Kenny was still clearheaded enough to note the uneasiness in Orrin's voice. So he wasn't necessarily sold on his buddy's meanness after all. Somehow that didn't surprise Kenny. But he was here, all the same. He'd gone along with Billy, whether he liked the idea or not. As far as Kenny was concerned, that made him just as bad.

Maybe just not as dangerous.

"Billy? What are you gonna do?" Orrin asked again.

"What do you *think* I'm going to do?" Billy said with an ugly laugh. "I'm going to teach Little Red Riding Hood here some respect. I told you, get him out of my way."

Kenny nearly gagged on the rage boiling through him as Orrin came and took him by his good arm. He shook him off, forcing the older boy to switch sides. When he did, Kenny slipped his hand into his pocket, palmed the knife and flicked it open. As Orrin bent to grasp him, Kenny twisted around, brought the knife up and plunged it in, then out, of Orrin's leg.

The boy screamed and fell backward. Kenny scrambled away from him, knife still in hand as he lunged toward Billy, who was standing over Maggie.

"Maggie! Run!"

But Maggie couldn't run. Billy was too fast. With amazing aim, even in the darkness, he blocked her and then he pivoted and kicked out at Kenny's arm, knocking the knife out of his hand and sending it clattering across the floor.

Then he cursed at Kenny and again kicked him in the head.

The last thing Kenny heard before the darkness swallowed him whole was Orrin shrieking like a girl and Billy cursing them all as he crashed across the room to get the knife.

Pip was on his knees, shivering as much from fear as the cold, when he heard Kenny yell. It got quiet for a couple of minutes, and then someone yelled again, only this time it wasn't Kenny. It was a terrible sound, like someone was hurt and hurt bad.

Pip didn't think but clambered to his feet and took off running as fast as he could toward the road. Not for the first time, he wished he were big. Big and strong like his papa had been. He wished he still had both hands. He wished he hadn't got lost and made Maggie and Kenny come looking for him.

They had been so nice to him, both of them. And now when they needed help, he was useless.

But he could still run. His papa always said he could run like a wild jack rabbit.

So Pip ran. He would run all the way into town if he had to, but somehow, somewhere he was going to get help for Maggie and Kenny.

Twenty-Nine

A Call for Heroes

Unbounded courage and compassion joined
proclaim him good and great,
and make the hero and the man complete.
Joseph Addison

Where were they?

Jonathan had been pacing the road beneath the tipple for more than ten minutes now, but there was still no sign of the children or their fathers.

He'd brought a lantern but left it dark, not wanting to announce his presence. At least not yet. Earlier the night had been clear, and he'd been able to see well enough, but clouds had now begun to gather, and he feared that soon he would have to light the lantern even if it did give him away.

Nearly sick with worry, he again scanned the railroad yard and the grounds beneath the tipple but found the entire area still deserted.

The shift would have ended nearly an hour ago; apparently, no one lingered long after the whistle blew.

Chilled, he was tempted to go back to the buggy and wait for the others but then decided against it. He couldn't see nearly as well from where he'd parked the buggy up the road, and he didn't want to risk missing the children.

He tried to feel hopeful. Perhaps Billy Macken and the Gaffney boy had given up their malicious plan and Maggie and Kenny were safely home by now. If nothing happened soon, he'd try to think of an excuse to stop by one or the other's house, just to make sure.

Somehow, even though he wanted to believe that scenario, he couldn't quite convince himself that was what had happened. The heaviness that had been pressing in on him throughout the day hadn't lifted; if anything, the oppression had only grown darker. During the ride here, one appalling image after another had inserted itself in his mind, until by the time he arrived he was half nauseous with dread.

He didn't know what else to do except to wait. Surely, Matthew and Judson Tallman—

Just then he saw Tallman coming around the side of the hill from his office. Relieved, he watched the mine superintendent approach. The man was half running in a stiff, straight-legged gait, one arm hanging close to his side, the other hand holding a lantern.

He moves like the person he's said to be, thought Jonathan. *He seems like such a rigid, unyielding sort of man.*

He reminded himself that he really didn't know Judson Tallman, although his recent encounter with the man had done nothing to dispel his earlier impression of him. Still, he should at least make an effort to be charitable. Especially under the present circumstances.

"They're not here?" Tallman said as soon as he reached Jonathan.

"No sign of them yet," said Jonathan. "I've been here for several minutes now, and I haven't seen anyone, except for a few men who were leaving just as I arrived. I don't know what to think."

He fished in his pocket for the matches he'd brought, struck one and lighted his lantern.

"What about MacAuley?"

Jonathan shook his head. "I haven't seen him. I'm sure he'll be here soon—"

Tallman interrupted with a gruff sound of impatience. "Likely you misunderstood the whole situation. You probably didn't hear what you thought you did."

Jonathan bristled. "I'm not given to poor hearing, Mr. Tallman. I know what I overheard, and it was exactly as I described it to you and Matthew MacAuley."

"Well, you can see there's no one here," Tallman said tersely. "Including MacAuley."

But just then Matthew MacAuley *was* there. The big miner, still in his work clothes, his face black with coal dust, came hustling down the hill, swinging a lantern in one hand.

"Sorry," he said when he reached them. "There was trouble with the cage—that rattletrap should have been replaced months ago." He shot a pointed glance at Judson Tallman before going on. "Anyway, we were late getting up. I tried—"

Before MacAuley could finish, a frantic cry split the stillness of the night.

Jonathan whipped around to see a boy breaking out of the edge of the trees across the railroad tracks, wildly flailing his arms and shouting as he ran toward them.

"It's Pip!"

The three of them took off running, but Matthew MacAuley quickly passed Jonathan and Tallman. Before Jonathan could make it across the road, he had to slow his pace; his heartbeat was severely erratic, the pain in his chest intense.

But Pip didn't stop for Matthew MacAuley or Tallman. Instead, he came running directly to Jonathan. The boy was clearly panicked, his dark eyes wild with fear, his breath coming in sharp, quick gasps.

Jonathan caught him by the arm. "Pip, what is it?"

"Over there!" He spun around and pointed toward the woods. "Maggie and Kenny!"

Matthew MacAuley and Tallman had retraced their steps and now stood behind the boy, listening. He was shaking badly when Jonathan took him by the shoulders. "What *about* Maggie and Kenny? Where are they?"

Again the boy pointed to the woods. "They're hurting them! Those boys—those boys from school—they took them to a house—"

"Slow down, Pip," said Jonathan. "What house? Where?"

But Matthew MacAuley was already moving, and there was nothing to do but follow him. Judson Tallman went at a run behind MacAuley, while Jonathan had all he could do to walk.

He felt a tug at the sleeve of his coat, and when he looked down, Pip took Jonathan's hand and placed it on his own narrow shoulder. "I'll help you, Mr. Stuart. You lean on me, okay?"

Jonathan swallowed, unable to speak. But he did indeed lean on the little boy at his side. Together, they followed the two fathers at a distance, Pip explaining how they'd become separated and what he had seen in the woods—and Jonathan praying silently, frantically all the way.

Holding the lantern up to see, Matthew didn't hesitate. He kicked the door in and charged inside, with Tallman right behind him.

He saw Kenny first, crumpled in a corner, a narrow trickle of blood streaming down the side of his face. Orrin Gaffney, his face white and stark in the flickering glow from the lantern, sat crammed against one wall, holding what looked to be a bloody glove over his leg. He took one look at Matthew and shrank back against the wall as if he were trying to vaporize.

Then Matthew saw Maggie.

A groan of despair tore from his throat. They had *gagged* the girl! She was sprawled on the filthy floor, her coat bunched up about her knees, kicking that animal, Billy Macken, in the legs.

He was laughing at her. And he had a knife.

Matthew snapped.

Billy Macken saw him and stopped laughing.

Matthew rid himself of the lantern by setting it carefully to the floor. He then straightened, and took a step toward Macken. After only the slightest hesitation, the boy bolted toward him, clearly intending to escape through the open door.

Matthew blocked him with his body. The boy raised the knife, but Matthew wrested it from him with one vicious motion, trapping him with an arm against his throat as he pitched the knife over his shoulder and out the door into the night.

The Macken boy was big and heavy-built, but Matthew toppled him as if he were nothing but a reed in the wind. When the boy went down, Matthew yanked him upright again, wrenching his bad arm hard enough to send pain shooting all the way up to his neck.

He grabbed the boy by both shoulders, shaking him as if he were no more than one of his girls' rag dolls.

His blood pounded, his heart hammered like a wild thing, and a rage he had not known since he was a boy thrummed through him, setting off a roaring in his head that shut out everything around him.

The young devil was crying now—crying, the simpering coward—and then begging, but Matthew had nearly crossed the line from mercy to madness. He took the boy's throat in his hands and began to squeeze.

"*Matthew!* No! Stop before you kill the boy!"

Jonathan Stuart's voice finally sliced through the storm of rage that had caught Matthew up in its vortex. He stared at the Macken boy, whose jaw had gone slack, his eyes panicky and wild, for Matthew still had him by the throat.

And as if his hands had suddenly caught fire, Matthew released the boy, who tottered backward.

"You get over there," Matthew ordered, his voice like gravel as he pointed to the opposite corner of the room. "And don't you move. Don't you even roll your eyes, understand?"

The boy's eyes now glittered with hatred, but, rubbing his throat and hacking, he stumbled over to the corner where his white-faced cohort with the bloody glove still cowered.

Matthew shook his head to clear it and saw that Jonathan Stuart had knelt down beside Maggie. The gag was gone, and the teacher was holding her as she sobbed against his shoulder.

He glanced at Judson Tallman, who had pillowed his boy's head in his lap and was wiping the blood from his face. Kenny appeared to be conscious now, but his skin was ashen, and he was moaning with pain.

The wee Pippino boy was on his knees at Kenny's side, his gaze going back and forth from the boy to Judson Tallman, solemnly watching them both.

Finally, Matthew turned and went to Maggie. He dropped down beside her, and Jonathan Stuart very gently turned her away from him and handed her over to her father.

He held his daughter to his heart, carefully so as not to bruise her with the force of his relief and his love, though he sullied her with his coal-dusted miner's hands. As he held her, he rocked her and stroked her wild red hair, so much like his own, and murmured a promise, over and over, that no one would ever hurt her again.

Please, God…

He glanced across the room then to see Judson Tallman pass a hand over his son's face in a gesture much like a blessing.

"Is your boy all right?" Matthew said.

Tallman looked up, his expression somewhat stunned, his eyes damp.

Perhaps he did care, after all…

"His arm is broken, and he's been beaten…again," Tallman said, his voice unsteady. "But, yes, I believe he will be alright." He paused. "And your daughter, MacAuley? How is she?"

Matthew gazed down at the top of Maggie's head and then at Tallman. "She'll be just fine." He hesitated and then added, "Thanks to your son."

Their eyes locked for a long moment before each turned back to his child.

Thirty

A Future and a Hope

"For I know the thoughts that I think toward you,"
says the LORD, "thoughts of peace,
and not of evil, to give you a future and a hope."

Jeremiah 29:11 NKJV

On the night before his birthday, Jonathan Stuart forced himself to make what was probably the most difficult decision of his life.

For days now he had been wrestling with a matter that threatened to break his heart every time he confronted it. Tonight he had faced the truth without shrinking, had resigned himself to the reality—and the finality—of his deteriorating physical condition, and had somehow come to terms with what he must do.

In the dim solitude of his small study, with icy, wind-driven snow pelting the windows, despair overcame his spirit as fatigue had overcome his body. So weak had he grown over the past weeks that he virtually dragged himself to and from the schoolhouse each day. The smallest tasks had become trying, to the point that exhaustion had become a way of life for him.

He would never understand how he had endured...and survived... the past few days. By all rights, the recent events would have consumed what little stamina he had left. The ongoing tension and worry, and then the harrowing night of Maggie and Kenny's rescue, had been as enervating as days of rigorous physical labor, perhaps even more so.

Yet he was still here, albeit depleted, still able to function if not well, at least enough to get by. And no matter what the ordeal had done to him, some remarkable things had come out of it. He had seen the end of Billy Macken and Orrin Gaffney's bullying the other children. Both boys had been spared a jail sentence in lieu of a year's stay at an institutional farm for wayward boys in the next county. One could only hope they would emerge from that experience more inclined to contribute to society rather than defy it.

According to Matthew MacAuley, Maggie and Kenny were both recovering nicely. Kenny was still resting at home, as was Maggie, but Matthew had assured Jonathan that both would be back to normal soon.

As for Judson Tallman, Kenny's father seemed to have had a much-needed awakening. Apparently, he had come to realize that his cold, uncompromising method of raising his son had nothing to do with instilling courage and a sense of manhood in a boy; indeed, such traits were already present in his son. What Kenny needed most was attention and love, and although Jonathan suspected that Tallman would never find it easy to be lavish with either, he could only hope the man would eventually learn how to provide both.

As for himself, he had made two new friends: Matthew MacAuley and Pip. The latter had become his shadow, showing up at his house every day during the Christmas vacation from school to see what might need fixing or what errands Jonathan might assign to him—or simply to talk his ear off while he "kept him company." Matthew, of course, was far too busy at the mines to enjoy the luxury of an idle visit now and then, but he stopped by when he could, often with some treat from his wife's kitchen.

Jonathan was almost beginning to feel somewhat spoiled by all the rest and attention. But at the edge of his mind there was the constant awareness that the present sea of calm was only temporary, that looming closer and closer was a time when his life would have to change.

Tonight, after hours of prayer and searching the Word, he could almost believe that he had finally made peace with his warring emotions and could follow through with what he'd known he must do for some time now. Although the decision had scarred his very soul and challenged his faith in a way nothing else ever had, he had, as much as possible, accepted the future that awaited him.

When the New Year arrived, he would resign his teaching position at the school. Shortly thereafter, he would leave Skingle Creek.

He felt a grim irony in the fact that he would be retiring from his career at an age when many other men were only setting out on their life vocations. He was still a fairly young man; tomorrow he would turn twenty-eight, not exactly a milestone. But he felt as if he had the worn-out heart...and of late the worn-out spirit...of a much older man.

For weeks now—no, more like months—he had known himself to be failing badly. The medication wasn't nearly as effective as it had once been, and the additional hours of rest his Lexington physician had prescribed no longer seemed to make any appreciable difference.

He had been a fool to believe that he could go on as he had been. For one thing, he was cheating the children; they deserved a teacher who was fit, strong, and healthy enough to do the job as it ought to be done. It simply wasn't right to delay any longer.

He had already decided that he wouldn't return to his family home. He had no intention of putting his parents through the ordeal of watching him die. The doctor in Lexington had told him about a place—a kind of sanitarium—where those with serious illnesses could go, supposedly for continuous treatment and rest, though Jonathan suspected it was more a retreat where the hopelessly ill could await the end.

He had to face the fact that finances could be a problem. Because his teaching salary was spare, to say the least, he had managed to accumulate only a modest amount in savings. And with both his flute and his gold watch gone, he no longer had anything of real value to sell.

But God had been faithful in the past to take care of his financial needs. He would simply have to trust Him to do so in the future.

He sighed, kneading his temples as he began once more to search his Bible for comfort or at least some word of affirmation. For even with his decision settled, the peace he sought still eluded him, especially when he thought about leaving his students.

His children.

He knew they would be far better off with a teacher who wasn't ill and exhausted most of the time. Still, he found himself riddled with doubts and an excruciating sadness. He had prayed and searched the Scriptures most of the evening for some assurance that would put his mind and heart at rest, only to become more confused than ever about what, exactly, God might be trying to say to him...

> My strength and my hope is perished from the LORD... my soul melteth for heaviness; strengthen thou me according unto thy word.

Where had those thoughts come from? Puzzled, Jonathan flipped through the pages, staring at the passage to which his reading had taken him:

> It is of the LORD's mercies that we are not consumed, because his compassions fail not. They are new every morning: great is thy faithfulness. The LORD is my portion, saith my soul; therefore will I hope in him.

Hope? Jonathan removed his glasses and rubbed a hand over his eyes. How long had it been since he had felt any real hope, other than the ultimate hope of heaven?

And yet he had always hoped in the Lord—in His goodness, His love, His promises. And he still hoped in Him.

Didn't he?

After a moment he replaced his reading glasses and renewed his search, thumbing through his Bible as if an unseen hand were guiding him.

> I know the thoughts that I think toward you, saith the

> Lord, thoughts of peace, and not of evil, to give you an expected end.

"Dear Lord, I have resigned myself to the fact that I most likely have no future...except eternity with You," Jonathan whispered. "And I'm at peace with that. I *am*."

But was he?

> Hast thou not known? Hast thou not heard, that the everlasting God, the Lord, the Creator of the ends of the earth, fainteth not, neither is weary?...He giveth power to the faint; and to them that have no might he increaseth strength...they that wait upon the Lord shall renew their strength; they shall mount up with wings as eagles; they shall run, and not be weary; and they shall walk, and not faint.

Jonathan felt a sudden stirring in his spirit, a kind of breathless expectancy. He was only vaguely aware that he was trembling, that his tired heart was racing. Confusion merged with anticipation, and he found himself wholly caught up in the Word of God as he had not been in weeks, perhaps in months...

> The Lord is my strength and song...

But he had no strength. And the song of his soul seemed long forgotten...

> He hath put a new song in my mouth...

A new song? But he had *no* song. There was no longer any music in him...

His singing voice had always been a disappointment to him at best. But as long as he'd had his flute, he had never much minded his inadequate voice. The praise and joy of his heart had found a clear and shimmering voice in the golden notes of the flute. Most mornings, and evenings too, he had let the music of his soul pour forth in unconstrained melodies of praise. The very act had been as much a part of his worship as the hymn singing on Sunday mornings and his daily prayer time and Scripture study.

But the flute was gone, and with it every vestige of his music...

> The LORD is my strength and song...

Jonathan's eyes locked on the verse he had read only moments before. He read it again. And then again.

His hands were shaking on the fragile pages of the Bible. Carefully, he removed his glasses so that the tears burning his eyes might flow freely.

And then, still questioning, still seeking, he went to his knees. He made no petition, neither for himself nor for others. He did not plead. He did not speak. He scarcely breathed. He merely waited in the silence, listening...

Much later—he could not have said how much later—Jonathan saw again, as if before him on the tapestry of his mind, the same words of conviction and promise. He saw them, heard them, and felt them reverberate throughout his entire being as though plucked on the strings of his spirit:

> The LORD is my strength and song...

A wave of awareness, like the dawn coming up over a fog-veiled valley after a seemingly endless night, rose up in him. And in his spirit, Truth whispered:

> *The music of life is within you...not in the world, not in circumstances or external things...and not in an instrument.* You *are the instrument, and* I *am the music. Whatever road you walk in this life, it is because I have set your feet upon it. Whatever trials you encounter, whatever struggles you endure—your joys, your sorrows—these, too, are My will. I would have you, through the life you live with Me, show these children...these people...that the music of life is within, not without...that it comes from Me. I am your hope...your strength...your song. I, the Lord, am your music.*

It was almost first light on the morning of his birthday when, for the first time in a very long time, Jonathan Stuart found the strength to lift his hands toward heaven and praise his Creator-Father-God with a melody only the soul can sing.

Thirty-One

A Surprise for Mr. Stuart

That man is great, and he alone,
Who serves a greatness not his own...

Owen Meredith (Lord Bulwer Lytton)

On the evening of Mr. Stuart's birthday party, the students and their parents arrived well ahead of time, as Maggie had requested. Her mother and older sisters had brought the cake in earlier, setting it up to display nicely with the punch that Mrs. Woodbridge had made.

To Maggie, it was an odd sight entirely to see her mother working alongside Lily's mother, the two of them being from opposite sides of town and probably having never brushed elbows before tonight. Maggie couldn't help but notice that Mrs. Woodbridge actually seemed much kinder and sweeter-faced up close than she appeared at a distance.

In truth, many parents had surprised her, including her own. It was as if something had happened among the grown-ups, something altogether unexpected. Once they learned how hard the children had worked on the collection for Mr. Stuart—only to give it up for a greater need—they had begun to pitch in and do whatever they could to help: gathering clothes and food and additional funds for the needy of the community, as well as lending their efforts to the birthday party. And from what Maggie had been told, most of the families in town had decided to donate what little they might have spent on Christmas presents for themselves to help others like the Crawfords and the Widow Hunnicutt.

Her da seemed different too, and in a most unexpected way. He hugged her a lot more these days—as he did Eva Grace and Nell Frances. And at bedtime, he had taken to telling them all he loved them.

Imagine *that* from Da.

She turned her attention back to the party. It seemed that everyone was here tonight. Even Judson Tallman had shown up with candy and fruit for all the students, which had left Maggie almost speechless.

According to Kenny, though, his father had been different ever since what she had come to think of as "the night of the rescue." It sounded as though Mr. Tallman was paying more attention to his son these days, even taking an interest in his ship models. Of course, Kenny said he wasn't so sure but what his father wasn't just pretending to be interested, but Maggie could tell Kenny was happier than he'd been since she'd known him.

It seemed that both their fathers had done a bit of a turn around.

One thing was for certain. Kenny looked as dashing as a ship's captain with his arm in a sling and a bandage at his temple.

This, plus some of the other changes she'd heard about, made Maggie wonder if maybe things hadn't worked out for the best after all. At least for some.

Her own heart still carried an ache that just wouldn't go away. The nightmare with Billy Macken and Orrin Gaffney had left a scar that she knew wouldn't go away for a long time. She still had bad dreams, and sometimes, when her mind wandered back to everything that had happened that awful night—and the trouble that had gone before—she would feel chilled all over again and sick to her stomach.

It would take time, her mother kept telling her. "Give yourself time, Maggie."

Maggie expected her mother was right, for already she could see that some days she hardly thought about that terrible time at all. But more than the horror she and Kenny had endured that night, the real pain in her heart was because of Summer.

Without Summer to share in the good things that were happening, there was no real excitement in any of it for Maggie. She stayed busy, so she had little time to dwell on how much she missed Summer. But when she did think about her friend, it hurt something fierce. Even now, she often felt as though she were simply dragging through the days, putting one foot in front of the other to keep moving, to get things done as Summer would have expected of her, but without any real joy.

The thought of getting things done reminded her that she still had things to do before Mr. Stuart arrived, and instead of standing around woolgathering, she'd better get busy. She went to find her da, and the two of them moved the teacher's desk and chair toward the center, not only to make more space for the party, but also to afford the guest of honor a clearer view.

As always, Mr. Stuart's desk was neat and orderly, with only two or three books propped up on one side and a cup of pencils and the attendance register on the other. Maggie placed the handmade birthday cards from the students and their families on the desk and then stepped back. As she stood inspecting her work, she clutched the brown-paper-wrapped gift she'd brought tonight to her heart, as if its contents might somehow bring her absent friend closer. When her vision blurred, she turned away and went to give the others their last-minute reminders.

Maggie caught her breath when Pastor Wallace stepped inside the darkened schoolroom, pausing to hold a lantern aloft. The plan was that the pastor would invite Mr. Stuart out for a birthday supper, but suggest that they first stop by the school to borrow some paper and paint for the church's Christmas pageant.

On cue, those parents who had earlier been assigned the task now hurried to light oil lamps and lanterns, setting some in place, holding others. For a moment, Maggie was afraid something had gone wrong and Mr. Stuart hadn't come. But then the teacher appeared, framed in the doorway.

Thin as he was, he still looked handsome and rested in his dark blue suit and light blue necktie, his flaxen-colored hair freshly cut and neatly combed. As he walked in, the schoolroom seemed to glow with light, and everyone cried out a greeting in unison: "Happy birthday Mr. Stuart!"

Maggie's heaviness lifted a little when she saw the teacher's face. Obviously, they had pulled off the surprise. He was clearly stunned. Laughter broke out around the room, and then applause, as Mr Stuart stood gaping at them.

They continued to applaud as Pastor Wallace patted him on the back and led him toward the front of the room to his desk. Mr. Stuart turned to face them with a bewildered smile. He appeared, Maggie noticed, greatly flustered and obviously embarrassed by such attention.

The applause finally subsided, and Pastor Wallace began to speak.

Jonathan heard only random fragments of Ben Wallace's greeting, but enough to realize that apparently all this was for him. He found the idea nothing short of astounding.

The small schoolroom was crammed with what appeared to be all his students and their families, plus numerous other members of the community as well. There was even a table with a cake and other refreshments.

His curiosity sharpened at the sight of a varied array of musical instruments in the corner of the room.

He saw the crowd of well-wishers through a thin haze, as if he stood at a great distance from them, observing them through a veil of heat rising from the ground. Every face seemed to be smiling at him with good-natured enjoyment of his surprise.

Years of teaching had instilled in him the ability to grasp a situation, assess it, and then react rather quickly. But at the moment Jonathan was having difficulty focusing, much less trying to form an appropriate response. He felt almost dizzy and even a little disoriented.

But through the fog of confusion and astonishment, he managed to hear enough of Ben Wallace's address to understand that the children themselves had planned all this—the entire affair—in his behalf, enlisting the help of their parents as needed. Without his knowing it, there had apparently been widespread speculation about his health and his continuing on as their teacher, for Ben had much to say about how the community appreciated Jonathan—and how hopeful they were that he would see fit to stay in Skingle Creek "for a long, long time."

They couldn't have known of his decision, of course, but even so their affirmation evoked a bittersweet stirring within him. If only he could stay. If only he were well enough to stay.

There was mention of his efforts on the children's behalf, efforts that had, according to Ben, "benefited the entire community," and, finally, an explanation that his students were desirous of giving him a very special birthday gift: the gift of music.

Jonathan blinked at Ben Wallace's closing words, watching as Maggie MacAuley, her face still ravaged by her recent ordeal, stepped up. She gave Jonathan a brave smile, and then she began to speak, precisely and clearly, as if her words had been well-rehearsed.

"The class wanted you to know how sorry we are about what happened to your flute, Mr. Stuart."

Jonathan's head finally began to clear. He studied the slim red-haired girl standing so straight at his side, clutching a brown-paper package tightly against her as if she feared someone might attempt to tear it from her arms.

"We took up a collection some time back," she went on, "meaning to buy you a new flute and give you back your music. But when we heard about Mrs. Hunnicutt—"

She stopped, darting a glance around the schoolroom. Jonathan had already seen the Crawfords among the crowd. To Maggie's credit, she didn't mention their names.

"When we heard about...those who needed help," she continued, "we decided the collection should go to them."

She paused again. "We thought that's what you would want us to do, if we were to ask."

The collection. The jar they had filled with money overnight...

A knot swelled in Jonathan's throat as the girl continued squeezing the words together in a rush as if to get them all out before she forgot anything. "Since we couldn't replace your flute, we tried to figure a way we could still give you back your music."

She stopped, caught a breath, and then went on. "And, well, that's our birthday gift to you tonight, Mr. Stuart. If you'd like to sit down and relax, we'll be getting started now."

Poor little wren. Her heart was still aching over Summer, Jonathan knew. He smiled into her eyes, hoping to encourage her, and then he sat down.

Lily Woodbridge came up now, with a paper in hand. She gave Jonathan a big, expectant smile, and then she shot Maggie a look that plainly said they were to trade places.

With a stiff little nod in Jonathan's direction, Maggie scurried off into the crowd, still clutching the brown parcel to her heart.

Jonathan couldn't help but wonder what was in the package Maggie was guarding with such diligence. But he had no time for further conjecture, for just then Lily commenced her role as announcer...and the party began.

Thirty-Two

A New Song

The Lord is my strength and my song.

Exodus 15:2

If Jonathan had thought himself overwhelmed at the beginning of the evening, by the time the third "gift" had been presented, he was positively stunned.

So far, he had been treated to a trio comprised of Matthew MacAuley on the melodeon; Ezra Tyree on the banjo; and Ezra's son, Junior, on the "bones." Next, Dr. Woodbridge had rendered a somewhat nervous but surprisingly sweet tenor solo of "Barbara Allen." And Caleb Crawford had stumbled up to the front on crutches to shake the tambourine, while his twins, Dinah and Duril, offered, if not an entirely melodic, at least a lively vocal duet of "Camptown Races."

It was a veritable delight for Jonathan to see the boisterous twins actually taking part in something besides mischief.

It was even more satisfying to see their father sober on a Friday night.

He also had the comforting awareness that, although Mrs. Hunnicutt wasn't strong enough to attend tonight, she was recovering nicely by now in her own home. Her pantry had been stocked, her coal supply replenished, and she was being cared for by another widow from town, Mildred Ramsay.

As the evening wore on, he felt himself almost overcome with a kind of paternal pride and pleasure. To see his students exercising such an impressive display of talent, and to realize that they were offering it all to him as a gift, made his heart swell nearly to bursting. Truly, tonight was the finest gift he had ever received, no doubt the finest gift any man could ever receive. He could not imagine that anything would ever surpass it.

The event wasn't without its plaintive moments, however. Whenever he happened to glance at Maggie MacAuley, her somewhat drawn, unusually sober countenance grieved him deeply. The girl stood near the front, watchful and heartbreakingly solemn, holding her precious package—for surely it must be very precious to the child, judging from the way she continued to guard it—and looking as if at any moment she might run from the room weeping.

Without the usual light in her eyes and the slightly tilted smile, she looked too old and dejected for her years. He still worried about what she and Kenny Tallman had gone through, what sort of long-term effect it might have on them. Yet, there was a strength in those two that Jonathan believed would eventually prevail over any emotional damage, and he prayed to that effect daily.

Knowing Maggie as he did, Jonathan suspected that she had been the instigator of this entire event. He also believed that, more than the horrible experience she'd just come through, something else was responsible for the sadness in her eyes tonight. He thought it likely that she would find it difficult for some time to come to enjoy *any* occasion because Summer was no longer a part of things.

With all his heart, he wished he could give Maggie a gift tonight—one that would somehow return the light to her eyes and the smile to her face. But he knew only time and God's comfort could accomplish that.

A stirring in the crowd brought him back to his surroundings. As Jonathan watched, the students—every one of them—stepped up to form two rows directly in front of him. At the same time, Dr. Woodbridge came forward and, after a quick nod and a quirk of a smile, turned and began to direct this unique choir in Foster's "Hard Times," followed by Jonathan's favorite hymn, "Amazing Grace."

Jonathan felt dangerously close to choking on the emotion that welled up in him. Those same feelings very nearly overpowered him as Herb Rankin, Summer's father—who had been standing directly behind the children—plucked his harmonica from his shirt pocket and began to accompany the hymn.

Jonathan had been surprised, and exceedingly moved, when he realized that Summer's entire family was in attendance tonight. Now, as he watched the children and Herb, whose grief was still so sharply etched on his gaunt face, the pain of his loss still so achingly apparent in the lonely wail of the harmonica, it was all he could do to maintain his last shred of composure.

Yet in the midst of his convulsive emotions, he was acutely aware of the words of the stirring old hymn as the children's sweet, albeit imperfect, voices filled the schoolroom:

The Lord has promised good to me,
His word my hope secures;
He will my shield and portion be
As long as life endures.

Jonathan sat there, the words and music penetrating to his very soul as he looked out upon the unlikely group of adults and young people who had come together to give him gifts on this evening of his birthday. And in that moment, he was moved with such love and gratitude he simply could not contain it. Despite his best efforts, he could no longer control his tears, and while such an unrestrained display of emotion would have humiliated him at any other time, tonight he was only vaguely aware of it.

Through many dangers, toils and snares
I have already come;
'Tis grace hath brought me safe thus far,
And grace will lead me home.

When the last stanza had ended, the children stood quietly as Herb Rankin went on playing the melody through once again. This time, the harmonica no longer keened but seemed to soar in a solitary affirmation of faith and hope and a kind of triumph.

At last the music ended. The children and Herb dispersed, melding with the others in the crowd. Jonathan drew a deep, unsteady breath, and, sensing the end of the evening at hand and knowing he would be expected to say something—as he certainly should—he stood, waiting.

But instead of Lily moving to close the program, Maggie MacAuley walked up. The girl's eyes were red and shadowed, her smile uncertain, and she still hugged the brown-paper package to her heart. For a moment she stood staring up at Jonathan. Then, in a gesture as protective as if she were handing him a valuable family heirloom, she extended the parcel to him.

"This is for you, Mr. Stuart," she said, her voice pitched low. "It's from...Summer and me, the two of us. I'm not one bit musical, as you know, and since Summer couldn't be here..."

Her face threatened to crumple, and Jonathan reached out a hand to steady her. But after a moment the sharp little chin lifted, and she went on. "It was all Summer's idea...the gift, I mean. I just wanted to make sure you knew that it's from both of us—but mostly from Summer."

She practically shoved the package into Jonathan's hands but made no move to leave; instead, she stood watching him with unnerving intensity. Jonathan looked from Maggie to the parcel. His hands were shaking badly as he loosened the string and carefully removed the paper wrapping. His throat threatened to close, and he was trembling so that he had to place the box on top of the desk before he could go on.

He glanced at Maggie. Her gaze was locked on his hands as he opened the lid of the box and examined the contents.

Maggie drew a long sigh of relief and satisfaction to finally see the birthday gift safely in Mr. Stuart's possession.

Her mother had helped her wrap it, had even used a scrap of silk from her precious stash at the bottom of her sewing box. Maggie knew Summer would have approved of their efforts.

She watched Mr. Stuart closely, trying to gauge his response. But his expression was hard to read, as if his feelings might be made of more questions than answers.

It suddenly occurred to Maggie that she had forgotten something. "Mr. Stuart?"

He straightened and looked at her in a most peculiar way. Maggie saw that his eyes were damp, and it shocked her for an instant. But then she realized that those tears in his eyes weren't unhappy tears because his face seemed to be shining.

"I just thought you should know," she said, "that Ezra Tyree—Junior's daddy—made it from a picture Summer drew. He worked real hard to get it exactly the way she sketched it."

Mr. Stuart gave her a long look and then turned back to the open box. He lifted a hand, wiped it across his eyes, gave a small nod, and bent his head over the gift.

Jonathan's heart threatened to explode as he finally managed to take in what had to be the most unusual gift he could have possibly envisioned. Cradled on what appeared to be a small doll's pillow that had been covered in shiny green silk was a bright new tin whistle—a penny whistle. In some inexplicable, wonderful way the primitive instrument resembled his missing flute.

He studied the piece of scarlet ribbon gracefully threaded over and around the tin whistle. After a long moment in which he struggled to get his breath, he removed the penny whistle from the box, complete with its emerald green pillow and scarlet ribbon, and carefully extended it toward the parents and students.

"This...is a gift from Maggie MacAuley...and Summer Rankin," he choked out.

There was a collective intake of breath among the students and their families, followed by some speculative murmurs. Then a hush fell over the entire schoolroom as everyone watched Jonathan...and waited.

Had he ever played a penny whistle before tonight?

Jonathan couldn't remember. Perhaps, when he was a boy. He thought he could manage. The technique shouldn't be all that different from playing the flute, after all.

More to the point, did he have the breath or the strength to play it?

He must. He must do this, at least once. For the little girl with the wounded, watchful eyes...for Maggie. And for the one who was very much with them tonight, in their thoughts and in their hearts. He must do it for Summer. Indeed, he wanted to play for all of them—his children, his people, his family.

And for Me...play for Me, Jonathan...

Give me the strength, Lord.

I *am your strength...I am your strength and your song...*

With painstaking care, Jonathan lifted the penny whistle from its pillow, and, after removing the scarlet ribbon from it, brought the instrument to his lips.

One long, steadying breath. And then he began to play. Tentatively, at first, then with mounting confidence. For a moment, he didn't realize that his breath was coming in a pure, fresh rush, or that his strength was increasing, new and flowing, as if a well had been uncapped from which he was free to draw all he needed. He was conscious only of the music trilling from the penny whistle.

And yet it *wasn't* coming from the penny whistle, not really, for surely the narrow little instrument was pitifully inadequate for the pure, golden notes cascading from it, sweeping and soaring over the room. No, the music seemed to be coming from his heart…from his soul.

It was new—a new song—each note bubbling up and spilling out *from* him, only to be caught by the penny whistle and flung out to all those in the room. Even as he played, God's love for him—and his love for God and every person in the schoolroom—was somehow transposed into the music.

What had begun as a gift to him—to Jonathan—now became a gift from him—to his students and their families. A gift poured out with indescribable love and turned to something of glory by the Giver of all gifts.

Jonathan closed his eyes and played on, lost now in this glorious music he knew had little to do with the instrument or with himself, but everything to do with the One for whom he played.

He has put a new song in my mouth…

The LORD *is my strength and song…*

"And you will sing that new song and play the music I give you for as long as it is My will that you do so. I was with you at the beginning of your journey, and I will be with you until your journey's end. Your days, your times, are in My *hands."*

Jonathan went on playing, his eyes open now. He saw the stares of wonder and astonishment, mingled with love, fixed upon him. He felt the wonder and amazement inside himself, and at the same time received the love of the people and offered them *his* love…and the music.

"Play on, Jonathan. Play your music. My *music. Sing your new song. For* I *am your hope, your strength, your song. I, the Lord, am your music."*

Maggie had slipped back into the crowd the minute she saw that Mr. Stuart meant to play the penny whistle. Watching him, she thought he might be praying, for his eyes were closed as he played a kind of music she had never heard before. It was the most beautiful, rare, and glorious music! Indeed, the penny whistle didn't sound as if it had been made from a sheet of junkyard tin at all, but more as if it had been crafted from the finest silver, fashioned by the very hands of God's angels.

Summer, can you hear? Mr. Stuart is playing the penny whistle! You knew he would, didn't you? You knew! He's playing it, Summer, and the music is a glory, a wondrous thing entirely! He's playing for us, Summer, and the music is more grand than anything he ever played on his expensive silver flute! Oh, Summer, I hope you can hear it, all the way up into heaven. I hope you can hear it!

Maggie could not think how such a small and simple thing as the homemade penny whistle could give forth such sound—like a pure crystal sea of heavenly music!

And then Mr. Stuart opened his eyes and looked directly at her as he went on playing. Maggie suddenly realized that she was weeping, but at the same time smiling, smiling through her tears...smiling and almost laughing out loud at the new joy and strength...and *hope* she could see shining in Mr. Stuart's eyes as he played—a hope that seemed to reach out and draw her in, along with her family and all the families in the schoolroom. It was as if God was putting His arms around them all.

The penny whistle itself looked to be aglow. It had caught the light from all the lamps in the schoolroom, and now it blazed and shimmered like pure silver as it dipped and swayed in Mr. Stuart's hands. And for the first time in what had seemed like an endless age, Maggie could feel the music washing away the coal dust and grime from Skingle Creek. The town...and her heart...were being washed clean of their dust and pain and sorrow—cleansed and made new by the music from Mr. Stuart's penny whistle...the penny whistle and God's love.

In that moment, Maggie MacAuley knew that the music had come back to Mr. Stuart...and to Skingle Creek...this time to stay.

Epilogue

Homecoming

Memory is a pilgrimage that takes me home.

From the diary of Jonathan Stuart

June 17, 1904

It was June in Kentucky. The air was warm and sweet-scented with wildflowers and the rich, pungent fragrance of newly mown grass and freshly turned earth.

With classes now dismissed for the summer, the school yard was empty and unnervingly quiet. The building looked much as Maggie remembered it, except that a new wing had been added. But the siding was the original white clapboard, which looked to have been recently painted, and the bell still hung suspended from the iron frame near the steps. The old rusting gate had also been replaced. The new one was wider, with hinges that didn't creak and groan when she opened it.

Because of the travel expense and her lack of free time, Maggie's visits home had been few and far between over the years. Once before she had come to the school, only to find it empty. There had been flood damage, and the children were being transported by wagon to the school in Fletcher. Years later, she came again, but that time he had been away in Lexington, visiting his parents.

Over the years, he had written to her, as had her mother, of the additions to the school and the moderate growth of the town. Somehow she had expected a more drastic change. But other than the new wing, the building appeared the same plain but sturdy structure she remembered from her childhood.

As she followed the path up the school yard, she could almost hear her own childish voice mingling with others from the past. Without warning, memories came rushing in on her like a summer storm, long-forgotten images of an earlier, simpler time she had foolishly thought would go on forever.

Where are the others now? she wondered.

Some she had kept in touch with, at least during the first few years away from home. Later, her mother's letters had brought her occasional news. Kenny Tallman, to everyone's surprise and no doubt his father's despair, had gone to the mission field. They had lost touch over the past year, but the last she'd heard from him, he was somewhere in South America. His father, Judson Tallman, was still superintendent at the mines.

Junior Tyree, in partnership with his father, had started a lumber mill outside of town and, last she'd heard, had become relatively prosperous. Poor Lester Monk had died in the worst mine accident in the history of the county—the same accident that had lamed her father. Lester had died a hero, though, saving the life of Orrin Gaffney, who had left school and gone into the mines upon his release from the wayward boys' farm. The thought of Orrin brought back another dark memory, that of Billy Macken, who, after spending a year at the same institution, had returned to Skingle Creek only long enough to collect his belongings and leave town. As far as Maggie knew, he hadn't been heard from since.

As for Lily Woodbridge—and now Maggie could only smile—Lily had decided early on, before they ever graduated from high school, that she would become a nurse and marry a doctor, in that order. True to form, she had accomplished both goals.

By now Maggie had reached the front doors of the schoolhouse, which stood open in invitation to the balmy weather. She entered, and as if the sound of her footsteps might somehow intrude upon the past, found herself walking on tiptoes.

She saw him immediately. He was sitting at his desk—the same desk he'd used a dozen years ago, she was certain—writing something, perhaps grading papers. She remembered the fine hand that had graded her papers so carefully, the precise script, the slight, unexpected flourish with which he always crossed the final *t* of his name.

Even though she had hoped he would be here today, she was completely unprepared for the emotion that welled up in her at the sight of him. The head bent over the desk was still flaxen, though she caught a glimpse of a few strands of silver here and there as it caught the light. As always, he was wearing glasses, and he appeared to be deep in thought as his pen scraped the paper.

She heard him sigh, and she couldn't help but smile. He had often sighed back then too, most usually when faced with a particularly inadequate test paper.

She was about to knock on the door frame when he looked up. His expression was questioning but pleasant, a smile quickly forming.

For a moment she found herself unable to speak. Only now did she realize how very young he must have been all those years ago. Why, he was *still* a young man. He hadn't been old at all back then, but merely ill—terribly ill.

Obviously, that was no longer the case, had not been the case, as she recalled, for many years now. The lean face glowed with good health, and the dark eyes behind the glasses were warm with intelligence and kindness—and the same glint of humor she still remembered.

Ever the gentleman, he got to his feet. "May I help you?"

For some ridiculous reason, Maggie's eyes started to fill, and she felt suddenly shy. She blinked, and then blinked again as she slowly walked the rest of the way into the room. "Hello, Mr. Stuart," she managed to say.

He inclined his head to one side a little, regarding her closely.

It gave Maggie an inordinate amount of pleasure to watch his expression gradually change from curiosity to recognition, and then to what was obviously delight. "Maggie? Why, it is, isn't it? Maggie MacAuley!"

He came quickly around the desk to greet her, clasping her hand between both of his—which were warm and strong, stronger than she might have expected. All at once, she was laughing. It was just so good, so incredibly good, to see him again, to hear him call her "Maggie" again. Over the years she had become "Meg" to her friends. But she had never quite left "Maggie" behind.

"I'm so glad to see you, Mr. Stuart!" she said.

"Well...Maggie." He studied her, openly shaking his head as if he couldn't believe his eyes. "Goodness, you make me feel old!"

Only then did he release her hand.

Again, Maggie laughed. "And *you* make me feel very young again. But how did you recognize me so quickly?"

His glance flicked to her still untamed red hair. Maggie rolled her eyes and nodded.

He motioned for her to take the chair near his desk. "I want to hear everything about you," he said, waiting for her to sit down before returning to his own chair across from her. "I see your parents often, you know."

She feigned a stern frown. "But you haven't written to *me* for ages."

He shook his head. "I'm sorry. I really am. I wasn't sure—"

He seemed to change his mind about whatever he'd meant to say. "I have kept up with you, though, through your family. And Ray's one of my students, of course."

"Then you know I'm a teacher."

He positively beamed. "And I'm quite sure a very good one."

Maggie smiled at him. "As a matter of fact, I am. But only because

I had such a fine example to follow." She paused. "Not to mention the scholarships you made possible for me."

He shook his head. "The scholarships were entirely your doing, Maggie. You were bright and you worked hard. All I did was submit your name and your records."

"You wrote letters—and you made two trips to Cincinnati on my behalf," she said quietly. "I know all about it, Mr. Stuart."

They talked for a long time, but as always, he spoke little about himself, instead plying her with one question after another about her life, the entire time leaning forward with evident interest in her answers.

At one point Maggie found herself wondering—and not for the first time—why Jonathan Stuart had never married. According to her mother, there had never been anyone in his life, at least not since he'd come to live in Skingle Creek.

The common assumption seemed to be that his singlehood was due to his poor health, but Maggie wasn't so sure. The man across the desk from her looked anything but unhealthy these days.

She thought it more likely that he had simply given his life to the school, to the children. *His* children, he'd always called them. And in a very special way, they were his children.

"Mother wrote me that you're the principal now," Maggie said. "That's wonderful, but I confess it's difficult for me to think of you not teaching."

"Oh, I still teach," he assured her. "We can't afford a full-time principal. To tell you the truth, I don't really like the job all that much. I prefer the classroom. But they couldn't seem to find anyone else for the position, and I was here, so—"

He shrugged, smiling. "But I want to know more about you, Maggie. You're still living in Chicago?"

Maggie nodded.

"And you work with one of the immigrant societies, your father told me. In addition to your teaching?"

"Actually, it's a part of it. I work at a settlement house," Maggie explained. "Hull House, it's called. I trained under Miss Jane Addams, the founder. Mostly, I teach immigrant children. And I teach classes on citizenship for their parents as well."

He regarded her with a look of approval. "I always knew you would do something special with your life. And I wasn't in the least surprised when I learned you were working with children. You were always so good with the younger students in the classroom."

He hesitated, and then he said, "I often think of Summer. I imagine you do too."

Again Maggie nodded. She had a secret she'd intended to keep but suddenly couldn't. She wanted him to know. "I...wrote a story about Summer last year. It's to be published as a children's book in a few months."

"Maggie, that's wonderful! I hope you'll send me one of the first copies off the press."

She promised him that she would. What she didn't mention, however, was that the book carried a dedication to him. Or that it was titled *The Penny Whistle.* She thought she would keep that much to herself for the time being.

She decided then to ask him the question she had wanted to ask for years. "Mr. Stuart? I've often wondered...did you ever find your silver flute?"

He smiled a little and then shook his head. "No," he said quietly, looking away. "I never did."

Maggie murmured a sound of sympathy.

When he turned back to her, his expression was anything but regretful. "It doesn't matter. In fact, I think it's best that I never learned what happened to the flute."

"But why?"

He pointed then to something behind her, and she turned to look. Only now did she notice the small, glass-enclosed cabinet mounted on the wall. There, behind the glass door, resting on the small green pillow and draped with the scarlet ribbon, was the penny whistle she and Summer had given him so many years ago.

Tears scalded Maggie's eyes as the memory of that winter night came to her again. She could almost see the schoolroom aglow with the light from the lanterns and the faces of the children and their families as they stared in wonder, watching a miracle. After all these years of holding it in her heart, that night still seemed like a dream that couldn't possibly have happened.

But it had happened, and her life had never been the same.

Neither had Jonathan Stuart's. She dragged her gaze away from the penny whistle and turned to face him. The very fact that he was still here in Skingle Creek, teaching "his children," was evidence enough that that night had changed his life too.

As if he'd read her thoughts, he rose and walked over to the window, where he stood, hands clasped behind him, looking out. "That night, the penny whistle changed my life." After a moment, he added, "I think perhaps it may have saved my life."

He turned back, offering a reply to Maggie's unspoken question. "I still play it, you know. I play it for the children, for each new class at the beginning of term—and on special occasions during the year. And when I play, I tell them a story. A story about two very special young friends who gave their teacher a precious gift from God."

Maggie swallowed hard against the knot in her throat. "Mr. Stuart, what really happened that night, with the penny whistle? I've never understood."

He removed his glasses and stood studying her for a moment. "I don't suppose I understand what happened either, Maggie. But I choose to believe that what happened was hope."

The look she gave him must have been questioning because he went on to explain. "That was your gift to me, Maggie—yours and Summer's. In your innocence, your unselfish desire to help me, you actually enabled me to find my hope again."

He stopped, and when he finally went on, Maggie had the sense that he was speaking more to himself than to her. "It's strange, but I can still remember that in my early years here the need I sensed most in the children was the need for hope. I resolved that somehow I would give them that hope. Yet, as it turned out, it was the children...two in particular...who ultimately restored the gift of hope to me."

He passed a hand over his eyes and then replaced his glasses. "That winter was a terrible time for me—for many of us. I was all but dead, at least in my spirit. For the most part, I was simply waiting...to die. At first I attributed the deadness of my spirit to illness. Later, I somehow deluded myself that it was a result of having the flute stolen."

He looked at her. "Music had always been such a...necessary thing to me. It was almost as if the absence of music—or perhaps my inability to make music—was responsible for my decline."

He shook his head, his smile faint and rueful. "I was so terribly, terribly wrong. It was the absence of *hope* that had stolen my music, not the loss of the flute. I was living a hopeless life, because I hadn't...taken God into account. I had simply given up."

His expression was thoughtful as he went on. "But God apparently hadn't given up on me. He had another plan. Through you and Summer and the other children—and the penny whistle—He reminded me of something I already knew but had temporarily lost sight of. He reminded me that hope is the real music of the soul. Without it, the human spirit cannot soar, cannot rise above the things of this earth and...sing."

As Maggie watched, his gaze again traveled to the penny whistle in the cabinet on the wall. "I can't begin to explain why or how it all happened. But I'm convinced that none of it was altogether for me, but that it was somehow meant for the entire town."

He looked at Maggie. "There were changes after that," he said, his voice low. "Subtle, gradual, most of them—but changes all the same. In the town, in the people—and in me."

Again he shook his head. "All I really know for certain is that on that night, God showed me that hope is, above all else, a gift—His gift. A gift that in reality has nothing at all to do with one's circumstances, but everything to do with His love. His love...and our willingness to trust that love. That's what hope is: the music of the heart. The music of life."

The long, searching look he now turned on Maggie held a depth of fondness and affirmation that warmed her heart. "Do you know, Maggie," Jonathan Stuart said quietly, "it would seem to me that in *your* life, He may well be composing an entire symphony. A symphony of hope."

What God Says About Hope

"Though he slay me, yet will I hope in him" (Job 13:15).

"The eyes of the LORD are on those who fear him, on those whose hope is in his unfailing love" (Psalm 33:18).

"Why are you downcast, O my soul? Why so disturbed within me? Put your hope in God, for I will yet praise him, my Savior and my God" (Psalm 42:5).

"Find rest, O my soul, in God alone; my hope comes from him" (Psalm 62:5).

"For you have been my hope, O Sovereign LORD, my confidence since my youth" (Psalm 71:5).

"There is surely a future hope for you, and your hope will not be cut off" (Proverbs 23:18).

"Those who hope in the LORD will renew their strength. They will soar on wings like eagles; they will run and not grow weary, they will walk and not be faint" (Isaiah 40:31).

"Those who hope in me will not be disappointed" (Isaiah 49:23).

"'For I know the plans I have for you,' declares the LORD, 'plans to prosper you and not to harm you, plans to give you hope and a future'" (Jeremiah 29:11).

"Hope does not disappoint us" (Romans 5:5).

"Command those who are rich in this present world not to be arrogant nor to put their hope in wealth, which is so uncertain, but to put their hope in God" (1 Timothy 6:17).

About the Author

Widely recognized for her award-winning historical fiction, BJ Hoff is the author of the American Anthem trilogy and the Emerald Ballad series. Her bestselling historical novels have crossed the boundaries of religion, language, and culture to capture a worldwide reading audience. Although she writes of early America and the people who helped to build the country, her stories of faith and love and grace are timeless.

The author of twenty novels and a number of inspirational gift books, when asked about her own story, BJ points to her family: "They're my story. My favorite, most important story."

A former church music director and music teacher, BJ and her husband, James, make their home in Ohio, where they share a love of music, books, and time spent with family.

If you would like to contact the author, you may write to BJ care of:

Harvest House Publishers
990 Owen Loop North
Eugene, OR 94702

Or visit www.bjhoff.com